THE LAW CLERK

A Novel

SCOTT DOUGLAS GERBER

OHIO NORTHERN UNIVERSITY

Ada, Ohio

KENT STATE UNIVERSITY PRESS
Attn: Rights and Permissions
PO Box 5190
Kent, OH 44242-0001

Individual Sales. This book is available through most bookstores or can be ordered directly by calling (419) 281-1802 or online at www.kentstateuniversitypress.com.

Quantity Sales. Special discounts are available on quantity purchases by corporations, associations, and others. For details, contact the "Special Sales Department" at the distributor's address above.

Printed in the United States of America

Library of Congress Cataloging-in-Publication Data
are available from the distributor.
ISBN 978-0-87338-903-7

Permission to use a portion of the following copyrighted nonfiction material is gratefully acknowledged: Robert J. Stoller and I. S. Levine, *Coming Attractions: The Making of an XRated Video* (Yale University Press, 1993).

Cover photograph by A. T. Willett
Cover design by Kira Fulks
Author photograph by Sandra F. McDonald

This book is a work of fiction. Names, characters, places, and incidents are either the product of the author's imagination or are used fictitiously. Any resemblance to actual events or locales or persons, living or dead, is coincidental.

For Leslie O'Kane and Bruce Comly French

Also By Scott Douglas Gerber

Fiction
The Ivory Tower: A Novel

Nonfiction
The Declaration of Independence: Origins and Impact (editor)
First Principles: The Jurisprudence of Clarence Thomas
Seriatim: The Supreme Court Before John Marshall (editor)
*To Secure These Rights: The Declaration of Independence and Constitutional
    Interpretation*

"Pornography sells women to men as and for sex. It is a technologically sophisticated traffic in women."

— Law Professor Catharine A. MacKinnon

"One man's vulgarity is another man's lyric."

— U.S. Supreme Court Justice John Marshall Harlan II

PROLOGUE
(October)

"Cut!" *Philmore Bottoms shouted. He yanked a Rhode Island Rams baseball cap off his head and pitched it to the floor, knocking over a can of Sprite that sat at his feet. An awkward lurch allowed him to elude the stream of soda rushing at his bargain-basement jogging shoes.* "Jesus Christ, Tiffany, I'm sick and tired of your bullshit! We're supposed to be getting people off here. Look at Peter. He needs to be fluffed again. Jesus Christ. Let's take five, people! . . . And someone clean up this fucking soda." *A forceful kick sent the Sprite can clanking across the room.*

The instant Bottoms called for a break, Tiffany jumped up from the bed where she was lying and wrapped herself in the terrycloth bathrobe that was draped over the chair behind the light standard. She was crying so hard her entire body shook. She ran upstairs to the dressing room at a pace that would have made an Olympic gold medalist proud.

Peter Boy stood naked beside the now-empty bed. He stared blankly into space. "Who's gonna fluff me?" *he asked.*

"How the hell should I know! I'm only the director!" *Bottoms answered, still at the top of his lungs. He paused to compose himself.* "Why don't you ask Vivianna? She's getting paid fifteen hundred bucks. A fluff is the least she can do. She hasn't been in a scene all day. At this rate, she never will be."

Peter Boy reached for a towel and tied it around his taut waist. He left the set in search of Vivianna. He always did what Bottoms told him to do. The Ovulator was a big-time shoot—a two-day shoot with more than one location— and if Bottoms liked him, he might put in a good word for him with Joey Mancini.

And that might lead to more work, including on Co-ed Fever, which was scheduled to shoot next Monday and Tuesday.

A mousy-looking camera guy and a strung-out still-shot guy headed over to the makeshift plywood table next to the EXIT sign and scrounged among plastic dishware and congealed Danish for something to eat while this latest catastrophe on the set was being resolved. First it was Stacy: she didn't seem to want to do two guys. Now it was Tiffany: she didn't seem to want to do anybody. The crew didn't mind the delay, though. They were being paid by the hour.

But Joey Mancini did mind. He shoved his coffee cup into the startled cameraman's hand and made a beeline for the bed where Tiffany and Peter Boy had been performing before Tiffany freaked out.

Bottoms was picking up the goose-down comforter that Tiffany had knocked to the floor in her haste to leave the set.

"What's the problem now, Philmore?" Mancini said. "You know I can't afford these goddamn delays. We're over budget as it is."

Bottoms placed the comforter back on the bed. He switched off the camera lights. He wiped beads of sweat from his brow with the back of his doughy hand. "It's Tiffany," he finally said. "I knew we shouldn't have used her again after Law Clerks in Love." He shook his head in disgust. "I warned you then that she was bad news. Let's send her home. We'd still have Jennifer, Stacy, and Vivianna. They're hot, and Vince and Sal managed to change Stacy's mind about the three-way."

"Tiffany stays on this shoot," Mancini said. "Under no circumstances are you, or anyone else, to send her home. Do you understand me?"

"Yeah, whatever." Bottoms popped open another can of Sprite. He took a long drink. "No offense, Joey, but what's your hang-up on this girl? Sure, she's got a great body—she's got the best legs I've ever seen—but I can find you dozens of pretty girls. And they'll fuck."

Mancini reddened. He jabbed an index finger into his director's chest. "Don't you worry about my so-called 'hang-up,' Philmore. In case you forgot, you no longer have a say in casting decisions. Does Lord of the Flings ring a bell? What a piece of craggy-faced shit that was. It's my goddamn money. You'll use who I tell you to use. Besides, I'll go and have a chat with her. You said that Stacy came around. Tiffany will, too. I guarantee it."

Joey Mancini exited the set to find Tiffany. He ordered Vince Patrone and Sal Chilleri to accompany him.

Philmore Bottoms remained behind, preparing—he hoped—for the next take.

"What the fuck are you doing in here!" Mancini shouted as he burst through the dressing-room door.

Stacy raced from the room.

Vince slapped her on the back of the head when she flashed by.

Sal laughed.

Tiffany was sitting on the floor, sobbing uncontrollably, and staring distantly into the hallway. She pulled shut the collar on her bathrobe. Now only her legs were exposed: her fabulous legs. "Please, let me go home," she whispered. "I won't say anything. I—I promise."

"We've had this conversation already," Mancini said. "Do you want me to have Vince and Sal here pay that boyfriend of yours a visit? He's not difficult to find. I see him every goddamn day. You're costing me money, you stupid bitch, and you're embarrassing me in front of my employees and you're keeping my customers waiting. Law Clerks in Love was a smash. They want more."

"But I only agreed to make one." Tiffany's eyes met Mancini's. Tears caused her mascara to run.

"Things change." Mancini threw Tiffany a towel. "Listen. I'm only gonna say this once: Clean yourself up and be back downstairs in five minutes. If you do well, two might be enough." Mancini turned to leave.

"Do you want us to have a talk with her, boss?" Sal asked, grinning. "You know how much Vince and me like to talk . . . Stacy's bruises barely show."

Vince laughed this time.

"That won't be necessary." Mancini pointed to Tiffany, who was still sitting on the floor. "But if she's not on the set in five minutes, I want you two to go and pay that boyfriend of hers a visit. You know where to find him."

Five minutes later, Tiffany was back on the set.

The camera guy and the still-shot guy grabbed their equipment—a Sony CCDTRV328 camcorder and a Canon EOS digital camera, respectively—and took their places next to the bed where the scene was to be shot.

Tiffany removed her bathrobe and draped it over the chair behind the light standard. She knelt on the bed. She was completely naked.

A still-shot snapped.

Mancini smiled. He moved to within five feet of the bed, barely out of camera range. "That's a good girl." He stared at Tiffany's voluptuous body. *I was right to think I could make her a star,* he said to himself.

Peter Boy pulled Vivianna to her feet, patted her on the behind, and said, "Thanks, babe." He tugged on his erect penis as he made his way across the room. He positioned himself at the edge of the bed, just above Tiffany.

"Facial!" Bottoms said. "Let's make this one a facial!"

Tiffany looked terrified. She turned to Mancini.

"Do it," he said to her.

Tears returned to Tiffany's eyes.

"AAGGHH!" Peter Boy cried out.

Mancini smiled again. He pulled a cigarette from his shirt pocket. He tamped it end over end. "Beautiful. Just beautiful, Tiffany. You're a good girl after all." He threw Tiffany another towel. "Now, if you'll excuse me," he said to his cast and crew. "I've got to get back to Providence. Court starts at 9:00 A.M., sharp."

PART I
Preliminary Motions

CHAPTER ONE

(Four Weeks Earlier)

It was 8:15 on a Monday morning and Sam Grimes was about to head out the door. He'd been up since 6:30. He'd had some coffee and a couple of bagels, and he'd read the *Providence Journal*. The Red Sox had won again last night. Curt Schilling had pitched, so the win came as no surprise to Sam. At 15–3 it looked as if Schilling was well on his way to a second consecutive Cy Young Award. Manny Ramirez got three hits, including a home run. That gave him thirty-six homers on the season. One more and he would be tied with Alex Rodriguez for the American League lead.

Yes indeed, Sam thought, this was shaping up to be quite an exciting couple of months.

Chad Smith was still sleeping, however. He groaned when Sam banged on his door at 7:30 and again at 8:10, but that was about it. He gave no indication of whether he knew why Sam was banging on his door, but they had been through the drill enough that Sam figured he did. Sam had done his duty as a roommate and a co-clerk. He wasn't about to just walk into Chad's room and wake him up. He had tried that once and was embarrassed to find Chad otherwise engaged with some woman he had met at The Hot Club—a local watering hole with the most ridiculous name imaginable—the night before. After that memorable moment, Sam and Chad had agreed that Sam should just bang on Chad's door and leave it at that. Chad Smith wasn't a morning person, and no one—apparently not even their boss, U.S. District Judge Artur Reis—was about to change that.

Sam and Chad lived in an apartment on Thomas Street. Chad was the one who had found it. Sam was grateful that he had. It was a fabulous place. It was directly across the street from the spot where Roger Williams had established the first Baptist congregation in America in 1639 when he had come to Rhode Island to escape religious persecution in Massachusetts. Ever since 1775 the spot had been occupied by the tall, graceful Meeting House of the First Baptist Church in America, designed by Joseph Brown. Roger Williams may have founded Rhode Island, but the Browns, who were leaders in the China trade, had made it flourish. The church, which copied one of several alternative Georgian designs for St. Martin-in-the-Fields in London, was capped by a 185-foot steeple.

The steeple was a breathtaking sight. Legend had it that the builders of the church were out-of-work ship's carpenters, unemployed because of the closure of the port of Boston after the Boston Tea Party. Their knowledge of masts and rigging had enabled them to build the steeple with sufficient sway to prevent it from being blown down in either the gale of 1815, which had devastated Providence, or the hurricane of 1938, which had washed away much of coastal New England. For a history buff like Sam, it was a thrill to look out his window every morning and see such a symbol of the nation's commitment to religious freedom.

Sam made it to the courthouse in time for the 8:30 A.M. pretrial conference on the Mancini case. Another great thing about Sam and Chad's apartment was that it was less than a quarter of a mile away from the big gray slab of concrete where they worked. Consequently, it was an easy jaunt down the hill from their apartment to their place of employ. Sam was certain this fact hadn't been lost on Chad when he had gone apartment hunting the previous summer. Chad was late enough from a quarter of a mile away. Sam shuddered to think how late his roommate would be if he had to drive through rush hour traffic every morning.

Carolyn, Judge Reis's secretary, buzzed Sam into the Judge's outer chambers.

Sam said good morning to her, and then asked if the Judge was ready for the Mancini conference.

"Good morning, Sam," she said. "Yes, he's ready. But one of the lawyers isn't here yet."

"Which one?" Sam asked.

"John Marone, the cute one," she answered with a glint in her eyes.

In addition to being Joey Mancini's lawyer, John Marone was also the son of Anthony Marone, chief justice of the Rhode Island Supreme Court. At least he *was* until he had been forced to resign the previous winter after the ·Providence Journal printed a photograph on page one that showed the esteemed Chief Justice leaving the home of a well-known socialite—not his wife—at two o'clock in the morning, noticeably disheveled. For years, many people had suspected that Anthony Marone did more than play gin rummy with some questionable types on Federal Hill. His resignation, therefore, was greeted with relief by many at the bar and, gossip had it, by most of the Chief Justice's colleagues on the state high bench. The former Chief Justice was now in private practice with his son John. They special-ized in defending the Joey Mancinis of the world.

John Marone was married with three kids, but he was also known to share his father's fondness for the ladies. Given that he had the dark good looks of a movie star, a prominent family name, and money, it had come as no surprise when Sam had learned that Marone did quite well in this regard. Indeed, Sam himself had seen Marone lunching more than once with an attractive young woman. And it was never with the same woman twice.

The Judge popped his head out of his office and said good morning to Sam and to Steve Sutton.

Sutton was an assistant U.S. attorney. An "Attorney for the United States of America," as he, like most AUSAs, liked to remind juries when-ever he got the chance. Sutton was a young guy—he looked about twenty-seven or twenty-eight—so Sam was surprised when he had learned that Lincoln Jenkins, the *real* U.S. Attorney for the District of Rhode

Island—the one appointed by the president—had given Sutton primary responsibility for prosecuting the Mancini case. After all, everyone knew who Joey Mancini was. Sam had expected Mr. Jenkins to assign one of his senior deputies to the case: someone like Lyle Richards, or perhaps Peggy Langston. They had both handled a number of high profile cases in the past, although admittedly none as potentially explosive as *U.S. v. Mancini*.

Perhaps Sutton got the case because he was Mr. Jenkins's son-in-law, Sam said to himself. This was Rhode Island.

"Where's counselor Marone?" the Judge asked. He was in his shirt sleeves. With his broad shoulders and well-defined biceps, the Judge's days as a college sports star didn't seem as long ago as they actually were.

"He's not here yet," Sam answered, standing to his feet. "He must be stuck in traffic. You know how Providence can be on a Monday morning."

Sam had no idea why he was covering for Marone. He had never even met the guy. It must have been habit talking . . . He wondered whether Chad was awake yet.

The Judge looked agitated. Judge Reis was a man of remarkable composure, but one thing that always got his goat was when a lawyer was late. He never said anything about it, but Sam could tell it bugged him. The courts were backlogged enough as it was and stuff like this only made matters worse.

"Carolyn, please give a call to counselor Marone's office to make sure he's on his way," the Judge said. He then went back into his office and closed the door.

Sam and Sutton—and Carolyn, too—sat and waited for John Marone to grace them with his presence.

CHAPTER TWO

Marone arrived at 8:50 A.M. and apologized to Sam and to Sutton for being late. "There was a wreck on Atwells," he said, noticeably short of breath.

Marone may have been short of breath but, Sam thought, Carolyn was right: he also looked like he could give the male models in GQ a run for their money. Sam shot Carolyn a quick wink, and then knocked on Judge Reis's office door and announced that Marone had arrived.

"Good. I'll be with everyone in a few minutes," the Judge said.

This was standard procedure. The Judge always made the lawyers wait a few minutes—even if he wasn't in the middle of anything. Sam suspected that the Judge did this because he wanted to remind the lawyers that *he* was in charge and that the case would proceed in accordance with *his* schedule. A power thing . . .

At precisely 9:00 A.M., the Judge invited them in: Sam, Sutton, Marone, and Holly Curran.

Holly was Judge Reis's courtroom and docket clerk. When she was in the courtroom, she was responsible for delivering the proclamation that opened every court session and for cataloging and securing the exhibits, evidence, and documents that were presented by the lawyers. When she wasn't in the courtroom—like now, for instance—she kept track of the pleadings, motions, orders, and judgments that constituted the Judge's docket, and she also made sure his calendar ran smoothly.

Sam didn't see how it was possible to do all the things Holly had to do, but she managed to do them and do them well. He found it remarkable how she seemed to have the status of every case on the docket committed to memory. He had never, ever seen her need to refer to her notes. *Never, ever.* She made him feel as if he had Alzheimer's.

"Good morning, all. Nice of you to join us, Mr. Marone." There was a hint of sarcasm in the Judge's voice, and it wasn't difficult to tell at whom it was directed.

"Sorry I'm late, Your Honor. There was an accident on Atwells. It was slow going this morning." Marone sounded apologetic, but not intimidated.

"Very well. Let's get to it." The Judge signaled for everyone to take a seat.

He sat behind a big, brown oak desk. It was the same desk he had used when he was a state court judge. It was beat up, but he insisted on keeping it for sentimental reasons. He had the American flag over his right shoulder and a gold oar over his left. The flag told everyone they were in a federal court. The oar symbolized the Court's admiralty jurisdiction. Given that Rhode Island was next to the ocean, the Judge had a number of admiralty cases on his docket.

Marone and Sutton sat in burgundy leather roundabout chairs across the desk from the Judge. Sam and Holly sat on the tan corduroy couch at the other end of the room. It was a big room, so they were pretty far away. The distance reflected their roles. When Sam's and Chad's clerkships had first started and the Judge had informed them that he wanted them to sit in on the pretrial conferences for the cases to which they were individually assigned (Sam and Chad split the cases), Sam had asked what they were supposed to do in the conferences.

"Just listen. So you know what's going on with your case," the Judge had said.

"Should we say anything?" Sam had asked.

"No. Be quiet as a dormouse."

And so Sam was.

The Judge began each pretrial conference by quickly summarizing for everyone what the case was about. Obviously, the lawyers already knew what it was about—they were the ones litigating it—but the Judge wanted them to know that *he* was on top of things. Another power thing, Sam had concluded. Actually, every Friday afternoon the Judge had Sam and Chad brief him on the cases for the upcoming week. *They* summarized the cases for *him* and *he* asked *them* questions about the cases. For Sam, this was one of the best parts of the job, though. The Judge had been a wonderful lawyer, and it was amazing to watch him as he tried to anticipate how the cases were going to unfold. The Judge also knew everyone in the Rhode Island bar. *Everyone.* In fact, the first thing he always wanted to know in the Friday briefings was who the lawyers were. After Sam and Chad told him, he would proceed to give them a quick rundown on the particular lawyer: what his or her specialty was, what his approach was, what his tricks were, and, to be blunt, whether they could trust what he said. There had been many a time when the Judge had told Sam and Chad that they—Sam and Chad—would have to do most of the legal research for a case, because the particular lawyer's brief would undoubtedly be slipshod, if not downright misleading. And the Judge was right. Sam had quickly discovered that some of the briefs were better suited for a creative-writing class than they were for a court of law.

"The defendant, Joseph Paul Mancini, is charged with violating the RICO statute by making and distributing pornographic videos in the New England area. Is that correct, Mr. Sutton?"

"Yes, Your Honor. The grand jury returned an indictment on Wednesday."

"Mr. Marone, how long will the defense need for discovery?"

"A year, Your Honor. We can't possibly be ready in less than a year. Of course, we would ask that Your Honor permit Mr. Mancini to be released into my custody in the interim."

Sam sat quietly—like a dormouse—and watched the Judge roll his eyes.

"You don't really need *a year*, do you Mr. Marone? This strikes me as a straightforward case. First, are the videos obscene? And, second, if they are obscene, did Mr. Mancini produce and market them? There doesn't appear to be anything groundbreaking here. And I assume Mr. Sutton will be quite cooperative in providing any materials you may need to protect your client. Am I representing the government's position fairly, Mr. Sutton?"

Sutton straightened in his chair and answered, unequivocally, "Yes, Your Honor."

Marone interrupted. "With all due respect, Judge, this is a very complicated case. For one thing, we plan to file a motion to dismiss on the grounds that my client has a First Amendment right to produce and market the videos in question. If we lose that motion, we intend to show at trial that Mr. Mancini wasn't involved in producing and marketing any tapes that might fall within the purview of the obscenity law. Both of these defenses will require substantial preparation."

Marone was engaging in the classic lawyer's ploy: he was arguing in the alternative. In other words, if one of his arguments didn't fly, that was okay because he was also arguing the exact opposite . . . Ain't the law grand? Sam said to himself.

"All right, gentlemen," the Judge said. He leaned forward in his chair. "The Court will permit two months for discovery. The Court also sets this Friday morning at 9:00 for Mr. Marone's motion to reconsider the Magistrate's detention order. Is my schedule clear at that time, Holly?"

"We have a motion to dismiss in *Sullivan v. Bank of New England*, Judge," Holly reported from the far reaches of the room. "Nine-thirty should work."

Sam noticed that, once again, Holly hadn't referred to a single note. Not one goddamn note.

"Fine. Nine-thirty it is. That's Friday, September 19th, at 9:30. Is that all, counselors?"

"Yes, Your Honor," Marone and Sutton said.

It would likely be the only time they were in agreement during the entire case.

"Good day then, gentlemen. I'll see you on Friday."

As everyone was leaving, the Judge called Sam back.

"Close the door a minute, Sam. We need to discuss a few things."

The Judge made his way to the overstuffed easy chair across from the couch where Sam and Holly had been sitting. Sam returned to the couch. Just as the Judge sitting across his desk from the lawyers was the routine during pretrial conferences, the more casual arrangement Sam now found himself in was the practice when the Judge was meeting with him or Chad. No power thing needed here. They were on the same team.

"I expected Mr. Marone to announce he was going to file a First Amendment challenge," the Judge said. He traced a fingertip across a coaster-sized bald spot on the crown of his head, as he often did when he was thinking. The bald spot was the only outward concession the Judge had made to his fifty-five years on this earth, and Sam knew how sensitive he was about it. Ex-jocks didn't age without a fight. In the Judge's case, that fight undoubtedly was being waged with daily doses of Rogaine and Propecia. "When you have a moment," he went on, "I'd like you to put together a short memo—one or two pages should suffice—on obscenity and the First Amendment. Nothing fancy, you understand. I'd just like to start my mind working on the question."

"No problem," Sam said. "I should be finished with the McShann memo by the end of the day. I'll jump on this one first thing in the morning. I'll have it to you by Wednesday."

"Great. Of course it goes without saying that we'll want to take even more care than usual with this one. Everyone will be watching. Holly is already getting calls about the case. The combination of sex and the Mob—you know who the defendant's father is—is apparently too much for the press to resist." The Judge looked concerned.

"I understand, Judge. I'll do my best. I'm really looking forward to this one. If memory serves, they taught us in constitutional law class that obscenity is a question of fact for the jury. That means Mr. Marone has no legs for his motion. More importantly, it means we get to watch some movies. I'll bring the popcorn. Do you take butter on yours?"

The concern disappeared from the Judge's face like ice from a thawing street, and he couldn't help but laugh a bit. "Be good now, Sam," he said, shaking his head. "I'll see you later." He reached for his bald spot again. "Oh. One more thing. Please tell Chad I'd like to see him. I want to find out where he's at with the Norwegian Cruise Line case."

◆ ◆ ◆ ◆

"It's show time!" Sam said as he strolled into Chad Smith's cluttered office. There were law books everywhere, including on the floor and the windowsill. "The Judge wants to see you. And guess what? I've been invited to quite a Hollywood screening. It looks like we're going to have to play the videos for the Mancini jury. And since that's my case, I'll have to watch, too."

"You bastard!" Chad said. "I'm working on some friggin' admiralty case and you get to watch stag films. What a gyp." He tossed the case reporter he was reading onto the chair next to him.

Sam couldn't help but notice that his co-clerk and roommate looked awfully tired sitting there behind his overflowing desk with his twenty-four-ounce coffee and two jelly doughnuts. But, clearly, the magic of the moment wasn't lost on him: *U.S. v. Mancini* was the best case on the docket and Sam got it.

"Don't worry, big guy," Sam said. "I'll let you know when the good stuff is on. Besides, this'll be the closest I've been to a woman since Karen and I split up. I could use the company. You're more than covered in that area, as I recall. How is Sherry, by the way? Her name is *Sherry*, isn't it?"

Chad flushed. He nearly elbowed his coffee to the floor. "Hey! Keep it down. I don't want *that* getting around. Suzanne might find out." Chad paused, regained his composure, and said with a grin as big as the dough-nut in his hand, "Besides, you're one to talk. Everybody knows about you and Mary Jackson."

CHAPTER THREE

The Colonial-style house at the end of the cul-de-sac wasn't the largest in the neighborhood, but it was sizable nonetheless. This was The Hamptons. Local zoning regulations forbade the construction of any house with fewer than six bedrooms and four baths. The doctors, lawyers, business executives, and celebrities who called The Hamptons home had made sure of that.

The little girl's room was in the back of the house. Her father had said that the back of the house provided better views of the horse barn. The little girl loved horses. However, that wasn't the real reason her father had put her room in that part of the house.

The little girl's mother had gone up to bed early for the night. She had complained of a headache—she got *lots* of headaches—and had left her husband and daughter alone in the den watching the series finale of M*A*S*H.

The little girl's parents' room was in the front of the house. That was where her mother was now.

The little girl tried to pretend that she was concentrating one hundred percent on the TV show, but she knew that her father was looking in her direction. He usually was, at least when her mother wasn't around. The little girl had purposely chosen to sit on the smallest seat in the room.

Her father clearly didn't approve of the choice. "Why don't you come over and sit on the couch with Daddy, sweetheart?" He cupped a snifter of cognac between his powerful surgeon's hands.

There was no response from the little girl. She continued to stare at the television.

"Did you hear me?" her father said.

"Yeth, Daddy." The little girl had recently lost her first tooth and she had trouble pronouncing her s's. She grabbed her teddy bear by the arm and joined her father on the couch.

Hawkeye Pierce and B.J. Hunnicut were engaged in a poignant conversation about how much each had meant to the other.

The little girl wished that she had a friend who cared that much about her. Friends like that would do anything for one another.

It always started the same way. The little girl's father would put his arm around his daughter and pull her close. Lots of fathers did that. The little girl had seen her uncle do it a bunch of times with her cousin. Her cousin didn't seem to mind, and it made the little girl feel bad that she minded when her father did it with her. It made the little girl feel even worse when her father would tell her that she was a bad girl for not wanting to snuggle with him. She always relented, though. She didn't want to be a bad girl.

The little girl's father also would tell her that she was a bad girl for not wanting him to kiss her goodnight. "All good girls let their daddies kiss them goodnight," he would say.

She always ended up letting him kiss her.

"All good girls let their daddies put them in their jammies," he would then say.

She always ended up letting him undress her, too.

However, she had resisted the first time her father had tried to touch her in her special place. "Mth Ward said no one ith supposed to touch uth there."

Mrs. Ward was the little girl's kindergarten teacher. New York law mandated that all kindergarten students were to be instructed about what to do if an adult tried to touch them in their special places. No separate instruction had been provided if that adult was the child's father.

"It's different if I'm your father, sweetheart. You don't want to be a bad girl, do you?"

"No, Daddy," a six-year-old Mary Jackson had said in a voice barely loud enough to hear. "I wanna be a good girl."

◆ ◆ ◆ ◆

Sam Grimes arrived at the courthouse early on Tuesday morning. He was excited about work. The Mancini trial promised to be the trial of the decade in Rhode Island—perhaps in all of New England—and he was intimately involved with it. The case was straight out of Hollywood: sex, gangsters, a flamboyant lawyer, and, no doubt, plenty of surprises.

Sam bought a cup of coffee from the courthouse snack bar, dropped off his briefcase in his office, and then headed up to the law library to work on the bench memo for Judge Reis.

The courthouse library was an extensive one. It occupied two large ornate rooms and was lined with case reporters and law journals. It also was equipped with five computer terminals. In this day and age—the age of Microsoft, Intel, AOL, Cisco Systems—almost all essential legal research materials were available on computer databases, specifically on Lexis and Westlaw. The databases were expensive but efficient. With a couple of well-constructed keyword commands, countless hours of wading through law books could be avoided. It was quite a system. Sam preferred the old-fashioned law book approach, though. There was just something strange to him—something artificial—about reading a judicial opinion or a law journal article from a computer screen and turning pages by pushing a button on a keyboard or, worse yet, by clicking a mouse. As the son of an English professor, Sam had been taught to love *books*. Indeed, almost his entire life had revolved around books. At home with his parents, in college and law school, and now here in Providence: Sam Grimes always had been surrounded by books.

Sam began his research on the constitutional status of pornography with a quick review of Laurence Tribe's hornbook on constitutional law. Tribe taught con law at Harvard, and his hornbook was first-rate. Hornbooks were legal encyclopedias. They provided a good overview of a subject, especially a subject as widely debated as pornography and the First Amendment. Obviously, Sam wouldn't want to limit his research to Professor Tribe's hornbook, but it was a good place to start. It would help to shape his thinking on the question. He would then go on and read the relevant cases, many of which were discussed in the hornbook. In an area such as pornography, the U.S. Supreme Court had said a lot. Naturally, those were the cases to which Sam would turn, given that the Supreme Court was the highest court in the land. All lower courts—including Judge Reis's—were required to abide by the Supreme Court's decisions, even if they didn't like them.

Sam found the law to be pretty much as he had told the Judge after yesterday's pretrial conference. Consequently, after only eight or nine hours of reading cases, he was ready to write the bench memo. He went back to his office with his notes and began.

MEMORANDUM

TO: Judge Reis
FROM: Samuel D. Grimes
DATE: September 16
RE: United States v. Mancini

Facts

The defendant, Joseph Paul Mancini, is accused by the United States government of making and distributing pornographic videos in violation of federal law. Mancini has been indicted under the federal Racketeer Influenced and Corrupt Organizations Act (RICO), a statute designed to curb organized crime. RICO prohibits any individual associated with an enterprise from engaging in racketeering activities. In essence, Mancini is accused of using his company, "Midnight Productions," to make dirty movies and sell them all over the region. "Joey" Mancini is the son of "Iron" Mike Mancini, the alleged crime boss of New England. Justice Department reports reveal that the making and selling of "adult" movies is a five-billion-dollar-a-year business in the United States and that organized crime controls much of that business.

The FBI has confiscated some five hundred videotapes and DVDs from video stores in every state in New England. The videos bear Mancini's "Midnight Productions" imprint. They are alleged to portray all sorts of hardcore sex acts, ranging from explicit scenes of sexual intercourse between a man and a woman to so-called crimes against nature involving women and various animals. The videos in question have titles such as "The Wedding Night," "Star Whores: Episode II," "Paris Hilton: Uncensored," and "A Girl and Her Dog."

Law

One of the most difficult tasks the U.S. Supreme Court has undertaken over the years is that of determining the First Amendment limitations on local, state, and federal laws regulating the production, advertisement, distribution, and sale of obscene books, magazines, films, and videos. Prior to the Supreme Court's entry into this field in 1957, most American courts had adhered to a legal definition of obscenity derived from the 1868 English case of <u>Regina v. Hicklin</u>. The <u>Hicklin</u> test was "whether the tendency of the matter charged as obscenity is to deprave and corrupt those whose minds are open to such immoral influences, and into whose hands a publication of this sort might fall." By the mid-twentieth century, this standard was widely regarded as unduly restrictive of artistic and literary expression. The primary objection was that the test sought to measure obscenity with reference to its supposed impact on the most vulnerable members of society (e.g., children). Under the <u>Hicklin</u> test, James Joyce's <u>Ulysses</u>, to name but one notable example, was banned.

The Prurient Interest Test

In <u>Roth v. United States</u> (1957), the Supreme Court handed down new legal guidelines for obscenity. Writing for the majority, Justice William Brennan expressed the view that obscenity is "utterly without redeeming social importance" and thus entitled to no First Amendment protection. He rejected the essence of the <u>Hicklin</u> standard, however, and stated the new test as "whether to the average person, applying contemporary community standards, the dominant theme of the material taken as a whole appeals to a prurient interest."

In spite of its apparent simplicity, the <u>Roth</u> test drew the Court into an interpretive quagmire from which it has not yet emerged. Virtually every term in the new obscenity test proved elusive. For instance, the Court could never reach full agreement on what constitutes an appeal to a "prurient interest." The term "redeeming social importance" also failed to generate consensus. A majority of the Court, in the years immediately following <u>Roth</u>, could not even agree on whether the term "community" referred to the nation as a whole or to individual states and localities. Although most of the justices believed that hardcore pornography was not entitled to First Amendment protection, they were unable to define its meaning. Justice Potter Stewart's well-known retort, "I know it when I see it," illustrates the difficulty of precise definition in this area. However, the Court did agree that the First Amendment prohibits making mere private possession of obscene material a crime. See <u>Stanley v. Georgia</u> (1969). In other words, the Court said that a person could *possess* obscene materials in his home, he just couldn't *acquire* them—if that makes any sense.

The Miller Test

When Chief Justice Warren Burger came to the Supreme Court in 1969, he was determined to limit the protection afforded to pornography. In <u>Miller v. California</u> (1973), Burger developed a more restrictive test than <u>Roth</u>. He explicitly rejected the "utterly without redeeming social importance" standard advanced by the Warren Court, for example. (The pornography industry had boomed under <u>Roth</u>, primarily because almost nothing could be said to be *utterly* without redeeming social importance.) Nevertheless, the new Burger Court guidelines were far from clear. The Court had indicated that the applicable "community standards" under the new test were local, or at most statewide, standards. But when authorities in a rural Georgia town attempted to ban the Jack Nicholson/Ann-Margret movie "Carnal Knowledge," the Court said local standards could not do that. See <u>Jenkins v. Georgia</u> (1974).

Conclusion

The Supreme Court's obscenity jurisprudence is a mess. This much is clear, however: Whether something is obscene or not is, initially, a question of fact for the jury. The Court—even the conservative Rehnquist Court—has *always* held that. This means the videos must be played for the jury.

S.D.G.

It was 10:30 at night by the time Sam finished the Mancini memo. He had gotten so caught up in it that he forgot to eat. He was starving. He printed three copies of the memo on the LaserJet. He placed one copy in his own file and left another in the Judge's in-box. He put the third copy on Chad's desk. He grabbed a meatball sub from Zero's sub shop, and headed for home to eat and unwind. Chad was watching TV when he arrived.

"Where have you been?" Chad asked.

"Working on the Mancini memo. I guess I lost track of time." Sam opened the refrigerator and noticed that Chad had bought a six-pack of JW Dundee's Honey Brown Lager. A cold beer sure would go good about now, Sam thought. "Chad," he called out. "Can I bum a beer? It would definitely hit the spot with my meatball sub."

"Help yourself."

Sam knew Chad would say that. There was an unwritten rule among roommates: share the beer. Milk, orange juice, Pepsi: except in dire straits, you drank only what you bought. But beer was different, especially after a long day at the office.

Sam carried his sandwich and beer into the living room to watch TV with Chad.

Chad was watching the Red Sox game. "How'd the memo go?" he asked, without averting his eyes from the screen. The score was tied 2-2 in the bottom of the ninth.

"Pretty well," Sam answered. He took a bite of his sandwich, and then washed it down with a gulp of beer. "I left a copy of it on your desk. As you'll see, the law is pretty straightforward. Sexually explicit material is usually protected by the First Amendment, but it can't rise to the level of the obscene. Whether something is obscene or not is initially a question of fact for the jury. That means we've got to show the videos. Or at least selected examples of them. That should draw a crowd in the courtroom."

"Yeah. We should sell tickets. Especially if we show Paris Hilton's bedroom tape. I heard Howard Stern call it 'the greatest movie ever made' on the radio the other day. That guy's a genius. And Miss Hilton ain't too shabby herself." Chad looked at Sam and smiled. "By the way," he added, "some of the guys are meeting at The Hot Club for a drink at eleven. Billy is going to try to beat Alan at pool again. There's twenty bucks on the game. Do you want to go?"

David Ortiz singled in the winning run the moment Chad finished his question.

"No thanks," Sam said. "I'm beat. Have fun, though. But don't do anything I wouldn't do."

Chad rose from his chair and smiled again. Sam knew his roommate wasn't smiling about Ortiz's hit. No, Chad was smiling because he knew Sam knew he was going trolling for women.

Sam was going to bed. It had been a long day—a productive day, but a long day nonetheless.

He glanced at the clock above the television. It was 11:05. He thought about calling Mary, but decided it was too late.

◆ ◆ ◆ ◆

"Two nights in a row, huh?" Billy Hewitt said.

"Yeah." Chad Smith took the seat across from Billy. "Where's Alan?"

Billy and Alan Hewitt were the brothers of Chad's girlfriend Suzanne. Billy said, "In the VIP room."

"Why are you sitting here, then?" Chad wiggled out of his jacket and placed it on the seat next to him.

"Because he's got company."

"Who?"

"'Rebecca,' I think her name is. She's new. Does it matter?"

"I guess not." Chad searched the room. "It isn't Sherry, is it?" He reddened.

Billy laughed. "You got a thing for Sherry?" He signaled for a waitress. "Like I said, it's a new girl. Sherry's been here for almost a year."

"How do you know that?"

"Because I spend a lot of time here."

A waitress pushed her way through the crowd. She had more guys grabbing for her ass than a running back during the Super Bowl. She never stopped smiling, though. It was her job to act as if she liked it.

She reached the booth at which Chad and Billy were sitting. She smiled for real this time. "I was hoping I'd see you again."

It was Sherry.

Billy said, "I'm here all the time."

"I meant *him*." Sherry's eyes were locked on Chad's. She placed a gin and tonic on the table in front of him.

Billy laughed again. "I don't know, Sher. He is dating my sister."

Sherry said, "Who said anything about dating?"

Chad almost lost it right then and there.

Billy said, "You wanna lap dance, Chad? My trea—"

"Sure," Chad said.

Billy said, "Don't be afraid to take a minute to think about it."

Chad waited a beat. "S-U-R-E." He rose from his seat and followed Sherry into a private room.

Thirty minutes later, Chad rejoined Billy in the booth.

Billy asked, "How was it?"

Chad answered, "Unfuckingbelievable."

"I'm glad you enjoyed it."

"Where's Alan?" Chad reached for his gin and tonic. The ice had melted in the time he had been away. He could barely taste the gin at this point.

"Still in the VIP room. I doubt we'll see him again tonight. He likes to sample the full menu."

Chad sat back and enjoyed the show. A statuesque blonde in a skimpy navy uniform shook her butt to 50 Cent's *In Da Club*. She took a full minute to unbutton each button. She removed her shirt and twirled it in the air like a cowboy doing rope tricks at a rodeo.

Chad leaned over and said to Billy, "Sam doesn't know what he's missing."

CHAPTER FOUR

Camille's Roman Garden was situated on Bradford Street in a large mid-nineteenth-century Italianate house that had served as a restaurant since the early 1920s. Camille's was a typical old-style Italian restaurant. It was cluttered with statues and paintings, and it had numerous private dining rooms behind trellises on which artificial grapevines grew. There were many superb Italian restaurants on Federal Hill, but Camille's was the landmark.

Chief Judge Francis Conigliero arrived at the restaurant at 7:15 P.M. He was precisely on time. Clearly, even a federal judge knew better than to keep Iron Mike Mancini waiting.

The Chief Judge informed the maitre d' whom he was meeting for dinner. He was promptly escorted to a private dining room in the rear of the restaurant. It was Iron Mike's special room. The walls were lined with photographs of the legendary Mafia boss dining with all manner of New England politicians and business leaders. The table at which Iron Mike dined at least three times a week was clothed in traditional red-and-white checkerboard linen, and it was decorated with three softly burning candles. For added elegance, a single red rose in a thin crystal vase served as a centerpiece.

The room was off-limits to everyone but Iron Mike and his special guests. It was here, over vintage bottles of Chianti and steady streams of Italian delicacies, where the powerful Don met with people who didn't feel comfortable being seen coming and going from The Players' Club around the corner. Chief Judge Francis Conigliero was clearly one of those people.

"*Buono sera*, Don Mancini," the Chief Judge said. He bowed his head slightly as a sign of respect.

"*Buono sera*, Francis," Iron Mike said. He signaled for Silvio Patrone to help the Chief Judge with his chair. "Please. Sit. Have some wine." Iron Mike took a long drag on a cigarette.

Silvio shook his head in disapproval.

Iron Mike smiled at the reaction. He said to his distinguished guest, "Silvio is worse than my wife when it comes to my smoking." He coughed, and then coughed again. "He's a good friend, though. He's got my best interests at heart. Good friends are hard to find these days." He took a sip of Chianti. "Now, what can I do for you, Francis? Why did you need to see me on such a lovely evening as this? You should be home sitting on the balcony with your beautiful wife, enjoying this beautiful weather."

The Chief Judge said, "*I* was supposed to get Ben Sizemore's seat when he retired. Artie Reis has been on the federal bench for less than two years. Can't something be done? It was supposed to be *my* seat. It's a natural progression for me."

Benjamin Nash Sizemore had occupied Rhode Island's seat on the U.S. Court of Appeals for the First Circuit for the past quarter century. The First Circuit was the court above the one on which both Francis Conigliero and Artur Reis served, the U.S. District Court for the District of Rhode Island. Iron Mike knew that much. However, he didn't know much else about which the Chief Judge was complaining.

Iron Mike studied the Chief Judge's face. He never did care for Francis Conigliero. He found him too power hungry and too caught up in the trappings of office. He had secured a federal district court judgeship for the man strictly as a favor to his wife's brother. Apparently, Conigliero used to be the lawyer for Iron Mike's brother-in-law. In Rhode Island, that was almost family.

"How do you know this?" Iron Mike finally asked. "And why do you care? It seems to me that you already have a nice position: a lifetime appointment as the chief judge of Rhode Island's federal trial court."

"Tommy—Senator Tomasino—told me this morning," the Chief Judge said. "As to why I care, it's because only Court of Appeals judges get appointed to the U.S. Supreme Court these days." The Chief Judge reached for his wineglass. His hand was trembling. Apparently, the mere mention of the possibility of a seat on the highest court in the land was more than his heart could bear. "Just think how much I could do for you there."

"Perhaps Senator Tomasino can be of some assistance," was all Iron Mike said about the matter. He nodded to Silvio. "Please tell Camille that we're ready for the first course."

"*Grazie*, Don Mancini," the Chief Judge said. "*Ringraziamenti*."

The two powerful men ate their dinner in silence. Nothing more was said about the First Circuit vacancy. Nothing more needed to be said.

After Chief Judge Conigliero had exited the restaurant, Silvio Patrone returned to Iron Mike's private dining room with John Marone in tow.

"Good evening, Don Mancini," Marone said. He, too, bowed his head as a sign of respect.

"*Buono sera*, John." Iron Mike motioned to Silvio, who quickly poured a cappuccino for the well-dressed lawyer. "How's your father? How's my favorite *avvocato*—my favorite lawyer?"

"He is well, Don Mancini. He is well." Marone stirred his cappuccino with a sterling silver sugar spoon, and then took a sip. He had always enjoyed Camille's cappuccino. It was the best in the city. "He says you and *Signora* Mancini must come to the house for supper soon. He says it has been too long."

"*Si*. It *has* been too long. Your father has always been a good friend to me, and to my family. As have you, John. As have you."

Marone bowed his head again.

Iron Mike continued, "I know you're busy, John. And I know it's late. But, please, tell an old man how things are shaping up with his son's case. My wife. She worries. Joey is still ten years old to her: still a little boy in short pants and tennis shoes. You know how mothers are."

"My mother is the same way with me, *signore*. And I've got children of my own now." Marone took another sip of cappuccino. "As far as Joey's case is concerned, I expect we'll win the motion to reconsider the detention order. But I've got to be honest with you, Don Mancini. I'm concerned about the trial. He did do it, you know. He did produce and market the videos."

The two men sat in silence for several awkward moments.

Iron Mike finally said, "Why does he do it, John? Why does he make those filthy movies?"

Marone clearly didn't know how to respond. He never before had been asked his *personal* opinion by Don Mancini. His *legal* opinion? Yes. Don Mancini had asked him for that on many occasions over the years. But his *personal* opinion? Never. *Iron* Mike was loath to reveal any weakness to anyone—no matter how trivial or how understandable—and requests for *personal* opinions did precisely that.

Marone said quietly, "I don't know why he does it, Don Mancini. Why do I drink ten cups of coffee a day? Why does my wife buy a new dress every time she passes *Signora* Lasorda's dress shop? Why do my children insist on eating peanut butter and jelly sandwiches for breakfast, lunch, and dinner? Why do any of us do anything?"

Iron Mike nodded, but said nothing more about this personal matter. "Let me know what happens at the hearing."

Marone said he would and then left.

Iron Mike reached inside his shirt pocket and pulled out a cigarette. Despite having been recently diagnosed with lung cancer, he couldn't quit smoking. Or at least he *wouldn't* quit. He turned to Silvio Patrone, who was once again shaking his head in disapproval, and said, "I want you to go down to the courthouse this week and get a feel for the place—for where Judge Reis's courtroom is, for how many marshals are on duty. Those sorts of things. The information might be useful to us."

◆ ◆ ◆ ◆

Vince Patrone lifted himself off the young woman and then fumbled for his pants. He hadn't bothered to remove his shirt. He had taken hers off, though. Her tits were too perfect to resist.

Don Mancini would never have allowed Vince to have had sex with the young woman, but Vince worked for Joey now. Joey didn't give a shit about that sort of thing. Joey didn't give a shit about anything, or anyone.

The only part of Vince's late-night escapade to which Joey might have objected was that Vince got to fuck the girl before Joey did. She wouldn't say anything, though. Vince was certain of that. Tiffany was a good girl.

CHAPTER FIVE

Sam Grimes headed out of his apartment at 7:30 A.M. He gave Chad Smith's door a quick bang before he did. As usual, there was no response.

As Sam crossed Main Street, he could see that reporters were already crowded around the front entrance to the courthouse. No doubt everybody wanted to make certain they got a good seat for the hearing. Joey Mancini's famed Enzo Ferrari—Chad had said it was the only one of its kind in the state—rested conspicuously in a parking lot full of Fords and Hondas.

Sam snuck around to the back of the building, emptying his pockets and saying hello to Jerry Cushing, one of the assistant U.S. marshals, as he walked through the metal detector that marked the rear entrance.

"It looks like we've got a circus on our hands," Sam said.

"You're telling me," Jerry said. He retrieved Sam's keys from a small wicker basket and returned them to the young law clerk. "Marshal Lawton wants us to triple-up on security in Judge Reis's courtroom this morning. You never know what might happen when a Mancini's involved. That family makes me nervous, if you know what I mean."

"I know what you mean." Sam stuffed his keys back into his pocket. "But the Judge wants us to keep a lid on that kind of talk. We don't want to give Mr. Marone an easy basis for appeal. I can hear him arguing to the First Circuit now: 'The trial was conducted in an environment of gossip and innuendo, which unfairly prejudiced my client.' The scary thing is, he'd probably win the appeal. That's why the Judge wants us to keep a lid on the loose talk."

"Got ya, Sam. I'll do my best to keep folks quiet."

"Thanks, Jerry. Now I've got to get to it. I'm giving odds that the Judge is already here. I'll see you in the courtroom a little later."

Sure enough, the Judge had arrived early to prepare for the hearing. He had spoken to Marshal Lawton the previous afternoon to arrange for extra security. He had issued clear instructions: Order was to be maintained in *his* courtroom. He wanted the assistant marshals to be particularly vigilant about keeping cameras—both TV and still—out of the way. To Judge Reis, this meant keeping them out of the courtroom altogether. The press would scream bloody murder and raise all manner of First Amendment objections, but the law was clear on the point: It was well within a trial judge's discretion to ban cameras from a potentially sensational trial. Not everything needed to be broadcast live and in living color. After all, the defendant's constitutional right to a fair trial was at stake. Judge Reis had told Sam earlier in the week that he predicted that one day soon most trials would be broadcast live on TV. "All those cable channels need something to televise," he had said. "We first saw evidence of that with the O.J. Simpson trial in the 1990s. The Scott Peterson and Michael Jackson trials confirmed it." But the Judge had also said he would resign before he would let his courtroom become a live feed for Court TV.

"Good morning, Sam," the Judge said the moment he saw his law clerk. "How does it look out there?"

"Good morning, Judge," Sam said, smiling. "I checked the courtroom a minute ago. It looks like Barnum and Bailey's, that's how it looks. There are more reporters out there than I expected. And I expected *a lot.* I think I even saw some national news people. I could swear I spotted Dan Abrams in the crowd. You know, the legal affairs correspondent for MSNBC."

The Judge's brows furrowed. "Well, they had better keep quiet, Dan Abrams included. I won't tolerate any disruptions in *my* courtroom. Are counsel here?"

Before Sam could answer, Holly Curran knocked on the door. The door to the Judge's private chambers was open, but Holly plainly wanted to show the appropriate deference nonetheless.

"Good morning, gentlemen," she said. "I just wanted to let you know that everyone is here and that we're ready when you are."

"Very well, Holly," the Judge said. "Is Judy here?"

Judy Bloom was the court stenographer. The Judge always wanted everything in place before he went on the bench, and today—especially today—was no exception.

"Yes, sir," Holly said. "Judy is here. The attorneys are here. Mr. Mancini is here. Three assistant marshals are here. Hey, we've even got dozens of reporters for your entertainment pleasure."

Holly issued these last remarks in her typical tongue-in-cheek manner. Given the pressures of the moment, Sam could tell that the Judge appreciated her good humor. The Judge and his staff could always count on Holly to cut the tension.

"Thank you, Holly," the Judge said with a warm smile. "I'll put my robe on and be right out."

◆ ◆ ◆

"Run, Forrest, run! Run, Forrest, run!"

Damn college kids, Silvio Patrone said to himself as he barreled down Angell Street on the east side of Providence. Brown University—one of the nation's most prestigious institutions of higher education—was on his left. Don't they have anything better to do than watch old Tom Hanks movies?

He, on the other hand, was wheezing so hard that he thought he might be having a heart attack. He was getting too old for this sort of thing. Sprinting down the street on the way to a job was a younger man's game, a game better suited for the likes of his brother Vince.

Silvio still hadn't figured out whether Vince had gone to work for Joey for the power or the women. Silvio knew that his younger brother had always resented the fact that he didn't have the access to Don Mancini that Silvio enjoyed. However, Silvio also knew that Vince—like Joey himself—had always liked the ladies.

It didn't really matter, though. Don Mancini had asked Silvio to scope out the scene at the courthouse, and what Don Mancini wanted, Don Mancini got. Nobody knew *that* better than Silvio Patrone.

CHAPTER SIX

Judge Artur Reis arrived in the courtroom through his private entrance at 8:30 A.M. (The motion to dismiss in *Sullivan v. Bank of New England* had been rescheduled. Again. One of the lawyers had asked for more time. *Again.*)

Sam Grimes scanned the courtroom to see who was present. Most of his fellow law clerks were in attendance. There was an informal commandment among the law clerks in the building—"Thou shalt keep thine brothers and sisters apprised of the exciting cases before thine judge"—and Sam had sent them all an e-mail to let them know about the Mancini hearing. No one had time to watch much of the action—no matter how exciting it might be—but they all liked to get a taste of what was going on. It was a great educational experience—not to mention great theater—and the main reason young lawyers wanted to clerk was for the educational experience. Sam even saw Chad in the audience. His hair was wet. He probably had been awake for all of ten minutes. He nodded as Sam caught his eye, and Sam replied in kind.

Holly Curran shot to her feet and cried out, "All rise! Oyez! Oyez! Oyez! All persons having business before the Honorable, the United States District Court for the District of Rhode Island, Artur Reis presiding, are admonished to draw near and give their attention, for the Court is now sitting. God save the United States and this Honorable Court."

The Judge took his seat at the bench. "You may be seated," he said to the capacity crowd.

Everybody sat.

The case was underway.

A tingle raced through Sam's body like electricity through a live wire.

"Madam clerk, may I please see the file for *United States v. Joseph Paul Mancini?*"

Holly handed the file to the Judge. It was already a thick file. The Judge thumbed through it. This was all for show. Everyone—especially the Judge—knew why he was there.

Judge Reis closed the file, placed it neatly on the leather blotter in front of him, and lifted his eyes to John Marone. "The Court is ready to hear the defense's motion to reconsider the Magistrate's detention order. You may proceed, Mr. Marone."

"Thank you, Your Honor."

Marone was looking good, as usual. He was wearing a brown Italian suit, an ecru cotton shirt, a tan silk tie with matching kerchief, and brown tassel loafers. His thick black hair was slicked straight back.

Sam could see that several women in the audience were whispering to one another as Marone was about to begin. They were undoubtedly talking about how good-looking the defendant's lawyer was.

"Maybe he does taxes, too," Sam thought he heard one woman say. "I could sure use an audit."

Marone gripped the podium. He directed his attention to the bench. "May it please the Court," he said in a strong voice. "The defense moves that Joseph Paul Mancini be released until trial. As this Court is aware, my client has been locked away in the Marshal's Office for over a week. There's no basis for this. Mr. Mancini has substantial ties to the community: he's lived in Rhode Island all of his life, he owns a home in the state, and his family resides here. There's no risk of flight. He's not charged with a violent crime. In short, there's absolutely no reason he should be forced to wait in a holding cell for what could be several months before he receives his day in court." Marone paused, brushed his hands through his thick hair, and then added, "We also request, Your Honor, given that Mr. Mancini has no prior criminal record and that he's not charged with a violent offense, that bail be waived. Thank you very much."

Marone released his grip on the podium. He strode back to his seat at the defense table. His argument had been brief and to the point. It couldn't have taken more than two minutes. Joey Mancini, dressed to the nines like his lawyer, sat expressionless during the argument. There was no way of knowing what he was thinking.

Sam took a quick sip of water, and then continued watching the best show in town.

"Mr. Sutton, does the government wish to respond?" the Judge asked.

Obviously, the government wished to respond. Judge Reis knew that, but it was his job to ask the question.

"Yes, Your Honor," Steve Sutton answered, rising to his feet. He made his way to the podium. "*The People* oppose the defense's motion to reconsider Magistrate Decordova's pretrial detention order. Mr. Mancini is a very wealthy man. We feel there's a substantial risk he'll take flight if he's released pending trial. Given who his father is—"

The Judge interrupted Sutton—*the People's* lawyer—in mid-sentence. "May I see both attorneys at the bench?"

It wasn't really a question, Sam knew.

Sutton and Marone knew it, too. They came forward. The courtroom grew silent.

The Judge spoke at sidebar in a hushed, yet forceful voice.

Sam was close enough to hear every word.

The Judge said, "Mr. Sutton, I hope you weren't going to say that Mr. Mancini's father is the crime boss of New England. He's never been convicted of that. I should know. When I was a state court judge, I presided over a trial on that very question. If you can one day secure a conviction along those lines, that's fine. But until you do, I won't tolerate gossip and innuendo in my courtroom. Mr. Mancini is charged with a federal crime, and the Constitution guarantees him a fair trial. I intend to make certain he receives one." The Judge paused, and then said, while looking Sutton directly in the eyes, "Am I making myself clear, counselor?"

"Yes, Your Honor. Perfectly clear." Sutton sounded as if he felt two inches tall.

"Very well," the Judge said. "You may return to your places, gentlemen."

Marone had already won one round, and he hadn't needed to say a word by way of objection. The Judge had obviously been serious when he had said this case would need to be handled with kid gloves.

Sam wondered if Iron Mike was in the courtroom. He didn't know what Iron Mike looked like, so he had no idea. He scanned the courtroom any-way, hoping to spot someone who looked like a crime boss . . . He had seen too many movies.

"As I was saying, Your Honor," Sutton said, plainly doing his best to appear unfazed by what had just transpired, "the People oppose the defen-dant's motion. We have reason to fear that a defendant of Mr. Mancini's wealth and station will flee if he's not held pending trial. Justice demands that the motion be denied. The People deserve to have this case come to trial. We respectfully request that you affirm Magistrate Decordova's well-reasoned detention order. Thank you very much."

The Judge disposed of the motion immediately from the bench. Sometimes he took motions under advisement, studied them, and then ruled at a later date. This motion was surprisingly straightforward, however.

"The Court finds that the defendant poses no substantial threat to the community and that there is no substantial risk of flight pending trial. The defense's motion for release pending trial is thereby granted, provided that a one-million-dollar bond is posted. This Court is adjourned." Judge Reis sounded his gavel.

"All rise!" Holly Curran cried out.

Everyone stood while the Judge exited through his private door.

Sam Grimes followed closely behind him.

Silvio Patrone watched from the back row while the Judge and his law clerk left the courtroom. The Judge was a large man, Silvio noted. He appeared to be about six feet two and to weigh about two hundred and twenty pounds. He wasn't fat, though. He was muscular—like an athlete. Silvio would need to use a gun, then. A gun didn't care how big a person was, or *who* he was. Experience—*plenty* of experience—had taught Silvio that.

◆ ◆ ◆ ◆

"I won't be needing these anymore," Joey Mancini said. He tossed a well-read stack of news magazines into the wastebasket behind the counter where Jerry Cushing was standing. He flashed the assistant U.S. marshal a condescending look, and then retrieved his wallet, watch, and keys from the plastic inventory pouch in Jerry's right hand.

Jerry didn't say a word.

John Marone entered the Marshal's Office. "I posted the bond, Joey. Are you ready to go?"

"Damn straight." Mancini glared at Jerry again. "I'll see you at the movies."

Marone grabbed Mancini's arm before his client could say something else he might come to regret. He led him to the door. "Let's go, Joey." He turned to Jerry. "Have a nice weekend."

Jerry said, "Thanks, Mr. Marone. I hope you have a nice weekend as well. You, too, Mr. Mancini. And please, stay out of trouble."

Mancini and Marone exited the Federal Building. They pushed their way through a throng of reporters. "No comment," Marone said more than once.

Mancini squinted from the sun. Ten days was a long time to be locked up. He said, "You got a cigarette?"

Marone reached into his shirt pocket and pulled out a pack of Camels. He lit one, handed it to Mancini, and then lit another one for himself. He took a drag on a Turkish Gold, sucking the nicotine deep into his lungs. After hearing about Iron Mike's cancer diagnosis from his father the night before, Marone had promised himself he would quit. Perhaps after the trial . . .

He said, "Jerry Cushing's advice back there about staying out of trouble this weekend is good advice, Joey. As your lawyer, I recommend that you take it."

Mancini grinned like a know-it-all brat in a high school class. "I always stay out of trouble, John. You know that. It's assholes like that shit-for-brains magistrate and that lard-ass guard back there that give me trouble, not to mention those prissy moralists over at the FBI. Can't they think of better ways to spend their time than harassing me about my movies? There's real crime out there. I should know. My father's up to his elbows in much of it."

Several minutes passed in silence.

"Here's your car," Marone finally said. He watched his client settle into the driver's seat of the $600,000 sports car and switch on the ignition. "What are your plans for the weekend?"

"Nothing special," Mancini said over the blaring engine. "Just a little business, that's all. Ten days is a long time to go without doing a little business."

CHAPTER SEVEN

Chad Smith was slapping together a stack of ham-and-cheese sandwiches when Sam Grimes burst through the apartment door.

"Where have you been?" Chad asked. "You're cutting it close. The game starts at one."

"I went for a quick jog," Sam answered.

Sam didn't want to give Chad any more ammunition to tease him with about Mary—like the fact that he had been trying to *hand deliver* a piece of chocolate cake to her on a Saturday morning!—so he decided not to mention *where* he had jogged to.

And Chad didn't press him on the matter. He was plainly too hopped up about the Red Sox game to care. "Are Billy and Alan out there?"

"Yeah." Sam stole a piece of ham from the counter and popped it into his mouth.

Billy and Alan Hewitt were going to the baseball game with Sam and Chad. Sam wasn't too excited about that fact, but they had asked Chad if they could go. Chad couldn't say no. He was dating their sister.

Billy and Alan were too much the spoiled rich kids for Sam's tastes. They lived off their father's fame and fortune. Billy was twenty-six and Alan was twenty-four, but they both still lived at home. Alan had flunked out of law school last year, and Billy had done the same the year before. Flunking out of law school was difficult to do—especially at Southern New England School of Law, where they had gone. Sam wasn't talking Harvard here. The tough thing about law school was getting in. Once you were in, you were pretty much set. Unless you were Billy and Alan Hewitt. It wasn't that they were dumb. They were just lazy. They were driving everyone to the game in one of their father's Rolls-Royces. At least that should be interesting. Sam had never ridden in a Rolls before.

Boston was only forty-five minutes from Providence. Consequently, they made it in plenty of time for the game. Sam used to go to Red Sox games all the time when he was at Harvard, but this was his first game since he had started clerking.

They parked the Rolls—a Silver Seraph with more gadgets in it than most people had in their houses—in an indoor garage about two blocks from the ballpark. They walked up Boylston Street, passed about a million vendors—sausage, peanut, pennant, ball cap: you name it and there was someone selling it—and then there she was. Fenway Park. She was as beautiful as Sam remembered her. Fenway—the oldest ballpark in the nation still in use—was a shrine to diehard fans like Sam. At Fenway, baseball was played as it had been meant to be played: there was no Astroturf and every seat in the house was a good one.

The Red Sox pummeled the Milwaukee Brewers 12 to 3, so Sam, Chad, Billy, and Alan were jacked. It didn't hurt that they were also plastered. They each drank about five cups of beer during the game.

Sam hoped that Alan was okay to drive them back to Providence.

"What a game," the younger Hewitt belched. "What do you boys say we spend the night at the brownstone? I'm a little too buzzed to drive home. Besides, I haven't had a night on the town in the big city in a long time. I've got a real craving for Pizzeria Regina, among other things." Alan smiled like the former frat boy he was.

"Sounds good to me," Billy said. He turned to Sam and Chad. "Are you guys up for it?"

"Sure," Chad said. "As long as roomie here wants to stay." Chad knocked Sam's Red Sox cap off his head.

"Sounds like fun," Sam said, retrieving his cap from a large pile of peanut shells. "But whose brownstone are we talking about, and where is it?"

"It's our folks' place in Louisburg Square," Billy said. "Let's grab some dinner first, though. I'm starving."

They arrived at Pizzeria Regina shortly after 8:00 P.M. By eight, the crowds that forced you to wait in line for a table had dissipated.

Pizzeria Regina was actually a chain of pizza restaurants, but the one in the North End at 11 1/2 Thacher Street was where it had all begun. The tiny brick building, from the well-worn wooden booths to the pressed-tin ceiling, looked and felt every bit its more than fifty years of hard service.

"We'll have one large mushroom and sausage and one large pepperoni and green pepper," Alan told the waitress, a young Italian woman who probably grew up and still lived in the neighborhood. "Two pitchers of beer—Michelob—too."

After they had placed their order, Sam excused himself for a minute and tried to find a pay phone.

From the moment they had left Providence, Sam had had a queasy feeling in the pit of his stomach. He knew why. It was Mary. He and Mary had had a terrible fight the previous weekend and he hadn't spoken to her since. He had bought her a piece of her favorite cake—German chocolate from Bearberries—as a peace offering, but she hadn't been home when he tried to deliver it. He had left it on the stoop outside her apartment.

It didn't help matters that there was a beautiful girl on the phone who looked an awful lot like Mary: about five-four, with a gorgeous wall of brown hair, brown eyes, fabulous legs, and curves in all the right places.

Man, Sam thought. He must have had too much to drink. Or not enough . . .

The beautiful girl smiled in Sam's direction as she hung up the phone. "All yours," she said, noticeably exasperated. "I hope you have better luck than I did . . . MEN!!!"

"I wouldn't bet on it," Sam said.

He dialed the number: 1-401-555-4362. After only two weeks of dating, he knew Mary's number by heart.

One ring, two rings, three rings. Suddenly, he was hoping—praying—no one was home.

Nobody was. The answering machine picked up. Sam panicked. He hung up the phone without saying a word. He rushed back to the table.

He felt like a fool—like he used to feel when he was in high school and he was trying to get a date for Saturday night. He was twenty-five years old and he was still too nervous to leave a message for an angry girlfriend. How sad was that?

He noticed that the beautiful girl who had been on the phone before him was looking in his direction again. The amused expression on her face suggested that she knew he hadn't had any more luck than she had had.

Man, she did look like Mary, Sam thought. She even smiled like Mary.

"Is everything all right?" Chad asked. "You look kind of pale."

"I'm fine," Sam answered. He didn't want to talk about it. It still hurt too much. "Just hungry. Where's the pizza?"

As soon as Sam had asked the question, their order arrived. The four of them—Sam, Chad, Billy, and Alan—inhaled the two large pizzas and two pitchers of beer. None of the airs and graces that were extended when girls were at the table were extended tonight. After all, most guys thought they had a finite supply of table manners: a supply they didn't want to deplete when there was no girl around to impress. No, guys thought, better to save up on that etiquette stuff for when it counted; namely, for when it might help get you laid.

◆ ◆ ◆ ◆

U.S. Senator Charleston Chase extended his hand as he made his way across the elegant room. "Sorry I'm late. The majority leader called an unexpected vote on the tax bill."

The Capitol Grille—the legendary haunt of D.C.'s movers and shakers—was just now beginning to fill up with overworked legislators. Saturday evening votes were par for the course in the nation's capital these days.

Judge Artur Reis pumped the Senator's large hand. "Think nothing of it, Chuck. It gave me a chance to catch up on some paperwork." The Judge closed the file folder he had been reading—the one that contained Sam Grimes's bench memo on *U.S. v. Mancini*—and returned it to his briefcase.

The Senator motioned for a waiter.

A tuxedo-clad gentleman rushed over with a pair of leather-bound menus. "Good evening. May I tell you about tonight's specials?"

"No, thank you," the Senator said. "We'll have two of your finest New York strips, please." The Senator directed his attention back to the Judge. "Are you still taking yours medium-rare?"

"I sure am," the Judge said. "When my wife lets me."

The two powerful men laughed.

"How is Eva?" the Senator asked.

"She's fine," the Judge answered. "Busy as ever, but fine."

"Please give her my best." The Senator took a sip of ice water. "I take it you saw the story in the *Providence Journal?*"

"Yes. I read it on the airplane." The Judge buttered a roll.

"What do you think? Are you interested?"

"What about Francis? I'm pretty sure he thinks the seat is his."

"He probably does. And Tommy Tomasino *certainly* does. He told me as much yesterday in the members' lounge."

The Judge took a bite of his roll. It was nice and warm. "There's the decision, then. Right?"

The Senator said, "Why? Just because Francis Conigliero has got more seniority than you do, and because Tommy Tomasino has got more seniority than me? We're talking about a seat on the U.S. Court of Appeals. We're talking about a steppingstone to the U.S. Supreme Court . . . I'm tired of all the politics. I'm tired of all the paybacks. Judge Sizemore's seat should be filled with the best-qualified candidate. That's you, Artie. There's simply no question about that."

U.S. District Judge Artur Reis gazed out the window onto the gas-lit street. It made him proud to think that Charleston Chase was actually concerned about the *merits* of the First Circuit appointment. It made him even prouder to think that the Senator considered him—the son of working-class Portuguese immigrants—to be the most qualified candidate. Only in America, he said to himself. Aloud to the Senator: "I'd be honored to be considered, Chuck. I think I'm ready. I know my law clerks are. I've got a couple of wonderful law clerks this year."

CHAPTER EIGHT

Many of the North End restaurants didn't serve dessert. Pizzeria Regina didn't. The cafés, most notably Caffe Vittoria, did a brisk business as a result.

Caffe Vittoria was located around the corner from Pizzeria Regina, at 296 Hanover Street. Like Pizzeria Regina, Caffe Vittoria had a quaint atmosphere: its latticework, marble floors, old photos of the neighborhood, and bevy of Italian grandfathers discussing world events over countless espressos made patrons feel as if they were in Rome. The mural of the Italian coast that dominated the main seating area added to the feeling. However, unlike Pizzeria Regina, Caffe Vittoria was widely suspected of being owned and operated by the Mafia. Indeed, before he had gotten sick, Iron Mike Mancini was said to have driven up from Providence on a regular basis to check on his Boston operations.

As usual, a Frank Sinatra song was playing on the jukebox when Sam Grimes, Chad Smith, and Billy and Alan Hewitt arrived. Billy signaled for a waitress, and then led the happy group to a table in the back.

"Four short ones and four cannolis, darlin'," he said.

The familiar tone of Billy's request suggested that he knew this young woman quite well. She was *definitely* a local girl, Sam said to himself. Only local girls worked at Caffe Vittoria. Mr. Bugialli—Caffe Vittoria's legendary owner—wouldn't have it any other way.

As soon as the espressos and cannolis arrived, Billy and Alan excused themselves from the table.

"Where are they going?" Sam asked.

"Don't ask," Chad answered. "Believe me, you're better off not knowing. I know I am. Just enjoy your cannoli."

◆ ◆ ◆ ◆

The dishwasher glanced up from a sink full of soapy water and dirty plates. He noticed a familiar figure standing behind him, smoking a cigarette. "*Buona sera, Signore* Mancini. You wanna me to tell *Signore* Bugialli you here?" he asked in his best broken English.

Joey Mancini flicked a cigarette ash onto the water-stained floor. "That won't be necessary, Adriano. I'm here to see someone else tonight."

A waitress entered the kitchen. She said, "I found them, Mr. Mancini."

"Thank you, sweetheart." Mancini opened his wallet and pulled out a twenty-dollar bill. He handed it to her.

"*Grazie*." She stuffed the twenty into the pocket of her apron. She picked up a fresh tray of cannolis and returned to the dining room.

"Where have you been, Joey?" Alan asked.

"What do you mean, where have *I* been?" Mancini answered. "*I've* been here. The more important question is, what the fuck are you doing with those two clowns?" Mancini motioned frenetically toward the dining room. "That Grimes guy almost saw me."

"So?" Alan said.

"*So?! . . . So?!*" Mancini said. "You two are even dumber than I thought you were. I'm on trial before Grimes's boss. Unlike you two flunkies, Grimes ain't no dumbshit. I don't want him to know why I'm in town."

"Sorry, Joey," Billy said, trying his best to stave off a confrontation between his impetuous younger brother and the even more unpredictable son of the crime boss of New England. "I guess we forgot that Sam worked for Judge Reis. The other guy—Chad Smith—is Suzanne's boyfriend. You know, our sister. We thought it would be fun to go to a ball game. It was a great game, too. The Red So—"

"Save the Red Sox wrap-up for Len Burton on the six o'clock news," Mancini snapped. "What did you find out about the shoot site for *The Midnight Rides of Paula Revere?*"

"We're thinking it would be best to shoot it up at our place in Louisburg Square," Billy said. "We ran the idea by Dad yesterday. He agreed. It would save us the site fee, and the place is late-eighteenth century. It's perfect."

Mancini stubbed out his cigarette on a soiled plate, and then turned to Adriano. "What do you think?"

Adriano startled. He dropped a wineglass on the floor. It shattered into a dozen pieces. "I—I no understand English *buono, Signore* Mancini. Mi— Mi *dispiace.*"

Mancini picked up on the fear in Adriano's voice, and took pleasure in it. "Adriano. Adriano, my good Sicilian friend. There's nothing to worry about. I'm only playing with you." He patted Adriano on the shoulder. He turned to Billy and Alan. "Louisburg Square it is. Good job, boys. You've restored my faith in you. We'll shoot it next Saturday and Sunday. Make sure everything's ready to go by then."

With his business done, Joey Mancini ducked out the back.

◆ ◆ ◆ ◆

Fifteen minutes passed with Sam and Chad alone at the table. They talked a lot about the baseball game. They agreed that Curt Schilling was the best free agent acquisition the Red Sox had made in years. They also agreed that they needed to make it to at least one more game before the season ended. Then the waitress who had seated them rushed over and whispered something into Chad's ear.

"Come on," Chad said to Sam. "Billy and Alan want us to meet them in the back."

The waitress led the two law clerks to a private room behind the kitchen. It was a small room. All it had in it were a stained pine table, four well-worn mismatched chairs, a battered old table lamp, and some dime-store paintings on the walls. The paintings were of religious scenes, mostly, although there was barely enough light in the room to tell.

"Have a seat, boys," Alan said.

The waitress closed the door on her way out.

Sam and Chad pulled up the two empty chairs, placing Billy's and Alan's espressos and cannolis on the table as they did.

Alan said, "It's very thoughtful of you boys to remember our coffee and dessert." He bit into his cannoli. "I think Billy's got a little reward for you."

Billy reached into his shirt pocket and removed a tinfoil packet. It was the size of a book of stamps.

Sam knew where this was going.

"Gentlemen," the older of the Hewitt brothers said. "It's time to begin the after-dinner phase of our festivities. As luck would have it, I happen to have here in my hot little hand some of the finest blow in the big city." Billy shifted in his seat and directed his attention to Sam. "My sister's betrothed informed me at the game that you're not averse, Sam. Are you in?"

"I'm in," Sam answered, almost before Billy had finished the question. "I wouldn't want to insult my hosts."

They all laughed.

"A true gentleman," Billy said as he unfolded the tinfoil. "A true gentle-man."

It had been awhile since Sam had done cocaine. He tried not to make a habit of it, but once in awhile it was a nice treat. It was difficult to avoid in the yuppie set he came in contact with. He and Chad had done coke together only once before: the night they had christened their apartment on Thomas Street. Sam had partaken a bit more often in law school. Karen, his girlfriend at the time, used to hate it when he did, but his room-mate always seemed to have a dime on him—and he hated to dine alone.

Alan handed Billy a small makeup mirror that he had apparently bor-rowed from the waitress, as well as the obligatory rolled-up dollar bill.

Billy proceeded to cut what looked to be a full ounce of cocaine. He exercised all the care of a heart surgeon. He expertly formed four symmetrical lines and left the remainder of the coke in a pile at the edge of the mirror. He offered the first line to Chad.

"Great shit," Chad reported after snorting his line. "It's the best I've had in a long time. Leave it to the Hewitt brothers to know where to get the best coke."

Sam went next. "Wow!" he said, registering his agreement with Chad's characterization of the Hewitt brothers' acquisition. "This is even better than the stuff I had last year at the Harvard Christmas party. And I thought law students had the best drug connections."

They all laughed again.

Slowly but surely the ounce disappeared.

"Is everybody ready to hit Venus de Milo?" Billy asked, licking what looked to Sam like dust—but what Billy apparently thought were the last remnants of the cocaine—from the mirror.

"Let's do it!" Chad and Alan said.

Sam said, "You guys go ahead. I think I'm gonna head back to Beacon Hill, if that's okay."

"Come on, Sam. The night is young!" Billy said. "Let's go find some women. Believe you me, there's more than enough tail to go around at Venus de Milo."

"No thanks, Billy. I've done the Venus de Milo thing before. It's a bit too wild and crazy for me tonight. I've been working like a dog on the Mancini case, and it's just now starting to hit me. You know, after the game and the beer and all. I'm really looking forward to a nice long walk back to Louisburg Square. Beacon Hill always looks so magical when you're high."

"*Come on, Sam!*" Billy said again.

Chad said, "Give it up, Billy. I know Sam. When he's got his mind made up, there's no changing it. Especially when it comes to trolling for women."

Billy said, "Okay. You win. Here's the key." He tossed the key to Sam. "Don't wait up."

"Don't worry, I won't," Sam said. "Have fun. And thanks for dinner, and for the game, and for everything else. I had a great time."

He really had. The Hewitt brothers had surprised him.

Perhaps they would again.

◆ ◆ ◆ ◆

It took Sam about fifteen minutes to walk from the North End to the foot of Beacon Hill. It was a walk he had made many times before, and it passed uneventfully. However, when he crossed Cambridge Street he found himself awestruck, as he always was, by the beauty of the Hill.

Beacon Hill was one of America's great architectural and historical treasures—a superbly preserved nineteenth-century district of red-brick townhouses and brownstones blended together harmoniously. Decoration was minimal: tasteful wrought-iron railings and fences, slender columns flanking doorways, delicate fanlights. Wealthy Bostonians later proclaimed their prosperity by building chateaux and castles along Commonwealth Avenue in the Back Bay, but on Beacon Hill the unspoken but unbreached rule was restraint. Indeed, if Sam listened closely enough, he could swear he could still hear the quiet grace of horse-drawn carriages being driven across the narrow cobblestone streets.

For some unknown reason—perhaps it was the restlessness from the cocaine—Sam found himself taking a detour to the Massachusetts State House: the crowning jewel of Beacon Hill. It had been a long time since he had walked through the streets of the Hill, and he had an urge to revisit his favorite spots—just like he used to do almost every evening after class at Harvard. It was a rare night that he would walk straight home from the sub- way station. The soft music of the Hill was calling to him then—and it was calling to him now.

Charles Bulfinch's architectural influence was everywhere on Beacon Hill, but the State House was his masterpiece. The majestic portico and resplen- dent dome embodied the values that the leaders of the late-eighteenth and early-nineteenth centuries had hoped would guide government from then on: dignity, restraint, and loftiness of purpose. The building was absolutely breathtaking. Standing in front of it on Beacon Street with his back to the Boston Common, Sam couldn't help but think how disappointed Mr. Bulfinch would have been to learn of the greedy self-absorbed politicians who occupied his beloved building today. More importantly, Sam couldn't help but think about Mary . . . Mary . . . Not even the beauty of Beacon Hill could make Sam forget about her.

CHAPTER NINE

Twelve-year-old Mary Jackson was in her room working on her geometry homework. Her door was shut. It always was. That wouldn't stop him, though. It never did.

She heard a car engine. She shot up from her desk and raced to the window. She watched while her mother sped down the tree-lined driveway. Her stomach knotted like a piece of jump rope during gym class.

There was a knock at her door.

She pretended not to hear it. But she always heard it. Always . . .

"Let me in, sweetheart," Dr. Edward Jackson said. "I can help you with your homework now." His voice was thick with alcohol.

"I—I'm fine, Daddy. I—I can do it."

"Let me in!"

She opened the door. Her father had a blank expression on his face. It was almost as if he didn't realize she was his daughter. Almost . . .

His eyes surveyed his daughter's bedroom. It was a room he had visited hundreds of times before, but almost never in the daylight.. He noticed a picture of Ricky Martin on the wall. It was next to a poster of the Backstreet Boys.

"My homework's over here, Daddy." Mary prayed that was really the reason her father had come to her room. She knew that her prayer wouldn't be answered, though. Her prayers never were.

She sat down at her desk and pointed to the geometry problem with which she was having trouble. Her textbook was full of schoolgirl doodles.

One doodle in particular caught her father's eye. "Who's this *Brendan*, sweetheart?"

Mary blushed. "N—Nobody, Daddy."

Dr. Jackson smiled. "He can't be nobody, sweetheart. You wrote 'Mary loves Brendan' in your math book."

"I was just playing. He—He's not my boyfriend or anything."

Silence filled the room.

The grandfather clock in the hallway struck four.

Dr. Jackson said, "If he's not your boyfriend, then someone will be soon. You're such a pretty girl. You look just like your mother." He caressed his daughter's cheek. Her skin was as soft as butter.

Mary began to tremble. She always trembled when her father touched her. He never seemed to notice, or at least he didn't seem to care if he did.

He said, "You'll need to know how to please your boyfriend, sweetheart, whether it's Brendan or some other lucky young man. Do you know how to please a man?"

More silence. Then, "N—No, Daddy."

"Let me show you." Dr. Jackson's pants were already unbuttoned. He had been rubbing himself the entire time his daughter had been trying to keep her eyes locked on her math book. He grabbed her head and turned her face toward his erect penis. "Open your mouth, sweetheart . . . That's a good girl."

◆ ◆ ◆

U.S. Senator Thomas "Tommy" Tomasino worked the crowd like it was Election Day. It always was. He shook hands, kissed babies, and inquired about nieces, nephews, and grandchildren. He had the patience of Job. He always had.

U.S. District Chief Judge Francis Conigliero was a different story altogether. He tapped his fingers on the table at the sidewalk café where he had been in the middle of an important conversation with the Senator before the Senator's constituents had so rudely interrupted them.

Thirty minutes later—thirty minutes *after* the Chief Judge was supposed to have been at the courthouse for a hearing—the Senator returned to the table. "*Dispiacente*, Francis," the Senator said. "I still have many friends in the old neighborhood."

They were on Federal Hill.

The Chief Judge nodded in reluctant acquiescence. He signaled to the waitress that the Senator was in need of a fresh espresso.

She brought it.

The Senator took a careful taste, and then said, "Don Mancini telephoned me last night. You've got his full support for the First Circuit seat. Needless to say, you've got my support as well."

"*Grazie*, Tommy," the Chief Judge said. "*Ringraziamenti*. But what about Artie Reis?"

The Senator polished off his espresso in one quick gulp. That was the best way to drink it: the *only* way to drink it. "Don Mancini said not to worry about Artie Reis. I won't, so you shouldn't . . . On a happier note, how's that pretty niece of yours? *Mary*, isn't it?"

"Yes. Mary Jackson. She's fine, I think. I don't see her as much as I should, or at least as much as her mother—my sister—would like."

"She's at the Rhode Island School of Design—RISD—is that right?"

The Chief Judge couldn't help but be impressed by how much the Senator knew about his niece. To the best of his knowledge, the Senator had met her only once—at a courthouse party welcoming the year's new batch of law clerks. It was the same party at which his niece had met Sam Grimes. The Chief Judge had yet to decide how he felt about Mary dating Sam. Although Sam seemed to be a pleasant enough young man, he was clerking for the competition. Aloud to the Senator: "She's a junior. She always did like to draw. Just like her mother did when she was a girl."

Sam Grimes slept better the night before the motion to dismiss than he did the night before the motion to reconsider the Magistrate's detention order. The motion to dismiss was far more important than the motion to reconsider—in the former type of motion the entire case was on the line because the defense was challenging the sufficiency of the government's charges as returned in the indictment—but Sam was becoming settled into the case, so he wasn't as fazed by it now as he had been in the beginning. He was still excited, but it was a controlled excitement—a focused excitement.

Judge Reis appeared more at ease with the case as well. Even he had been a bit off stride in the beginning. And that had surprised Sam, because the Judge was usually extremely self-confident. He wasn't cocky or arrogant. He was self-confident in a good way: he knew that he knew what he was doing. Sam would be self-confident, too, if he had excelled at everything he had ever tried.

Sam arrived at the courthouse at 7:55 A.M.

"Here we go again," he said to Jerry Cushing as he hurried through the back entrance.

The metal detector sounded.

Jerry laughed.

Sam handed Jerry his keys and tried again. This time he made it.

Jerry returned Sam's keys to him and said, "You know it, Sam. Don't worry, though. We've got things under control. Marshal Lawton decided that today would be the day to start using the new metal detectors. We don't wanna take any chances. They're state-of-the-art, as you just found out. The crowd last time was bigger than we expected, and it looks even bigger today. We're ready, though."

Jerry offered these remarks with the bravado that was characteristic of all the assistant marshals. Most of them previously had served as local street cops for a number of years. They still bore that edge, although it was muted somewhat by thinning hair and thickening waistlines.

"I noticed the crowd, too," Sam said. "I'm not worried, though. It looks like an orderly mob to me."

Sam knocked on Judge Reis's open office door and stepped over the threshold.

"Good morning, Judge," he said. "How was your meeting with Senator Chase? Was Kaitlyn Ashmont's story in the *Providence Journal* correct? Is Senator Tomasino really going to push for Chief Judge Conigliero?"

The morning's newspaper had been dominated by a long article about who might replace the retiring Benjamin Nash Sizemore on the First Circuit. The smart money was said to be on either Judge Reis or Chief Judge Conigliero.

"How was the Red Sox game?" the Judge said. "I see they won." The Judge smiled, and then pointed to the Mr. Coffee steaming in the corner. "Pour yourself a cup and grab a seat. Let's talk about the Mancini motion for a few minutes."

It didn't take a Supreme Court justice to figure out that the Judge didn't want to talk about his meeting with Senator Chase. And Sam knew it wasn't his place to press the issue, no matter how much he wanted to know what had happened. Consequently, it was back to the business at hand and to the morning's first cup of joe.

Sam took his usual seat on the corduroy couch, and the Judge took his on the overstuffed easy chair across from him. The Judge held the Mancini file in his right hand and a cup of coffee in his left. He was drinking out of his favorite UVA Law mug. He was so familiar with the mug that he seemed to know without looking where its chips and cracks were located. He steered clear of those when he brought the steaming mug to his lips.

"Thanks for the supplemental memorandum on *Jenkins v. Georgia*," he said. "It was very helpful." The Judge had asked Sam to do a little more digging on that case. "I was particularly impressed by your distinction between trial courts and appellate courts and the different responsibilities each bears vis-a-vis the jury. Most young lawyers, being fresh out of law school, wouldn't have picked up on the distinction. And heaven knows most law professors aren't aware of it. They think all courts are appellate courts. Your discussion of Professor Collins's article is proof positive of that fact."

Sam said, "I'm glad the memo was helpful."

The Judge rose from his chair and walked over to the coffeemaker. He refilled his cup. "If you don't mind some fatherly advice, I think you should consider becoming a law professor when your clerkship is over. You've got a scholar's knack for synthesizing complex material and for discerning the subtleties of the law. This has been apparent to me throughout your clerkship, and your *Jenkins* memo is more evidence of it. You certainly ran circles around Professor Collins. And he teaches at Yale." The Judge returned to his chair. "Of course it goes without saying that I'd write you a strong letter of recommendation."

"I have thought about teaching law one day." Sam leaned forward in his seat. He placed his cup on the table. "As you know, my dad teaches college. I guess it's true what they say: 'The apple doesn't fall far from the tree.' Obviously, a letter from you would carry a lot of weight."

"Just let me know when you need it," the Judge said. "I'll do everything I can to help."

"Thanks," Sam said. "Thanks a lot. Now, I'd better let you have a few quiet moments before the hearing."

◆ ◆ ◆ ◆

Sam searched the courtroom to see who was present, as he usually did before a hearing. Reporters had come in the same large numbers as they had for the motion to reconsider the Magistrate's detention order. Also like last time, there were quite a few support staff from the building, some local lawyers, and some regular folks from the community. Most important to Sam, many of his fellow law clerks had returned as well. Morris, one of Judge Sizemore's clerks, was sitting in the third row. He had made it back from the First Circuit session in Boston, just like he had said he would.

Chad was in attendance, too. Once again he sported the wet-headed look of someone who had just woken up. Suzanne was with him this time. Howard and Joanne, Chief Judge Conigliero's law clerks, were sitting in the back. David, one of Judge Sizemore's other clerks, was seated next to them. But Mary—she was nowhere to be found.

Sam had caved the previous night and left a message for her. He had apologized for being such a jerk the week before and he had invited her to the hearing and then to lunch afterward.

Where was she? Sam asked himself. And why hadn't she at least returned his call? With the exception of their stupid fight the previous week, things seemed to be going so well with them. From their very first date, things seemed to be going so well . . .

CHAPTER TEN

Finally, it was here: Sam's first date with Mary.

What was a "date," anyway? Was it any time a guy and a girl went out together alone? Did it have to be at night? Did the guy have to pay? Did you have to kiss at the end of the evening? Did you have to sleep together?

Sam had no idea. Sometimes one person thought it was a date, but the other person didn't. That was rare, though, and it usually happened only when the person who didn't think it was a date felt guilty about using the person who did. Of course, the person who thought it was a date found out it wasn't a date only after the other person who was using him went back to the obsessed rich guy she was trying to get away from in the first place. But that was a story for another day.

Sam was pretty sure he and Mary were going on a date: if the razzing he had been getting from Chad was any indication, they were. Shit, if Chad asked him one more time whether he was going to, quote, "do her," Sam was going to pop his roommate in the nose. He really was.

They were going to the Cable Car, which was over on South Main Street. The Cable Car Cinema and Café, as it was officially known, showed classic, foreign, and second-run films. Mary wasn't the pretentious sort, which was good, considering what the Cable Car looked like inside. When they had been trying to decide where to go on their date, Sam had mentioned that *Dead Poets Society* was playing at the Cable Car and that he really wanted to see it again. Mary had wanted to see it again, too—it was the tenth-anniversary director's cut—so she had said that was where they should go. When Sam had told her that the Cable Car was a pretty bare-bones movie house, she hadn't seemed concerned. She had said he could make it up to her by tak-ing her to Bearberries for coffee and cake afterward. Imagine, Sam had thought at the time, a low maintenance girlfriend. This could be a first in the annals of his dating history.

The front buzzer sounded at 6:45 P.M. She was right on time.

Even though it was a date, Sam and Mary had decided that because Sam's apartment was on the way to the Cable Car, Mary would pick him up. God bless modern women.

"Hell-o," Sam said as nonchalantly as he could when he opened the door. You know, kind of like the way Cary Grant used to say "hell-o" in those old romantic comedies that ran so often on the Turner Classic Movies cable channel. "You look nice," he said next.

He was lying. She looked *fantastic*. She was wearing a hip-hugging pair of Levi's, tan cowboy boots, and a man's work shirt tied at the waist. Her thick mane of wavy brown hair was bundled in a loose ponytail and she had placed a daisy above her left ear.

Some guys were attracted to women who looked sexy. Sam went for the cute-as-a-button type. Karen was that type, and Mary was, too.

"Are you ready to go?" Mary asked.

"Yeah," Sam answered. "Just let me grab my jacket. Come on up for a minute."

Sam led Mary up the stairs to his and Chad's humble abode.

"You weren't kidding on the phone the other day," Mary said when she reached the kitchen.

"What do you mean?" Sam said like the clueless straight man he appar-ently was.

"You and Chad *are* clichés. This place is a mess . . . What would your mothers think?"

Sam laughed. "Very funny. I'd be careful if I were you. If you don't watch out, I won't buy you any popcorn at the movies."

It was a beautiful New England fall evening—clear, crisp, and colorful—just like in the travel brochures. So Sam and Mary decided to walk to the movie theater.

Mary began the conversation. "It must be nice to wake up every morning and see Roger Williams's church from your window. The only view I've got from my apartment is of Foley's Dry-Cleaners. It hardly compares."

As Mary was saying this, Sam couldn't help but think how happy he would be to let her view the church for herself some morning—like, say, *tomorrow* morning.

He wasn't Chad, but he wasn't dead either.

"It is nice," he said, trying his best to suppress the guys-have-only-one-thing-on-their-minds quality that even he sometimes possessed. "I'm a history buff, so it means a lot to me. Frankly, I don't think Chad knows the church is there. I think he picked the apartment because it's close to the courthouse. He has trouble waking up some mornings."

"That's cute," Mary giggled. She brushed her soft brown hair from her angelic face. She was the most beautiful woman Sam had ever seen. She said, "Oh. We're here already. You guys really do live close to the theater."

"Two, please," Sam said to the box-office attendant. He handed the man a ten-dollar bill.

"Enjoy the show," the attendant said. He handed Sam the tickets and four dollars in change.

A *six-dollar* date! Sam sang to himself. Did he love this girl or what?!

They entered the lobby.

"Look at that," Mary said, pointing.

"At what?" Sam said.

"At that movie poster. *Breakfast at Tiffany's* is my all-time favorite movie. I love Audrey Hepburn, and I love that name."

"Which one: Audrey, or Tiffany?"

"Oh. And look at that," Mary said next, pointing again. "Popcorn!"

"I take it you'd like some popcorn." Sam was doing his best to keep up with Mary's child-like attention span.

"That would be great. I didn't have a chance to eat before I left. I'm starving."

"I'll get a large then."

"And some soda, if that's okay."

"That's fine."

It felt good for Sam to be doing something for a woman again, even if it was just buying her a ticket to the movies and some popcorn and soda. It had been awhile. Since he and Karen had broken up . . .

Fortunately for Sam, half the regular seats in the Cable Car had been replaced with overstuffed two-seater couches. With love seats, really. Sam had been to the Cable Car only once before, and that had been awhile ago: when he had first arrived in Providence. He had forgotten about the love seats. Really, he had. But he wasn't complaining. Really, he wasn't.

The theater was about three-quarters full. Mary found them a love seat about halfway up, right as the movie was starting. Sam sat down first. Then, Mary sat down closely—*very* closely—next to him.

Life was good, Sam said to himself.

The movie passed quickly, as most good movies did. Sam followed Mary out of the theater.

"Are you ready for some coffee and dessert?" he asked. He deposited their empty popcorn and soda containers into the trash receptacle by the exit.

"That would be great," Mary answered. "Should we go to Bearberries?"

"Where else? It's only about a ten-minute walk if we go up George Street. We'll pass by Brown on the way. Brown is gorgeous at night."

"Did you like the movie?"

"I loved it. Robin Williams is one of my favorite actors. He's so talented it's scary. Obviously, he's an amazing comedian, but movies like *Dead Poets* show how good he is in drama as well. Frankly, I don't think anyone is as talented as he is. He sure has come a long way from his *Mork and Mindy* days, although I have to confess that I tape that show every night off TV Land."

"I liked it, too. The *movie*, I mean. I've never seen *Mork and Mindy*!" Mary laughed, and then said, "Not only was Robin Williams great, but the younger actors were great, too. I especially liked the kid who played Todd Anderson. You know the one I mean. The shy one who Robin Williams helped bring out of his shell. I started to cry when Todd stood up on his desk at the end—before anyone else did—to say goodbye, and thanks, to his 'Captain, My Captain.'"

"That was a tough scene to watch. I can't believe how Robin Williams's character got screwed by the headmaster. It just goes to show that Leo Durocher was right: 'Nice guys finish last.'"

"I hope that's not true," said Mary smiling tenderly at Sam.

Maybe she thought *he* was a nice guy, too? They shared the silence of the evening. It was a wonderful moment.

Sam and Mary talked for at least two hours over coffee and, yes, several pieces of cake. She told him about her interests, her dreams, and her fears—and he told her about his. They had a lot in common, with the exception of the fact that she came from money and he didn't. College professors didn't get paid very much. Most of it was "psychic income," as Sam's father always said. Enjoying what you did for a living.

They held hands on the walk back to Sam's apartment. It felt great. It felt *right*. Sam didn't invite her in, though. He wanted to—again, she was unbelievably beautiful and he wasn't dead—but he wanted her to know that he cared about *her*, not about how she looked or about what she had. In talking to her, Sam had gotten the impression that most of the guys she had dated in the past were after her money or her body—and usually both. He thought she thought he was different. He did kiss her goodnight, however. It was a wonderful kiss. The first kiss was always special, but this one was more than that. It was magical.

CHAPTER ELEVEN

"All rise!" Holly Curran cried out.

Everybody did.

Sam Grimes snapped back to the moment.

"Please be seated," Judge Reis said. His eyes fixed on the defense table. "You may proceed when you're ready, counselor."

John Marone was wearing a beige Italian suit, a crisp white shirt, a mauve power tie, and his customary tassel loafers. Joey Mancini was seated next to him. Although Mancini was dressed in equally expensive clothes, his look paled in comparison to that of his lawyer. Everyone's did—for Marone was blessed with those one-in-a-million good looks and that impeccable sense of style that made everyone around him seem ordinary.

Marone began his argument the moment he reached the podium. This was a lesson he had learned from his father, Sam suspected. The former Chief Justice had been renowned in Rhode Island legal circles for getting right to the heart of the matter.

"May it please the Court," the younger Marone said. "The freedom of speech guaranteed by the First Amendment of the United States Constitution is the bedrock of our democracy. The United States is unique among the nations of the world in valuing, and protecting, the freedom of speech. And it is precisely *that* freedom—the freedom of speech—that distinguishes a free people from the subjects of a totalitarian police state." Marone paused, adjusted his tie, and then said, "My client, Joseph Mancini, seeks nothing more than the right to enjoy the cherished freedom the Constitution promises to him. Some may disagree with how he chooses to exercise that freedom, but the very purpose of the Bill of Rights, including its centerpiece, the First Amendment, is to allow individuals to express themselves without fear of retribution from the majority." Marone reached for his legal pad. "As U.S. Supreme Court Justice Robert H. Jackson reminded the nation many years ago: 'The very purpose of a Bill of Rights was to withdraw certain subjects from the vicissitudes of political controversy, to place them beyond the reach of majorities and officials and to establish them as legal principles to be applied by the courts. One's right to life, liberty, and property, to free speech, a free press, freedom of worship and assembly, and other fundamental rights may not be submitted to vote: they depend on the outcome of no elections.'"

Marone lifted his eyes from his legal pad, looked squarely at the Judge, and then offered his final remarks: "To permit the United States government to prosecute Mr. Mancini for expressing his artistic judgment is to read the freedom of speech out of the Constitution. It would be an affront to our democracy. It is an affront this Court must not permit. I respectfully request that this Honorable Court grant the defense's motion to dismiss the indictment in the case of *United States v. Joseph Paul Mancini*. Thank you, Your Honor."

All eyes were on Marone as he returned to his seat.

Sam could understand why: Marone's argument had been delivered with the passion of an accomplished actor. All good trial lawyers were good actors, and John Marone was one of the best. He had a presence about him that made people listen intently when he spoke. A movie star's charisma. It was a charisma that went beyond good looks, though. Good-looking actors were a dime a dozen, but only a handful had the magic that riveted your eyes to the screen. Tom Cruise had it. Harrison Ford still did, too. Gwyneth Paltrow had it. Jessica Lange still did, too.

And John Marone had it in the courtroom. He had proved it again today. Indeed, the power of his argument was a testament to the power of his presence, given that, as Steve Sutton was about to make clear, his argument was technically very weak. Image was *not* everything, Andre Agassi's well-worn statement to the contrary notwithstanding.

"Thank you, Mr. Marone," Judge Reis said. He turned to the prosecution table. "Mr. Sutton, I assume you disagree."

The Judge offered the remark with a playful intonation—with the deadpan of a David Letterman—that eased the tension of the moment. The courtroom erupted into a brief interlude of nervous laughter.

"Yes, Your Honor, *the People* disagree." Sutton approached the podium. "Mr. Marone's argument, passionate though it may have been, cannot withstand legal analysis. I refer Your Honor to *Miller v. California* for support. The essence of that landmark case is that obscenity is a question of fact for the jury, not a question of law for the Court. As a result, Mr. Marone's motion is completely out of place, attempting as it does to preclude a jury trial on the question of obscenity. If I may be so bold, Your Honor, this is *not* a complicated motion. Under current Supreme Court precedent, the motion to dismiss *must* be denied. *The People* respectfully request that you deny the motion. Thank you very much."

Sutton's argument had been considerably more pedestrian than Marone's, Sam thought. He did make his position clear, however, which was what a lawyer was supposed to do. Now it was Judge Reis's turn.

"The Court would like to thank counsel for both parties for framing the issue so clearly," the Judge said. "However, in the Court's judgment the matter is not nearly as straightforward as either side maintains. I will now explain why I must deny the defendant's motion to dismiss the indictment."

The courtroom came abuzz with "oohs" and "ahs."

The Judge quickly gaveled it to order.

He picked up his legal pad and began his explanation of why Joey Mancini would have to face a jury after all, First Amendment or no First Amendment.

"As Mr. Sutton correctly observed," the Judge said, "the essence of the *Miller* test is the Supreme Court's determination that juries be entrusted to interject their own views into each case as to what constitutes contemporary community standards. The Supreme Court's rationale is that such determinations, along with the others outlined in *Miller*, are essentially questions of fact. Because community standards play such an inextricable role in labeling material, quote, 'obscene,' the Supreme Court decided that a national standard of obscenity was unworkable."

The Judge tore off the top page of his legal pad, placed it neatly to one side, and moved on to page two. "Despite the sweeping statements in favor of jury resolution of issues in *Miller*, only one year later the Court restricted the discretion of juries in their administration of the *Miller* guidelines. To my disappointment, neither party picked up on this development."

Sam could see both Marone and Sutton flinch—literally, flinch—as Judge Reis chastised them, albeit politely, for overlooking the dispositive case. Overlooking the dispositive case was every lawyer's nightmare, and Sam strongly suspected that both Marone and Sutton were going to be having sleepless nights tonight.

The Judge explained the case. It was *Jenkins v. Georgia.*

He said, "After a jury in a rural Georgia community returned a conviction against the owner of a movie theater for showing the Jack Nicholson/Ann-Margret movie *Carnal Knowledge*, the Supreme Court in *Jenkins v. Georgia* reversed. The Court stated that, quote, 'as a matter of constitutional law' the film did not depict sexual conduct in a patently offensive way. Although *Miller* had left the question of obscenity to juries, the *Jenkins* Court held that while questions such as whether material appeals to the prurient interest or is patently offensive are essentially questions of fact, quote, 'it would be a serious misreading of *Miller* to conclude that juries have unbridled discretion in determining what is patently offensive.' Additionally, and most importantly for present purposes, the Court indicated its belief that First Amendment values are protected adequately only if appellate courts have the ultimate power to conduct an independent review of constitutional claims when necessary. Stated another way, *Jenkins* stands for the proposition that appellate courts should disturb jury verdicts when such intervention is necessary to vindicate First Amendment rights."

The Judge paused, flipped to page three of his legal pad, and then concluded with a flourish: "Put simply, *this* Court is a *trial* court, not an *appellate* court. If the First Circuit wishes to second-guess the jury findings that may be issued in this case, that's its prerogative under *Jenkins*. That does not mean, however, that *this* Court may keep the question from the jury. At the *trial* level, whether something is obscene or not is for the jury, not for the Court. The defendant's motion to dismiss the indictment is denied. This Court is adjourned."

The Judge sounded his gavel.

"All rise!" Holly Curran cried out.

The Judge disappeared through the private door to his chambers.

Sam Grimes followed quickly behind him. The courtroom was once again abuzz with chatter.

Silvio Patrone surveyed the area. He could do it, he said to himself. But not here—not in the courthouse.

◆◆◆◆

"I told you I thought highly of your memo," the Judge said with a wink and a smile. "Did you recognize a few of those lines? . . . George Hadley has got nothing on me."

George Hadley was the award-winning *Providence Journal* columnist who had been fired a few weeks earlier for plagiarizing another reporter's work.

"Yes, sir," Sam said, beaming. "A few of the lines did sound familiar. Like I said before, I'm just glad the memo helped."

The Judge turned serious. He poured himself a cup of coffee. He offered Sam a cup, and then motioned for his law clerk to have a seat on the couch. "I wonder how the press is going to handle the ruling."

Sam took a sip of coffee. He sunk into the couch. "My guess is they won't understand it. In my short time here I haven't been too impressed by the press's ability to grasp the subtle points of the law. They'll probably say that Mr. Mancini's motion to dismiss was denied, and then they'll concoct some simplistic explanation for why it was. We'll know soon enough. A couple of the TV stations were milling about in the hall. I've got no doubt they'll run the story on the six o'clock news."

"I agree with you, Sam. Unfortunately for us, not to mention for the general public, the reporters who are assigned to cover the courthouse have almost no background in law. Take Kaitlyn Ashmont, for example. She might as well be covering the annual Festival of Lights for the Style section."

"What's next?"

Sam knew, but he could tell that the Judge was getting annoyed thinking about how the press would screw up, so he decided to change the flow of the conversation.

The Judge straightened in his chair. He was back to his confident self, talking about matters he could control. "Now we've got to figure out the timing of the trial. Mr. Marone has got about a month left of discovery time. I want to empanel a jury as shortly thereafter as I can. I don't like cases sitting around on my docket, especially criminal cases where someone's reputation—not to mention liberty—is at stake."

"Do you think it'll be a long trial?"

The Judge lingered over the question, and then replied between sips of coffee. "It's always difficult to predict how long a trial will take. In a way, that's the most important task I face as a judge. There are so many cases crowding the docket in any court—including ours—that we need to keep them moving. Obviously, the shorter the trial the better, but I believe it's inappropriate for a judge to try to push for a settlement in a civil case, let alone for a plea bargain in a criminal case. Many judges feel otherwise, but I think the lawyers, together with their clients, should decide what the risks of proceeding to trial are. The parties have a right to their day in court. My job is to see that a fair trial is had, if one is desired, not to pressure the parties to settle or compromise."

Sam said, "Mary told me the other night that Chief Judge Conigliero twists arms in order to get a settlement or a plea."

"Mary's right about that. Francis is a fine judge. We simply disagree on this particular question. We've had some heated discussions about it, too." The Judge took another sip of coffee, and then asked, smiling, "By the way, Sam, what do you mean that Mary told you 'the other night'? Is there something you want to tell me about you and the Chief's niece?"

"I guess the cat is out of the bag, huh." Sam was blushing like a school-girl. "To be honest, there's not much to tell. At least not yet . . ."

On occasion, the Judge expressed interest in seeing Sam have some romance in his life. He knew that Chad had Suzanne, and he was plainly worried that Sam didn't have anybody. It was nice. It was sort of a fatherly gesture. In fact, Sam had come to realize over the past several months that there was more to clerking than learning about the law. It was about people—about life—too.

CHAPTER TWELVE

At first glance, the white clapboard house with the black shutters and the well-kept yard at the corner of Shrewsbury Avenue and Lloyd Terrace looked like any other of Pawtucket's scores of working-class homes. However, upon closer inspection the presence of five discreetly positioned but well-armed guards indicated that someone of considerable station lived in the house.

Joey Mancini had been urging his parents for years to move to the more upscale milieu of Benefit Street in Providence, or perhaps of Bellevue Avenue in Newport—heaven knew they could afford it—but they wouldn't hear of it. Michael and Theresa Mancini were born in Pawtucket, grew up in Pawtucket, met and fell in love in Pawtucket, and raised a family in Pawtucket. Besides, the father had often told the son, Pawtucket was both close enough to his office in The Players' Club on Federal Hill to oversee his business operations and far enough away to placate his wife of forty-seven years, who never had accepted her husband's decision of some thirty years earlier to replace his own father as the head of the most powerful crime family in New England. Theresa Mancini was a devout Catholic, and she wasn't at peace with what her husband did for a living.

"Hello, Silvio," Joey said as he exited his Enzo Ferrari. The sports car's sleek black finish sparkled in the afternoon sun.

Silvio Patrone placed a massive arm around Joey Mancini's slender shoulders. "It's good to see you again, Joey. It's been too long. Your father has been asking about you."

"I know," Joey snapped. With a quick flinch, he extricated himself from Silvio's powerful embrace. "Why do you think I'm here?"

Silvio Patrone, a man of considerable patience as well as girth, resisted the temptation to spar with the boss's tempestuous son. "Your mother says that Connie is preparing your favorite Sunday dinner: *polenta con salsicce.* She's serving it with *montevertine chianti sodaccio, crostini al ginepro,* and *buccellato alle fragole.*" Silvio's description of the Sunday menu drew a brief smile from the young Mancini. "It's good to see you smile again, Joey. Connie's cooking always makes me smile, too." Silvio patted his protruding stomach.

Joey said, "You always could make me smile, Silvio. Ever since I was a boy. I'll have Connie send you out a plate."

Silvio watched Joey walk toward the front door. He wanted to know— *needed* to know—how his brother Vince was doing. But he knew that there was a time and a place for everything, and that *this* time and *this* place were about Joey and Don Mancini.

The front door squeaked open. Some things never changed, Joey said to himself. He thought again of Benefit Street in Providence, and of Bellevue Avenue in Newport.

"Joey, is that you?" Theresa Mancini called out.

"Yes, Mama. It's me."

"Then come and give your mother a kiss."

Joey entered the dining room of his boyhood home and found his mother setting the table with the family's best bone china. Theresa Mancini always insisted on using the family's best china for Sunday dinner. Joey couldn't recall a single Sunday when she hadn't used it. "Sunday is God's day," his mother would always say. "We owe it to God to be on our best behavior on this, His day."

Joey bent down and kissed his mother on the forehead. She was wearing a tasteful emerald-green dress: the same dress, no doubt, she had worn to Mass that morning. Joey also couldn't recall a single Sunday when his mother hadn't attended Mass. A navy-blue pillbox hat sat on the chair next to the door that opened to the kitchen. The smell of red onions and Italian sausages scented the air.

"Hello, Mama," Joey said.

Theresa Mancini placed a crystal vase overflowing with pink roses in the center of the dinner table, and then turned to her son. "Where have you been, my son? We're a family. Families should spend time together. Your father and I haven't seen you in weeks."

"I've been in jail, Mama. You know that. John just got me out."

The color rushed from Theresa Mancini's heart-shaped face. She became as white as the linen tablecloth adorning her Chippendale table. "There will be no talk of jail in this house on a Sunday. Sunday is God's day. We owe it to God to be on our best behavior on this, His day. Now be a good boy and let me finish setting the table. Connie is making your favorite: *polenta con salsicce*." Theresa Mancini retrieved a set of linen napkins from the cabinet next to the Gustave Empreccio painting of a sun-blasted Sicilian village. "Your father has been asking for you all day. He's in his study. Go and pay your father the proper respect."

"Yes, Mama." Joey kissed his mother on the forehead again. "And thank you for asking Connie to prepare *polenta con salsicce*. I know how much time it takes to make."

A tear came to Theresa Mancini's tired eyes. "Connie would do anything for you, Joey. You know that. We all would. Now go and do as I say. Go and pay your father the proper respect. Dinner should be ready in thirty minutes."

Joey Mancini had understood ever since he was a small boy that his father's study was his father's sanctuary. It was to his study where his father would retreat to escape the pressures of running the Donetelli crime family. Classical music filled the room now, as it always had, and books lined the shelves now, as they always had.

"Iron" Mike indeed, Joey said to himself when he spotted his father sitting quietly, eyes closed, on his well-worn reclining chair. Sitting there, in a tattered cardigan sweater, reading glasses perched precariously on his nose, Michael Mancini looked to Joey Mancini more like a retired corner grocer than an unforgiving crime boss. But, Joey knew, in his father's case, looks *were* deceiving. Joey had seen his father order dozens of men killed during his many years as Don of the Donetelli family.

"It's business," Iron Mike would always say when his youngest son pressed him on how he could have men killed without any visible sign of remorse. "It's my responsibility to the family. I won't allow my family to be destroyed, as so many of the other families have been."

"Hello, Father," Joey said.

Iron Mike started. He closed the novel resting on his lap. It was Herman Melville's *Billy Budd*, a personal favorite. The Sunday paper lay scattered on the floor next to the recliner. The lead story was of Joey's recent release and pending trial.

Iron Mike rubbed the sleep from his eyes, and then turned to his son. "Hello, my son. Have you said hello to your mother? She's been worried sick about you." He reached for his pipe, filled it with his special-blend cherry tobacco, and struck a match.

The sweet smell of Iron Mike's pipe quickly found its way to Joey's nose. Joey had always loved the smell of his father's cherry tobacco. It reminded him of the quiet Sundays of his youth when his father would read aloud to him and his brothers. He forced himself to suppress a smile.

"Yes, Father," he said. "I saw Mama. She said dinner will be ready in thirty minutes."

Iron Mike studied the porcelain table clock that was jammed between a row of well-read books on the bookcase at the far end of the room. The bookcase had been a Christmas gift from Joey some ten years earlier. Joey had built it in shop class at St. Xavier's High School. It was lopsided, and more than a few of the boards were splintered, but Iron Mike wouldn't trade it for anything in the world. The clock read 1:35 P.M.

He said, "Thirty minutes? Very good. I'll need to put on something more appropriate than this old sweater, though." He tugged on a loose button. "You know how your mother is about Sunday dinner." He blew a perfect smoke ring into the air and watched it dissipate several feet away. "I talked to John on Friday. He's quietly optimistic about the trial. He says that Judge Reis is a cautious man, but a fair man. I know this to be true. I went before Judge Reis when he was a state court judge. He treated me with respect. He's not like that son of a bitch Decordova." Iron Mike's face flushed with anger, but he quickly calmed himself. "I shouldn't be using such language on a Sunday. If your mother heard such language, I would never hear the end of it. I apologize."

"There's no need to apologize, Father. I know you're upset about my trial. I am as well."

"I *am* upset about your trial. But, my son, I'm also upset about *why* you're on trial. Why must you involve yourself in such a filthy business? Come and work for me at The Players' Club. You know your brothers and I want you there. We could use your help. You've always been good with the books—with accounting matters."

"I want to make my own way, Father. I mean no disrespect. You know I've always shown you respect."

Iron Mike's face flushed again. This time, he began to cough and wheeze. He took several deep breaths, and then said, "Ha! Of my five children, only *you*, my youngest, don't show me proper respect. Your brothers, Michael Jr. and James, they show their father proper respect by coming to work for me in a business for which *my* father, God rest his soul, sacrificed his life. Your sisters, Alicia and Talia, they show me proper respect by marrying decent hardworking men and giving me, their father, six beautiful grandchildren. But *you*, the child I had to beg your mother to have after she said she wanted to bear no more children, show me *dis*respect. This pornography business—it disgraces the family. I tell you, if you want to show me proper respect, you'll quit this filthy business. You're a *Mancini*. We make our living in a better way."

Joey long had been expecting this flurry of disapproval from his father. It had been only a matter of when and where.

"A 'better way'?" he said. "I'm not a child anymore, Father. Airport cargo hijacking, labor racketeering, extortion, loan-sharking, bookmaking, illegal restraint of trade, counterfeiting, car theft. Are *these* a 'better way'? Is *killing* a 'better way'? My way is no worse than your way. You're angry because I've chosen *my* way. I'm *not* Michael Jr. I'm *not* James. I'm *my own* man. You've always known that."

Iron Mike could no longer control his famous temper, Sunday or no Sunday. "How *dare* you speak to me in that manner! I'm still *your father*. As head of the Donetelli family for thirty-two years, I've been approached many times about involving the family in that filthy business. But I won't do it. I won't involve the family in pornography, just as I won't involve the family in drugs. It's—It's just not right."

"That's *your* view, Father, and you're entitled to *your* view. But *my* view is that there's a lot of money to be made in pornography. Almost everyone rents it, although few will admit it. I bet you and Mama have watched it at least once."

"ENOUGH!" Iron Mike screamed. The ashtray on the corner of the coffee table crashed to the floor. "It's bad enough that you insult *me*, but I FORBID you to insult *your mother*. And in her own home, no less. LEAVE this house, and don't return until you have come to your senses and dropped this pornography business, this FILTHY pornography business."

Joey looked his father squarely in the eyes. Man to man, as the saying went. He had never done that before. "If that's how it must be, I'm gone. Say goodbye to Mama for me."

Joey Mancini exited the house—the house where he had been raised and where his parents still lived—as quickly as he had entered it. His black Ferrari flew out of the driveway before anyone knew what had happened.

Anyone, that is, but father and son.

CHAPTER THIRTEEN

As usual, Chad Smith was already home by the time Sam Grimes arrived. Last to get to the office in the morning, first to get home in the evening. Chad didn't have a bad thing going.

It was 6:30 P.M. Sam had spent the previous two hours tying up loose ends on some pre-Mancini matters. (The Mancini case wasn't Sam's only assignment, although it sure seemed like it was.) It felt good to be home.

"What's the smut report?" Chad deadpanned. He was sitting at the kitchen table drinking a beer and reading the latest issue of *Rolling Stone* magazine.

Twenty-four hours after losing the motion to dismiss, John Marone had invoked Joey Mancini's constitutional right to a speedy trial. Consequently, Judge Reis had closed discovery and set the case for trial.

Sam put his briefcase on the cooking island. He loosened his tie. "There's nothing to report," he said. "I was only in the courtroom for a little while this afternoon and no tapes were played. Judge Reis is still trying to seat the jury. He says it's been pretty tedious so far. From the little bit I saw, he's right."

Chad tossed *Rolling Stone* into the corner, and then reached for this month's *Car & Driver*. An Enzo Ferrari similar in style to Joey Mancini's car was featured on the cover. "Don't forget to let me know when things get good, if you know what I mean. This trial should save me a fortune in video rentals."

Unfortunately, Sam *did* know what Chad meant: his roommate was into skin flicks. Sam had learned this tidbit of information late last week when he had gone to retrieve his tennis racket from Chad's closet. Tucked away behind Sam's trusty Prince Tour NXG Graphite with the oversized head and calfskin grip had been a stash of porn videos. When Sam had queried Chad about the videos, Chad had said that Suzanne had turned him on to them. "Suzanne likes to watch porn before we get down to business," he had said. "It's all in good fun. We've been dating for a long time. We need *something* to spice up our relationship. Things can get pretty stale after three years."

Frankly, Sam didn't quite know what to make of the whole thing. He had been to a couple of bachelor parties where the hosts had shown porn videos, but he had never known anyone who had rented them—let alone *purchased* them—to watch at home. And Chad looked so normal, too, sitting there at the kitchen table in his white Oxford shirt and blue polka-dot tie.

"Don't worry," Sam said. "I promise I'll let you know. On another front, did Mary call?" The anticipation in his voice was palpable.

"Not since I've been here she hasn't. But I only got home about fifteen minutes ago. Check the machine. Maybe she left a message. And relax, buddy." Chad grabbed a second beer from the refrigerator.

Sam made his way across the cluttered kitchen to the hallway that separated the kitchen from the living room. That was where they kept the answering machine. He moved the newspaper that had somehow managed to end up on top of the machine. The little red light was blinking, so Sam knew there was at least one message. He rewound the tape, hoping against hope that it was from his favorite art student.

There was only one message, and it was from Suzanne. She was in Newport. She wanted to know whether Chad wanted to come down for the weekend. She said Sam was invited as well. Her mom and dad were throwing a party. It was a warm-up for their Halloween party at the end of the month.

Chad said, "What do you say? Do you want to spend the weekend in Newport? The Hewitts throw great parties. We can goof on the rich people . . . HELLO!!!"

"Sorry," Sam said. "What did you say? My mind was somewhere else there for a minute."

"I'll say it was." Chad inhaled the remainder of beer number one and quickly opened beer number two. He was drinking JW Dundee's Honey Brown Lager, his favorite. He went through the stuff like water. "I asked if you wanted to go down to Newport with me for the weekend. Who knows, you might meet some rich chick, fall in love, and get married. Then you'd be on easy street."

"Can I let you know tomorrow? It sounds like fun, but I'm worried about Mary. She never returned my calls."

"Damn. You've really flipped for that girl, haven't you? She's probably just working late and lost track of time. You do it yourself all the time."

"You're right. I did it today, in fact. Come to think of it, Newport sounds great. Let's do it." There was newfound resolve in Sam's voice.

"You won't be sorry," Chad said. "I've been to a few of the Hewitts' Newport parties before. They're wild and crazy. Rich chicks are as loose as they come. And you've already had a taste of the world-class blow. I can't imagine a party at the Hewitts' without more of the same. Billy and Alan wouldn't sit still for it."

Sam said, "I'm sure there'll be plenty of coke. But I've got to watch that a bit. Lately, I've been partaking of the coca leaf more than I probably should. Mary said something about it when I told her about the night we christened the apartment."

Chad glowered. He tossed his empty beer bottle into the recycle bin. "Twice in two months doesn't make you a cocaine addict. Have some fun. And for God's sake, don't let some girl tell you how to live your life. I don't care how good a fuck she is."

Chad's uncharacteristically disparaging remark about Mary made Sam feel worse than he already did. Sam and Mary had been dating for only a few weeks, and neither one of them had said theirs should be—let alone was— an exclusive relationship. But Sam couldn't help but worry. Mary was nothing if not considerate. He knew she wouldn't just ignore his messages.

◆ ◆ ◆

Joey Mancini sat, head drooped and shoulders slouched, at the opulent marble bar in Stanford's Bistro. A tumbler of Dewar's Scotch Whiskey was nestled restlessly between his palms.

Stanford's Bistro was on the ground floor of the Omni Biltmore Hotel. It was named for Stanford White, the famed architect who had designed the Rhode Island State Capitol, the Newport and Narragansett casinos, and the original Madison Square Garden.

A jazz quartet was conducting a sound check for the evening's perform-ance. The opening riffs of Dave Brubeck's "Take Five" danced through the room. No one was around to hear them except Joey Mancini and a solitary bartender.

Mancini was wearing a wrinkled pair of black jeans and a green-and-white checkered shirt. His most comfortable shoes—his suede Hush Puppies with holes in the soles—adorned his feet. His outfit was a far cry from the Newbury Street look he had sported in court a few days earlier.

The bartender, a Brown University graduate student who tended bar as often as he could so as to avoid falling more deeply in debt than he already was, didn't appear to recognize his famous customer.

"Should I bring the check?" he asked.

"No," Mancini muttered into the side of his glass. "Bring me a double. Neat, this time."

The bartender hesitated—Mancini had already had three drinks in the span of an hour—but he nevertheless refilled the tumbler with two generous shots of Dewar's. He placed the glass on the bar in front of his only customer. He glanced at him, but said nothing.

Mancini nodded in acknowledgment. He wiped his hands on the napkin that came with his drink, and then removed an envelope from his back pocket. The envelope contained a letter from his mother. He had woken from a heavy sleep shortly after noon and discovered it in the day's mail.

The jazz quartet broke into a rousing rendition of Charlie Parker's classic song "At the Blue Note."

Mancini downed the double Dewar's in one long gulp in the foolish hope that it would provide the courage he needed to open the envelope. He knew his mother was going to say something about Sunday's flare-up between him and his father.

Joey Mancini might not have cared about much, but his mother was always able to get to him. It must have had something to do with him being the youngest child, he said to himself when he tried to figure out why he cared so much about what his mother said to him. There was a special bond between a mother and her last-born, a bond that could never be broken.

He split the seal on the envelope with a plastic swizzle stick he retrieved from the bar. He pulled out the letter.

He would recognize his mother's pink-rose-pedals-on-lavender-background stationery anywhere. She had been using it ever since he could remember.

The letter read:

My Dearest Joey:

Your father told me that the Judge ruled you must stand trial. I am confident you will prevail. You are a good boy and God will protect you in your legal proceedings, just as he has protected your father over these many years.

How did your father know about the Judge's decision? Because he was in the courtroom, that's how. He put on a false mustache, a pair of dark glasses, and his favorite boccie cap, and he went. He didn't want to risk being recognized.

I don't know what happened between you and your father on Sunday. That is between the two of you. But remember, my son, he is still *your* father. He loves you very much, as do I. Please let him help you. He is a very powerful man. If you won't do it for him, please do it for me.

You are in my prayers.

Love,

Mama

"Another double," Mancini said. All the color had disappeared from his face. He returned the letter to its envelope, and then placed it back into his pocket.

The bartender put down the rag he was using to dust around the bottles that lined the shelf behind the bar. He looked at Mancini. He still didn't appear to recognize him. "Is everything all right, sir? You don't look well. Are you sure you want another drink?"

Mancini shot the bartender a cold stare. It was a stare he had been using a lot lately. "Another double," he said again, this time forcefully. "I'm here to drink, not to spill my guts. I never bought into that bartender-as-psychotherapist bullshit."

The bartender poured Mancini a double, then another, and then another.

Three-quarters of a bottle of Dewar's later and Joey Mancini was feeling no pain: no pain about his business, no pain about his trial, no pain about his family.

PART II
Trial

CHAPTER FOURTEEN

Judge Reis was taking Sam Grimes to the University Club for lunch. The Judge said it was a reward—for both of them—for suffering through two and a half days of unavoidably redundant *in camera* meetings with seventy-five potential jurors about whether they had been exposed to too much about the Mancini case in the media to be objective. After lunch the Judge was going to rule on the lawyers' respective challenges for cause and then seat the jury.

Sam wasn't sure whether the University Club was a part of Brown or a part of RISD. It was located in between them on Benefit Street. The Judge hadn't attended either school. Clearly, he had been invited to join the club because he was an important person in town, one of only five federal judges in the state. The Judge treated Sam and Chad to lunch about every two weeks, usually separately. It was over lunch where they had some of their most interesting conversations.

They arrived at 12:30 P.M. and took their seats in the main dining area. Sam was nearly snow-blinded by the white linen that dominated the room.

Judge Reis said, "The steak sandwiches are great here, Sam. That's what I'm going to have."

Sam said, "Sounds good to me."

"Waiter," the Judge called out. "We'll have two steak sandwiches, please. I'll have an iced tea as well. Sam, what would you like to drink?"

"Pepsi, please."

The waiter wrote down their orders, and left Sam and the Judge to talk.

Sam said, "In law school I took a course in which we studied pornography from a philosophical perspective. I was wondering what you thought about pornography as a philosophical matter."

"That's quite a question," the Judge said, smiling. "They teach courses on pornography at Harvard?"

Sam blushed. "No. It was a jurisprudence course. We talked about a lot of things. Natural law, capital punishment, strict liability in tort. A hodgepodge of stuff. Pornography was just one of the topics."

"I know." The Judge was still smiling. "I was just teasing you. But I've got to admit that I've never thought about pornography as a philosophical matter. As a matter of constitutional law, I think people should be free to watch whatever they want to watch in the privacy of their own homes. Eva and I don't watch it, obviously, but that doesn't mean other people shouldn't be allowed to. I don't think we should be legislating morality. And I'm a Republican . . . That's about as philosophical as I can get on the subject, I'm afraid."

The steak sandwiches arrived. The Judge took a generous bite from his, and then waved hello to a fifty-year-old-ish-looking gentleman in a gray pinstriped suit. His attention quickly returned to the conversation at hand, however.

"Fair enough," Sam said, nodding to the same gentleman. He had no idea who the man was.

"Why don't you tell me what you talked about in your jurisprudence class," the Judge said. "It's never too late to learn. I've never bought into that you-can't-teach-an-old-dog-new-tricks malarkey."

Silvio Patrone exited The Players' Club. He had received his instructions from Don Mancini. They were the most important instructions of his life.

Sam smiled this time. Who would have thought he would be teaching a federal judge about jurisprudence, let alone about the jurisprudence of pornography?

He started at the beginning. "It all starts with Catharine MacKinnon who, as you probably know, is the leading feminist legal scholar in the country. She teaches at Michigan. She was considered for a job at Harvard, but her application was blocked, some say, by men."

Judge Reis said, "I think I read about that in the *National Law Journal*."

Sam nodded. "The story received a lot of attention for an academic dispute. But what makes Professor MacKinnon's jurisprudential argument so interesting is that she attacks traditional liberal legalism head on. In her view, pornography isn't just another form of expression. It's a discriminatory practice. Consequently, the standard free speech analysis shouldn't apply, she says."

Sam glanced over at Judge Reis. The Judge had moved on to his steak fries, but he was also listening attentively.

"In short," Sam continued, "the reason Professor MacKinnon maintains that pornography is a discriminatory practice is that it fosters the notion that women are commodities for use by men. I can still remember one of her most evocative lines: 'Pornography sells women to men as and for sex. It's a technologically sophisticated traffic in women.'" Sam raked his hands through his hair. "She's quite a phrase maker. She also says that John Stuart Mill's famous argument that we should silence speech we don't like with other speech rather than with censorship won't work with pornography. As she puts it in yet another compelling phrase: 'Permitting pornographers to speak silences women by ensuring their subordination.'"

"That's fascinating stuff, Sam. Does she have anything else to say?"

The Judge looked genuinely interested, Sam thought. Here, the fact that Judge Reis was a student of the law, and not simply a politician in robes, was evident. Chief Judge Conigliero would have had no patience for a conversation such as this one.

Sam took a quick bite of his steak sandwich. It was getting cold, but it didn't matter. He was having too much fun to care.

"Yes," he said, mouth full. "She was the first to write about pornography's legal regulation based on the sexual abuse of women to make it. She also attacks obscenity law. You know, the stuff I talked about in my first bench memo. She insists that obscenity law is *not* neutral—that it's made by men and reflects male views. In fact, she characterizes Justice Stewart's famous retort, 'I know it when I see it,' as proof positive that the obscenity standard is based on what *men* see and on how *men* feel. She's got a point. After all, the defining characteristic of what can't be shown to stay within the R rating is the penis."

The Judge laughed when Sam said the word "penis." He clearly didn't mean to, but he did. That gave Sam a chance to taste his steak fries and to sneak a sip of Pepsi. Then, he carried on with his lesson.

"Perhaps most important to you, Judge, Professor MacKinnon also offers an interesting critique of the *Miller* test. I took the liberty of photocopying the relevant portion of her most famous book, *Toward a Feminist Theory of the State*. Ironically enough, the book was published by Harvard University Press. You know, by the same university that turned her down for a job. The book received a lot of attention in the law school community." Sam pulled the pages from his pocket. "She writes: 'Feminism doubts whether the average person, gender neutral, exists; has more questions about the content and process of definition of community standards than about deviations from them; wonders why prurience counts but powerlessness does not, why sensibilities are better protected from offense than women are from exploitation; defines sexuality, hence its violation and expropriation, more broadly than does any state law; and wonders why a body of law which cannot in practice tell rape from intercourse should be entrusted with telling pornography from anything less.'"

The Judge was listening more closely than ever. His eyes were riveted on the excerpt from Professor MacKinnon's best-selling book.

Sam cleared his throat, took another sip of Pepsi, and then quoted some more of MacKinnon's provocative argument.

"'In feminist perspective, one notices that although the law of obscenity says that sex on street corners is not supposed to be legitimated by the fact that the persons are simultaneously engaged in a valid political dialogue, the requirement that the work be considered as a whole legiti-mates something very like that on the level of publications such as *Playboy*, even though experimental evidence is beginning to support what victims have long known: legitimate settings diminish the injury perceived to be done to the women whose trivialization and objectification it contextual-izes. Besides, if a woman is subjected, why should it matter that the work has other value? Perhaps what redeems a work's value among men enhances its injury to women. Existing standards of literature, art, science, and politics are, in feminist light, remarkably consonant with pornogra-phy's mode, meaning, and message. Finally and foremost, a feminist approach reveals that although the content and dynamic of pornography concerns women—the sexuality of women, women as sexuality—in the same way that the vast majority of obscenities refer specifically to women's bodies, women's invisibility has been such that the law of obscenity has never even considered pornography a women's issue.'"

"That's certainly a powerful indictment of pornography, Sam," the Judge said when his law clerk had finished reading the excerpt. "But if I remem-ber correctly, in law school there's always two sides to every story. At least two . . . What do Professor MacKinnon's critics have to say?"

Silvio Patrone maneuvered his Cadillac Seville through the narrow streets of the east side of Providence. He reached inside the pocket of his sports coat to make sure his gun was loaded. It was. It *always* was.

"You're right," Sam said to the Judge. "Professor MacKinnon does have a lot of critics. Perhaps the most well known is Joel Feinberg. He's a legal philosopher at Cornell. He's also a *man*, as some feminists point out when defending her writings against his."

The waiter interrupted them for a moment. "Will you gentlemen be hav-ing dessert or coffee? Our dessert special this afternoon is blueberry cheesecake."

Judge Reis answered almost immediately. "I usually avoid dessert. But I'd like my law clerk here to finish briefing me. I can't think of a better way for him to do that than over a piece of cheesecake and a cup of coffee." The Judge turned to Sam and smiled. "I hope you won't make me feel guilty alone."

"Don't worry, Your Honor. I'll make the sacrifice. I'll force myself to eat a piece of cheesecake."

Was Sam Grimes a selfless fellow or what? Eating a piece of cheesecake with the Judge was almost as much of a sacrifice as kissing Mary on their first date had been.

Mary . . .

"Great," the Judge said. "We'll have two pieces of cheesecake and some coffee, please."

"Very well, sir. I'll be right back." The waiter scurried off to get the coffee and dessert.

The Judge said, "Please, Sam. Continue."

Sam finished the last two bites of his steak sandwich, and then took a long drink of ice water. Now it was Professor Feinberg's turn.

"Interestingly enough, Professor Feinberg points out that the original drive to ban pornography was led by social conservatives, but now it's led by feminists at the forefront of the sexual revolution. That historical anomaly aside, the key to Professor Feinberg's critique of Professor MacKinnon's position is the distinction he draws between so-called violent pornography, which he admits might harm women by encouraging rape, and what he calls ideal pornography, which emphasizes the joys of sexual pleasure. He provides some examples of violent pornography. They're pretty gross. For instance, he describes how a spread in one hardcore magazine showed a series of pictures of a woman covered with blood, masturbating with a knife. The title of the spread was 'Columbine Cuts Up.' He also points out that the widely circulated magazine *Hustler* once had a cover picture of a nude woman being pushed head first into a meat grinder, her thighs and legs poised above the opening to the grinder in a sexually receptive posture, while the rest comes out the bottom as ground meat. Professor Feinberg describes a movie called *Snuff* as well. In it, female characters—and, it's alleged, the actresses who portrayed them—are tortured to death for the sexual entertainment of the audience. The movie was shown briefly in a commercial theater in New York. There are countless other examples, but I think you get the picture."

"Indeed I do," the Judge said, noticeably disturbed. "I'm just glad the dessert hasn't arrived yet."

"Sorry about that," Sam said. "When I first read those examples in an article that Professor Feinberg published in the *Cornell Law Review*, I literally felt sick to my stomach. Importantly, though, he insists that most people watch pornography in order to fantasize about being worshiped, rather than to degrade someone else. The real problem, according to him at least, is the so-called cult of machismo, not pornography per se. In the cult of machismo, the macho male wins adulation and respect from his friends through reckless and insensitive behavior, particularly involving women as sexual conquests. Violent pornography is a symptom, not a cause, he says, and it appeals only to those psychologically disturbed types. It disgusts the rest of us. He says we need to cure this cult of machismo through counseling and education, not censorship. Even if violent pornography is a cause of rape and so forth, that doesn't mean we should ban all pornography, just violent pornography. Indeed, he believes that pornography might be sexual liberation for women, not sexual subservience. Some recent feminist critics of Professor MacKinnon's feminism agree. Succinctly put, not all feminists think alike, no matter how strenuously some feminists fight to present a united front against so-called male domination."

The cheesecake had arrived during the middle of Sam's most recent monologue. Clearly, the Judge hadn't been too disturbed by Sam's description to eat: His Honor had only one bite left!

Sam tied up his synopsis of Feinberg's argument. "Professor Feinberg makes two final arguments that I find intriguing. First, statistics don't support the notion that pornography increases rape and other sex offenses. For example, sex crimes are virtually nonexistent in Denmark, where pornography is freely available on commercial TV. Second, he rejects the group defamation argument at the heart of Professor MacKinnon's position. If everything were banned that portrayed women in a, quote, 'subservient' light, then there wouldn't be any soap commercials and, more significantly, many famous books and movies would be outlawed. In short, per Professor Feinberg, we shouldn't ban pornography because it offends some people. That's either legal moralism, which liberalism rejects, or you can simply avoid it by not renting the videos or buying the magazines."

Sam glanced at his watch. He had been talking almost nonstop for nearly forty-five minutes. He drained his ice water to soothe his throat.

"That was a highly sophisticated presentation, Sam," Judge Reis said. He reached for his coffee. "And it confirms my earlier point that you should seriously consider a career in law teaching after your clerkship is over. You're a natural."

Sam blushed. "Thanks, Judge. I think I would enjoy being a law teacher. Either that, or a writer. Who knows, maybe I could write novels about lawyers?"

"The next John Grisham, huh?" The Judge smiled and shook his head.

"A guy can always dream." Sam returned the Judge's smile. He glanced at his watch again. "Should we be heading back?"

"I'm afraid so. I've got to rule on the lawyers' challenges to prospective jurors."

Sam rose from his chair, placed his napkin neatly on the table in front of him, and said, "Thanks very much for lunch."

The Judge stood, too. "You're very welcome, Sam. I enjoyed your discussion about the jurisprudence of pornography. I learned a lot. I don't think I can get that philosophical as a working trial judge, but it's always important to try to understand the philosophical debate over a given legal question."

The Judge led the way out of the University Club. He waved hello to at least a dozen lawyers on the walk to the door. He told Sam who each of them was, but Sam told him they all blended together in his head.

"I'm good with ideas and theories, not names and faces," Sam said.

"That confirms it," the Judge said. "You should definitely become a law professor. You'd never make it in practice. These days, practice is all about politics—about knowing who the players are."

They stepped onto the street.

"Thanks again for lunch, Judge."

"You're welcome, Sam. Next week is Chad's turn. I think I'll take him to Burger King."

They both laughed. They also both were squinting from the bright sunlight that shot up the hill from the Roger Williams church to the sidewalk in front of the University Club like a bullet from a gun.

A *gun*.

CHAPTER FIFTEEN

The blinding sunlight was perfect for Silvio Patrone.

Perfect cover for his *gun*.

Silvio waited inside his Cadillac—a birthday present from Don Mancini—for the federal judge and his law clerk to give him the space he needed to do the job he needed to do.

"Nice car, man," a frat boy said from the sidewalk. "It's bigger than my dorm room."

Silvio flashed the kid a hard stare, and the kid raced off to a class he probably hadn't attended all semester.

"Fuckin' brat," Silvio said. He watched the kid fade from view. Then, his attention snapped back to the task at hand.

The Judge and his law clerk were about a block ahead.

Silvio exited his car. He tried to look as inconspicuous as he could, but that was difficult when you were a six-foot-three two-hundred-and-eighty-pound Italian in a part of the city overflowing with anorexic-looking college kids with names that ended in numbers (e.g., Philip Hunnington Wilson III, Kenneth Stephen Bryan V) rather than vowels (Patrone, Mancini, Marone).

The Judge and his law clerk kept walking, and Silvio kept pace behind them.

This was gonna be tough, Silvio said to himself. There were too many people around.

But Silvio Patrone had been working for Don Mancini for almost thirty-five years—he had started out as a numbers runner while he was still in high school and had progressed all the way to the Don's personal body man—and he wasn't about to disappoint his boss now. Nobody ever disappointed Don Mancini.

At least not *twice*. Silvio himself had made sure of that on more occasions than he could count.

The Judge and his law clerk continued to make their way down the hill in the direction of the courthouse. They were only about four blocks from the building. Silvio didn't have much time. It was now or never, as the saying went. But what if he hit the law clerk by mistake? Don Mancini hadn't told him to kill the law clerk, but that was a risk Silvio had to take. It just went with the territory. Sometimes, people were simply in the wrong place at the wrong time. The law clerk might be one of those people . . .

Silvio spotted a large oak tree at the crest of the hill. The tree would provide both a good angle and good cover to get a shot off. He would have time for only one shot, though. He had to make it count. Lucky for him, the street was nearly empty now. The students must be in class, he thought. Only the law clerk might get in the way . . .

Silvio pulled his gun from the inside breast pocket of his favorite sports coat. It was suede, and looked as if it had taken three cows to make. Vince had given it to him shortly before he had gone to work for Joey . . . Silvio fixed his aim a few feet to the right of a fire hydrant at the bottom of the hill. The Judge would be passing the spot in another hundred yards or so. Silvio closed his left eye and prepared to do what he got paid so well for doing. The Judge was almost in view. Thirty yards. Twenty yards. Ten yards. Fi—

"Sweet jacket, man!" another crazy college kid yelled out from a car passing directly behind Silvio.

Silvio pulled the trigger, but the distraction was enough to throw off his aim. The bullet hit the fire hydrant instead of the Judge.

"Duck!" Sam Grimes cried out. He pushed the Judge to the pavement and fell on top of him. He spotted a large man up on the horizon. "Stay down, Judge!" Sam's heart was beating a million times a minute.

Silvio Patrone sprinted off in the direction of his car. It was difficult to believe that such a large man could move so fast.

Three police cars, sirens blaring, came tearing around the corner. One screeched to a halt in front of Sam and Judge Reis. The other two raced on in search of the shooter.

"Are you okay?" a young police officer said as he jumped out of his squad car. "Ju—Judge Reis? . . . Holy shit. S—Sorry, Your Honor." The officer's face was as red as the light on the roof of his car. The rookie cop clearly remembered the Judge from a speech the Judge had delivered at the police academy during the summer. "Are—Are you okay?" he said again. "Do—Do you need to go to the hospital?"

The Judge stood to his feet. He wiped the dirt from his pants and jacket. "I'm fine, officer." He turned and motioned in Sam's direction. "Thanks to my law clerk, I'm fine."

Sam was blushing, too, albeit for a different reason than the police officer had been. "I didn't do anything, officer. All I did was fall on him."

The officer smiled and shook his head. "Sometimes that's all it takes. How about you, though? Are you okay? Do you need to go to the hospital?"

"I'm fine, too," Sam said. "Lucky for us, the guy wasn't a very good shot. Did you get him? Did you guys catch the son of a bitch?"

Silvio Patrone was panting like an old dog after a long run. He was getting too old for this shit, he said to himself.

He ducked behind one of the many ivy-covered buildings at Brown University to catch his breath. This was the closest he was ever going to get to college. At the moment, it was too close for comfort.

"Excuse me, sir. Are you lost?" a tiny female voice asked from over Silvio's shoulder.

Silvio turned and faced her. The top of her head barely came to his chest. "Er—No." He ran his hand over his breast pocket to make sure his gun wasn't visible. "I'm waiting for my daughter."

"You're up for parents' weekend, huh?" the tiny young woman with the tiny voice asked next. She adjusted the daypack draped loosely over her slender shoulder.

"Ye—Yeah. That's right. Parents' weekend. I'd—I'd never miss it."

"I wish my parents felt that way."

Silvio had no idea why the tiny young woman standing in front of him seemed so intent on having a conversation. And he didn't have time to find out. There was no telling where the cops were. He had to keep moving.

"Listen, sweetheart," he said to her. There was a surprising amount of tenderness in his voice. "I've gotta go. I wanna get my son a present before I see him."

Silvio started to walk away. His pace grew faster the farther away he got.

"Have fun, sir," the tiny young woman called out in her tiny voice. She adjusted her daypack again. Then, "*Son?* I thought you came to see your *daughter?*"

Sam Grimes held the door open for Judge Reis as the two men entered the courthouse.

One of the police officers who had arrived at the scene of the shooting was serving as an escort. He stopped on the outside of the door to stand guard.

Jerry Cushing came barreling down the marble stairs to meet Sam and the Judge. "Wh—What happened? Are you all right, Your Honor? Sa—Sam?" Jerry was almost to the point of hyperventilating.

The Judge said, "We're fine, Jerry. We're fine." He put his arm around his law clerk's shoulder. "Thanks to Sam."

Sam blushed again. "Don't listen to him, Jerry. I didn't do anything."

Jerry pointed to the city cop standing guard outside the courthouse door. "That's not what the police are saying. Marshal Lawton spoke to Chief Veltri a couple of minutes ago. He said you saved the Judge's life."

Sam was still blushing. "All I did was fall on him, Jerry." Then a broad grin captured his soiled face. "Even Chad could have done that."

"But Chad didn't, Sam," the Judge said. "You did."

Sam Grimes was growing increasingly uncomfortable with the praise that was being heaped upon him. Despite all the success he had already achieved in his young life—all-star athlete as a kid, scholarship student as a young adult, law clerk to a federal judge—his parents weren't big on paying him compliments. Like most accomplished people, Sam's parents had *expected* their son to succeed.

He asked, "Did they catch the shooter?"

"Not yet," Jerry answered. "But they're looking. They're looking hard."

Silvio Patrone peered out from around the corner of yet another ivy-covered building.

He *still* didn't see them. He *still* didn't see the cops. He knew they were out there, though. He had heard their sirens blaring in the distance. He had felt their eyes searching through the crowds.

Silvio Patrone had been chased by the cops many times during his fifty-three years on this earth. It had come with the life he had chosen to live.

But what *choice* had he really had? He had grown up in one of the poorest sections of East Providence. His parents had worked hard—day and night—but they hadn't had much education and they hadn't been able to find a job that paid much more than minimum wage. Consequently, Silvio had left home at fifteen to make his own way in the world. He had met Don Mancini the second week he had been on the street. The Don had taken a shine to the young man with the fists the size of loaves of bread and had given him a job—a good-paying job—running numbers for him on Atwells Avenue. Five years later, Silvio had begun working directly for the Don. And ten years after that, Vince had gotten Silvio's old job.

Vince . . .

CHAPTER SIXTEEN

"Did ya hear?" Sal Chilleri said. He burst into the room like a kid on a sugar rush. "Did ya hear about Vegas?"

Vince Patrone had his nose buried in the morning's edition of the *Providence Journal*. The lead story had captured his attention like one of the true crime books he enjoyed so much. It should have. It was about an assassination attempt on the life of U.S. District Judge Artur Reis.

Silvio, Vince said to himself when he had finished reading the story. Only Silvio would have the balls to try something like that. Aloud to Sal: "What?"

"Did ya hear about Vegas?" Sal handed Vince a cup of convenience-store coffee.

Vince popped the top off the cup. He took a quick sip. "What about it?"

"Joey's talkin' about goin' to the CES this year. You know, the Consumer Electronics Show. It's apparently the best place around to pitch adult videos."

"No shit, Sherlock. It's about time Joey figured that one out." Vince took another sip of coffee. "Is he bringin' us with him? I don't know about you, Sally, but I wouldn't mind spendin' a couple of days at the tables. I haven't been to Vegas in ages."

"He's bringin' one of us. But he said that someone's gotta stay with the new girl. You know, in case she gets cold feet."

Both Sal and Vince glanced over at Midnight Productions's latest discovery. Joey had told them her name was Tiffany. She was sleeping again. That was about all she ever did. That, and get . . .

"I'll do it," Vince said. He drained his coffee. He crushed the cup against his thigh and pitched it to the floor. "I'll stay with her."

"Really?" Sal said. "But you just said you wanted to go."

Vince was still looking—still *leering*—at Tiffany. "That's all right. I can go next time. You can go first."

"Are you sure? I don't mind stayin' behind. I'm not much of a card player."

"Yeah, I'm sure. I don't mind watchin' the girl. I don't mind at all."

Sal finally appeared to pick up on what Vince had in mind while he and Joey were making the rounds in Las Vegas. "You dog," Sal said, smiling. "You dirty dog."

◆ ◆ ◆ ◆

"Way to go, Sam!" the salesclerk at the snack bar said.

One of the custodians put down his mop and flashed an exuberant thumbs-up. "Yeah! Great job!"

Sam Grimes had just entered the courthouse for the start of a new day. He didn't quite know what to make of all the fuss. He had seen the story in the *Providence Journal*, but he had expected the matter to end there.

The two probation officers in the building began to applaud when Sam passed their offices.

"Thanks, guys," Sam said, blushing.

The entire staff from the Clerk's Office rushed into the hallway.

"There's my boy," the Chief Clerk said. He was a lifelong civil servant pushing sixty-five and, hence, about to enjoy a cushy retirement on the taxpayers' dime. "There's the man of the hour."

Sam smiled. He was still blushing.

"Nice job, Sammy," one of the assistant clerks said.

Not even Sam's mom called him Sammy.

Holly Curran said, "Look, ladies. It's James Bond."

Sam couldn't help but chuckle at that one. "Yeah, right," he said to the mischievous Ms. Curran. The smile quickly left his face, though. Chief Judge Conigliero was waiting for him at the foot of the stairs.

The Chief Judge extended his hand. "Well done, young man. Well done."

Sam shook the Chief's hand. He had never done that before. He had never been afforded the opportunity, not even at the reception during the first week of the new clerkship cycle. He didn't know what to do next. The Chief Judge had never said more than two sentences to Sam, and he had certainly never complimented Sam for anything.

Sam said, "Thank you, Your Honor. I appreciate that. But I really didn't do anything."

"That's not what Marshal Lawton said. And Kaitlyn Ashmont made you sound like Audie Murphy in the *Providence Journal* this morning."

Sam had no idea who Audie Murphy was, but he didn't feel it wise to ask. He figured the guy must have done something heroic in the past, probably during one of the wars. The Chief Judge was widely known to be an avid reader of military history, especially of Stephen Ambrose's books.

"Thanks, sir."

An awkward silence.

"Well, I've got to get going," the Chief Judge finally said. "I've got some briefs to read. Besides, it looks like Ms. Ashmont has got a few follow-up questions for you."

Sam spun around and found himself witnessing the arrival of a runaway train.

"Sorry," Kaitlyn Ashmont said as she bumped into a lawyer on his way to the courtroom. "Pardon me," she said to another attorney with whom she collided.

Sam tried to make a break for it, but the determined newspaper reporter wouldn't permit it.

"Mr. Grimes!" she said in a high-pitched squeal. "May I have a word?"

Before Sam could say no, Ashmont was on top of him. Literally. She had tripped on her heel and knocked him to the floor.

"This is so embarrassing," she said. Her nose was about an inch away from Sam's. "Are you okay?"

"Ye—Yeah. I think so. Now I know what Judge Reis must have felt like when I landed on him."

"That's what I wanted to talk to you about." Ashmont was still nose to nose with Sam.

"Can we get up first?"

"Oh, yeah. Sorry." Ashmont bobbled to her feet. She inspected her clothes for dirt. She didn't appear to find any. Why should she? Sam had cushioned her fall.

Sam, on the other hand, had dirt all over his suit. He started to brush it off.

"Sorry about that," Ashmont said. "I've never been too good with these things." She tugged at her four-inch heel. She nearly fell over again as she did.

Sam smiled, and then said, "What can I do for you?"

"My editor wants me to write a follow-up piece to the story I wrote for today's paper. Did you read it?"

"Yeah, I read it."

"Did you like it?"

"Yeah, I liked it. Although I think you made too much out of what I did."

"What do you mean? You saved the Judge's life."

"No I didn't. I just fell on top of him. It was instinct more than anything else."

"But your so-called 'instinct' saved his life. You can be as modest as you want to be, Sam, but you can't deny that."

Sam blushed again. "I can *try*, Ms. Ashmont. You might not believe me, but I can *try*."

Ashmont smiled. "I don't believe you, Sam. More importantly, my editor doesn't." She reached into her pocketbook for her tape recorder. It was the size of a Snickers bar. "He wants me to write a profile on you. You know, a story about where you grew up, where you went to school, your family. That sort of thing."

"A profile on *me?* Nobody would be interested in that. And even if they were, I don't think I should do it."

"Why not? What's the harm?"

"None, probably. But given who I work for"—not to mention *what* he was working on at the moment (the Mancini trial), he wanted to add—"I just don't think I should."

"Sam!" Jerry Cushing called out from the far end of the corridor. "Can you come here for a moment?"

"Besides," Sam said, pointing to Jerry, "I've gotta run."

"Thanks," Sam said. He and Jerry were standing in front of the entrance to the Marshal's Office. "You saved my butt back there. I wasn't sure I could say no to her."

Jerry smiled. He glanced down the corridor. "Kaitlyn Ashmont is as pretty as a picture, that's for sure. But she's not as pretty as Mary."

Sam felt as if he had been punched in the gut by a heavyweight boxer when Jerry mentioned Mary's name. The commotion of recent events had distracted him for a while from worrying about where she was. But now he was back in panic mode. He wasn't ready to talk about it with Jerry, though. He wasn't ready to talk about it with anyone.

He said, "What's in the bag?"

Jerry was clutching a plastic shopping bag in his left hand. "This?" He jingled it like a Christmas present. A broad smile captured his round face. "The guys and I wanted to give you something. Marshal Lawton did, too." Jerry reached a large hand into the bag and pulled out a plaque. He handed it to Sam. "Read it."

Sam read it. The plaque said, "IN RECOGNITION OF A JOB WELL DONE, I HEREBY CONFER UPON SAMUEL D. GRIMES THE TITLE OF HONORARY UNITED STATES MARSHAL FOR THE DISTRICT OF RHODE ISLAND." It was signed by Marshal Lawton. Sam's eyes teared a bit. "Thanks, Jerry. Thanks a lot."

"There's more," Jerry said, still smiling. He reached into the bag again. This time he pulled out a gold badge. "May I?"

"Of course."

Jerry pinned the badge to the lapel of Sam's blazer. "Marshal Lawton wanted me to give you this."

"Thanks, Jerry. And please thank Marshal Lawton for me. This means a lot to me. I don't deserve it, but it means a lot."

"I'll tell him. I'll go tell him right now, in fact."

When Jerry left, Sam was alone with his thoughts for the first time in two days. His thoughts were about Mary—about why he hadn't heard from Mary.

◆ ◆ ◆

"Cut!" Philmore Bottoms shouted. He wiped the sweat from his brow with a faded blue bandanna and quickly distanced himself from the heat of the camera lights.

Commotion returned to the set.

Two naked women untangled their arms and legs. They rose from a velvet couch and reached for a pair of bathrobes that were lying in a pile at the director's feet.

"Am I done?" the brunette asked. She tied the belt on her bathrobe. Her name was Vivianna. She was in her late twenties, pretty, but beginning to show signs of age, and she was also two or three pounds past perfect. She had the lead role in *Poke Me, Man: The Movie*.

Bottoms's eyes made a quick pass over Vivianna's body. He wasn't impressed. At least not like he used to be . . . "You can go," he said to her.

"Do you have anything for me next week?" Vivianna fumbled for her pocketbook. "I *need* something. My source is pressuring me to settle up."

"Let me get back to you on that. I'm not sure what Joey has in mind. Besides, I thought you said you weren't doing smack anymore?" Bottoms shot Vivianna a hard look. "As I recall, being clean was one of the conditions of your employment." He shook his head in disgust. "Risking AIDS for the art is one thing, but it's something altogether different when you're talking about a needle."

"I've cut way back. Really, I have. I—I wasn't high for my scene with Stacy."

"Next time, you had better not be high for *any* of your scenes. You missed two of my position changes in your scene with Peter Boy. Even he said something about it, and he doesn't complain about much. 'A fuck is a fuck' is his motto."

"Sorry. It won't happen again. I—I promise." Vivianna turned and exited the set.

Thank God Joey found Tiffany, Bottoms said to himself as he watched Vivianna leave the room. He hadn't met Tiffany yet, but she was all Joey could talk about.

◆ ◆ ◆ ◆

"Hi, sweetie," Suzanne Hewitt said. She stepped over the threshold into Chad Smith's apartment. "Where's Sam?"

"At work." Chad closed the apartment's door.

"Is he *ever* not working? Does he *ever* have fun?"

"He loves clerking for Judge Reis. It's fun for him." There was more than a hint of defensiveness in Chad's voice.

"I guess." Suzanne placed her purse and a small bag on the kitchen table. She primped her hair with her fingertips.

Chad said, "Why are you so hard on Sam? He's a good guy. He's certainly never said a bad word about you."

"I know. It's not that I don't like him. It's just that I've never seen him do anything but work."

"That's not true, and you know it. He's the captain of our softball team. He's also got a new girlfriend."

"Who? Do I know her?"

"I don't think so. She goes to RISD."

"So that means I wouldn't know her? 'Dumb old Suzanne. At least she's good for a roll in the hay.' I could've gone to RISD—or to Brown, even. It's just that my father wanted me to manage his law office. I'm not dumb, you know. My brothers aren't, either."

"Shit, Suzanne. Do we always have to talk about the same thing? I've told you dozens of times that I think you're smart. I know you could've gone to college. I just meant that Mary—that's Sam's girlfriend—runs with a different crowd than you do."

"Is she nice?" Suzanne's voice had brightened a bit.

"Yeah. She's kinda quiet, but so is Sam." Chad walked to the kitchen table. He had been eyeing the small bag that Suzanne had brought with her from the moment she had entered his apartment.

Suzanne said, "Take a look."

Chad opened the bag and pulled out three DVDs. He smiled.

"I thought you might like some new ones. We've watched yours about three times each. I've even memorized most of the dialogue."

Chad laughed. "Me, too. All thirty-seven words of it."

Suzanne grabbed Chad by the crotch. "Let's go see if they're any good."

CHAPTER SEVENTEEN

The black Enzo Ferrari screeched to a halt at 1231 Atwells Avenue. Joey Mancini was late for a strategy session with John Marone. Joey had come to dread these sessions. For one thing, Marone scheduled them for 8:30 in the morning, and 8:30 in the morning was a bit too early for someone who made his living after-hours. For another thing, Marone's office was only a block and a half from The Players' Club, and The Players' Club was where Iron Mike's office was. It hadn't happened yet, but Joey was convinced that one day soon he would walk into Marone's office and find his father in close counsel with his—Joey's—lawyer.

As usual, Joey was escorted by Gina Marchette to Marone's private suite on the second floor of the modest two-story brick building. This was the one part of the morning strategy sessions that Joey didn't mind, both because Gina—who Joey was convinced was sleeping with her boss—was drop-dead gorgeous and because Marone's suite overlooked Pancino's Bakery, which Joey remembered fondly from his boyhood days of hanging around The Players' Club while his father oversaw the Donetelli crime syndicate.

"Joey," Marone said with a nod of his handsome head. "Have a seat." He turned and addressed his secretary. "Thanks, Gina."

Gina Marchette exited the room.

Both Marone and Mancini watched her leave.

Then, Joey took a seat on the leather armchair next to Marone's meticulously organized desk.

A toilet flushed.

Out from Marone's private bathroom walked Iron Mike Mancini.

Joey jumped to his feet and rushed for the door.

"Wait!" Iron Mike said.

"Wait for what?" Joey snapped. "For you to insult what I do for a living? Or will you just be insulting *me* this time?"

"I'm here because your mother asked me to come," Iron Mike said. "She hasn't heard from you in days. She's worried sick about this trial. She's watched me suffer through many an unnecessary trial over the years. That was difficult for her, but she knew I was strong. But you, Joey, you're her youngest child. And no matter how old you get, and no matter how successful you may become, you'll always be to your mother her youngest child. So I ask you—for your mother's sake—let me stay. Let me help. Our differences about what you do for a living can be discussed after John gets you off."

An icy silence engulfed the room. Joey stared out of Marone's office window to Pancino's Bakery across the street. The smell of fresh pastries and bread seeped through the cracks and crevices of the bricks and windowpanes.

The silence was broken when Joey sighed an unintended sigh. "Very well, Father," he said. "I'll let you stay. I'll let you help. But, I swear on Grandpapa's grave, if you mention—even once—that you disapprove of what I do for a living—of *my* business—you must leave. And when you do, you can take your so-called 'help' with you. I'm doing this for Mama, and only for Mama."

"Excellent, gentlemen," Marone said, seizing the moment like a good lawyer should. "Please. Both of you. Have a seat. I'd like to explain what you should expect to happen this morning, for this morning is perhaps the most important day of the entire trial: opening statements."

Marone motioned to three wooden armchairs that surrounded a small conference table at the south end of his office. A fresh pot of coffee rested in the middle of the table, along with a plate of Mrs. Pancino's famous *pasta frolla*. A dusty portrait of Marone's father—Iron Mike's father's lawyer—stared down from above. Scores of mementos from the former Chief

Justice's long and controversial career as head of the Rhode Island state judiciary were strewn throughout the room.

"Coffee?" Marone asked. He considered his watch. "It's five past nine. We've only got a few minutes before we have to head down to Kennedy Plaza for the morning's court session." He reached for a *pasta frolla*—for a lemon one, his favorite—and then apprised his client—clients, plural—of the day's likely course of events.

He said, "During opening statements each side provides an overview of what it intends to prove and of the evidence it'll be presenting. Opening statements are important because jurors often make up their minds on the basis of them. People, jurors included, don't like to admit they're wrong— even to themselves—so once someone has formed an opinion about something it's difficult to get him or her to shake it. The prosecutor—Steve Sutton in Joey's case—has the advantage of making the first opening address to the jury, and for this reason I've got to be able to articulate a strong and persuasive statement of my own to dislodge any unfavorable ideas he may have placed in the jurors' minds. To make a boxing analogy— I know how much you both enjoy boxing—the prosecution is the hard-charging Felix Trinidad; the defense is the counterpunching Oscar de la Hoya. Sometimes Trinidad wins; sometimes de la Hoya wins. It all depends on who's fighting the best on a particular day. And believe me, gentlemen, this is going to be a fight."

"A fight you must win," Iron Mike said. "Have you thought about ways of increasing our chances for success?" He glanced at Marone. "Silvio has managed to obtain a copy of the jury list—"

"Mike, please," Marone interrupted with a wave of his hand. He almost never called Don Mancini by his first name. Nobody did. But he had a point to make. And it was an important one. "Let me try the case first. I haven't let you down yet, have I? We're what, four and o? Trust me: This case will make it five and o. My father didn't send me to Yale for nothing."

Of course Marone didn't have the nerve to ask Don Mancini the question to which he most wanted an answer: whether the Don had had anything to do with yesterday's assassination attempt on Judge Reis.

Iron Mike studied Marone, stone-faced. He was always careful not to reveal too much about what he was thinking, even to his longtime attorney.

"All right, John," he finally said. "We'll do it your way. I won't get involved—yet. But the moment I sense the trial is moving against Joey, I intervene. I promised Theresa. Now, say what you need to say. Let's hear what you learned on *my* dime. Your father is a fine man and a fine lawyer, but the Mancinis sent you to Yale."

Marone nodded deferentially to the old but still intimidating man—to the all-powerful Don. "Sutton—again, he's the lead prosecutor—asked Judge Reis if he could show a sample videotape during his opening statement. The Judge said yes." Marone paused. He ran a smooth hand across his chiseled face. Gina had done a fabulous job of shaving him this morning. Gina had done a fabulous job at a lot of things . . . "That could be a problem for us."

Joey glanced over at his father when Marone made reference to the videos being "a problem." True to his word, Iron Mike had resisted the temptation to lecture his son on the "evil" that was pornography.

"To overcome that problem," Marone said next, "I'm going to need to personalize Joey." Marone's eyes met those of his young client. He added, in barely more than a whisper, "I'll be speaking of Claudia and the girls. Is that okay, Joey? I think it's necessary. The jury has got to see you as the likable person we know you are."

Claudia Mancini was Joey Mancini's wife of three years. She had left him in February, and she had taken their twin daughters with her. She had left when she had learned of Joey's involvement with pornography. She, too, thought that pornography was a filthy business and she, too, wanted her husband to find another line of work. Her father owned the neighborhood funeral parlor, and she had always hoped that Joey would go to work for him.

Joey merely nodded in response to his lawyer's question.

Marone understood what that meant, however. His young client had given him permission to mention the unmentionable: Claudia and the girls.

Marone again considered his watch. It now read 9:25 A.M. "Court starts at ten," he said. "And I know how prickly Judge Reis can be about keeping a trial on schedule. We should get going. Does anyone need a ride?"

"I'm all set, John," Joey quickly said. "But I'd be more comfortable, for safety's sake, if Father rode with Silvio."

This time, Iron Mike was the one who merely nodded. The father clearly understood that the son's suggestion about who should ride with whom had nothing to do with a concern about safety.

CHAPTER EIGHTEEN

Sam Grimes entered the courtroom for the opening statements in *U.S. v. Mancini*. He was surprised to discover Chad Smith seated at the law clerks' table. Sam took the chair next to him.

"I thought I'd get a bird's-eye view of the openings," Chad said. "You don't mind, do you?"

Sam said, "Not at all. There are two chairs at the law clerks' table because Judge Reis has two law clerks. Besides, take a look around the courtroom. You couldn't find a seat out there if you wanted to." Sam gestured to the crowd. Then, he said good morning to Holly Curran.

Holly said, "Good morning, Sam. Good morning, Chad." She stood to her feet and cried out, "All rise!"

Judge Reis entered the courtroom, just as he had done on hundreds of occasions since Sam's clerkship had begun some three months earlier. Perhaps for the first time, however, Sam fully appreciated the magnitude of the Judge's job. Maybe it was because two hundred and fifty people stood to their feet the moment the Judge walked into the room. Maybe it was because the room had suddenly become so quiet that Sam could hear the buzzing of the overhead fluorescent lights. Or maybe it was because everyone on the Judge's staff had been bombarded with questions: questions from the press, questions from colleagues, questions from friends, questions from family . . . questions from lovers. Indeed, Chad had mentioned to Sam the previous night how curious Suzanne seemed to be about the case.

The Judge had devoted a considerable amount of time during the last several days to voir dire: the process of selecting a suitable jury. Both the subject matter of the trial—pornography—and the notoriety of the defendant—the son of the reputed crime boss of New England—had made the task difficult to accomplish. However, after asking the hundred-person jury pool more questions about sex and Mafiosos than anyone who wasn't involved in casting *The Sopranos* would care to remember, he had managed to accomplish it.

He turned his attention to the fourteen people who had made the cut—to the twelve jurors and the two alternates—and said, "Good morning, ladies and gentlemen. This morning you will hear Mr. Sutton's opening statement for the government in United States versus Joseph P. Mancini. Before he begins, however, I need to make certain that no one has discussed, read about, or otherwise given consideration to this case since I instructed you not to do so during yesterday's empaneling. If you have, please signify by raising your right hand."

Dead silence.

Nobody's hand went up.

The Judge made a note to this effect in his bench book. Then he said, "You may proceed, Mr. Sutton."

Steve Sutton nodded respectfully at the Judge. He rose from his seat and walked toward the jury box. He stopped about five feet in front of it: close enough to maintain eye contact with the jurors and to be heard easily by them, but not so close as to make them feel uncomfortable. Posture military-straight, he began in a somewhat nervous voice, "Good morning, ladies and gentlemen. My name is Steve Sutton, and I'll be prosecuting this case against Mr. Mancini for the people of the United States. The facts will show that the defendant, Joseph Paul Mancini, produced and distributed obscene materials in violation of federal law."

Sutton pivoted on his Cole Haan heel and faced Joey Mancini. He singled out the defendant with an exaggerated pointing of his left index finger. His eyes returned to the jury: the twelve most important people in his—and Mancini's—life. "The purpose of my opening statement is to provide you with an overview of the evidence to be presented so that you may more easily follow the proceedings and evidence as it is produced. By the nature of everyday life, many of the relevant events in this case occurred in a piecemeal fashion: at different times, in different places, involving different persons. By the end of this trial I will have done my best to tie these events together for you."

Sutton turned to the bench. "With Your Honor's permission, I'll read from the indictment." He waited for Judge Reis's okay.

The Judge didn't disappoint him.

Sutton read the indictment to the jury. He then proceeded to provide the jury with a narrative of what he expected the evidence to prove. "I'd like to begin with a brief overview of the Racketeer Influenced and Corrupt Organizations Act—commonly known in law enforcement circles as 'RICO'—the law Mr. Mancini is charged with violating. In 1970 Congress enacted RICO to combat the influence of organized crime in interstate and foreign commerce. The statute makes it unlawful for any person to use a pattern of racketeering activity or the proceeds thereof to invest in, acquire control over, or conduct the affairs of, any formal or informal interstate enterprise."

Juror number three's eyes were glazing over, Sam noticed.

Sutton clearly noticed it, too. He tried to simplify his description of the law for her—for all the jurors. His nervousness was gone. He was doing a surprisingly good job. Maybe nepotism alone didn't explain why he had been assigned the case.

"RICO was enacted in response to congressional concern over the infiltration of legitimate commercial enterprises by traditional organized crime associations, a concern that traces back at least to the time of the Kefauver Committee hearings in the early 1950s and that grew in the early 1960s with the hearings before the McClelland Committee and the testimony of Joseph Valachi regarding *La Cosa Nostra*."

Sutton paused, adjusted his tie, and then added in a strong voice, "It's important for you to keep in mind, ladies and gentlemen of the jury, that the People are not accusing Mr. Mancini of being a member of the quote-unquote 'Mafia.' Consequently, we don't need to prove that fact, even if we can. Instead, RICO was focused, not on the status of the person doing the infiltrating—in this case, Mr. Mancini—but on whether the infiltration either derived from or was implemented by a 'pattern of racketeering,' which is defined very broadly to include a long list of state and federal predicate crimes commonly committed by so-called mobsters. As our expert witnesses will testify, the adult film industry has long been controlled by organized crime."

Sutton again turned to the bench. "As Judge Reis will instruct you," he said deferentially, "an individual employs a pattern of racketeering activity when he or she commits two or more specified criminal acts having sufficient continuity and relationship to constitute a pattern." Sutton's attention returned to the jury. "Under section 1961 of the RICO statute, quote, 'dealing in obscene matter' qualifies as a predicate offense. In the case before us in this courtroom, federal agents Kevin Wright and William Mulkaski will testify that they seized from every state in New England more than *five hundred* pornographic videotapes bearing Mr. Mancini's 'Midnight Productions' imprint. That's substantially more than *two*. And as you'll now see, ladies and gentlemen, and as you'll see at length throughout this trial, these videotapes *are* obscene. They therefore qualify as a predicate offense for RICO purposes."

Sutton stopped.

Silence dominated the courtroom.

"With Your Honor's permission," he finally said, "I'd like to show the jury an example of the kind of material I'm talking about."

"Very well," the Judge said.

Sutton had already cleared—over John Marone's futile objection—his use of a sample video during his opening statement. He renewed his request now to add drama to the moment: to focus the jurors' attention on what they were about to see.

Jim Hodges, the junior-most member of the Providence-based U.S. Attorney's Office and Sutton's second chair for the Mancini trial, wheeled a TV/DVD player to the front of the jury box.

Holly Curran turned off about half the lights.

The video began to play.

Chad Smith leaned over to Sam and whispered, "It's show time."

CHAPTER NINETEEN

Sutton played the entire video, including the phone sex ads. In a way, Sam thought, the phone sex ads were the most damaging part. Bluntly stated, there wasn't anything "literary, artistic, political, or scientific"—which there needed to be under the Supreme Court's *Miller* test—about a prerecorded phone message asking the caller to "stick your thick rod inside my pussy." The telephone number itself—1-800-555-FUCK—didn't help matters.

The video Sutton had selected to play for the jury was titled *Sisters*. It starred Teri Body and Tara Body—stage names, obviously. Apparently, they were sisters in real life. They certainly looked alike. Both were very pretty, and both had fantastic figures. The only noticeable difference from where Sam was sitting was that the younger of the two was a redhead, while the older sister was a blonde.

Sutton said, "This video is merely an example. It's graphic, but not necessarily the most graphic. As you'll see throughout this trial, others are even more disgusting—plain and simple."

The video played on. As it did, Sutton apologized for the offensive nature of it, but given that Mancini's alleged RICO violations involved trafficking in obscene material, "that's unavoidable."

The first scene was set in a lawyer's office. The so-called plot seemed to be that the sisters' parents had passed away and only one of the sisters could inherit the family business. The family business was, not surprisingly given that this was a porn flick, a condom company. The parents' will stipulated that the first of the sisters to marry and, of course, to consummate the marriage, would inherit the company. Both sisters left the lawyer's office intent on getting married—and laid—first and, perhaps most tellingly, of doing whatever it took to keep the other one from beating her to the punch.

Sure enough, the second scene found the younger sister having sex with the older sister's newly acquired fiancé in order to keep him from marrying the older sister. Best of all for Sutton and the prosecution, the sex scene was extremely graphic. There was absolutely nothing left to the viewer's imagination. The camera offered countless close-ups of the performers' genitals, they did the nasty for about fifteen minutes in a variety of circus-like positions, and the sum and substance of the dialogue was grunts and groans. The scene climaxed—literally—with the fiancé ejaculating on the redhead's buttocks.

Variations on this theme were repeated four more times, with each scene alternating between the sisters engaging in explicit sex acts with a variety of different men and, in one case, with another woman. The video ended with the sisters splitting the inheritance. There must have been a tie, although that particular plot twist was never explained in the video. Nobody cared, though. Plot development wasn't what porn flicks were about, as Sutton reminded the jury during the concluding moments of his opening statement.

"Again, I apologize if the video was offensive," he said, standing to his feet. "But that was unavoidable. This trial is precisely about the People's right to live in a community free from such moral depravity. In closing, ladies and gentlemen of the jury, based on the evidence, and on the instructions of the Court, as I believe will be given to you, *the People* of the United States in the State of Rhode Island will ask you to return a verdict of guilty of violating the RICO law against this defendant."

Sutton turned on his heel and pointed to Mancini again. Then, he marched back to his seat. He looked pleased with his performance.

"Thank you, Mr. Sutton," Judge Reis said. "We'll break for lunch and then hear from Mr. Marone this afternoon. This Court will be in recess until 1:00 P.M."

The Judge rapped his gavel and exited through his private door. As soon as he was gone, the courtroom came alive with chatter. It was about the video. Sam made his way through the crowd to say hello to his fellow law clerks. "Doesn't that beat all," he overheard an elderly woman remark. "That wasn't so bad," someone else said. "How did they do that?" said another. "Those awkward positions, I mean."

"*Citizen Kane*-caliber entertainment," Sam said when he finally reached Valerie, Morris, and David. Judge Sizemore had obviously given them permission to watch the opening statements.

"Hardly!" Valerie said. "That's the first X-rated video I've ever seen. Frankly, I don't know quite what to make of it. It was disgusting, that's for sure. But as someone who believes strongly in the First Amendment, I've always thought that people should be allowed to express themselves in any way they see fit."

"It wasn't so bad," Morris said. "I've seen worse. Why, just last night . . ."

Valerie and David rolled their eyes at Morris's retort. Their co-clerk had once again displayed his uncanny knack for coming up with a zippy one-liner to fit almost any occasion.

Sam pinched Morris on the back of the neck. Then, he directed his attention to Valerie. "Before this case began, I would've reacted in the same way, Val. But I've become extremely skeptical of the First Amendment argument. What bothers me the most is the damage that's undeniably done to the performers—physically and mentally—in the porn industry. When I was preparing some background information on the case for Judge Reis I read the *Miles Commission Report on Pornography*, which was released last year. Among the many issues addressed in that 1,760-page opus was the first-ever discussion of the impact of pornography on the performers. Although the report can be fairly criticized for being biased by the conservative politics of the Commission members, I thought the discussion of the impact on the performers was convincing. Essentially, the Commission found that the performers are generally young, previously abused, and financially strapped; that on the job they find exploitive economic arrangements, extremely poor working conditions, serious health hazards, strong temptations to drug use, and little chance of career advancement; and that in their personal lives they often suffer substantial injuries to relationships, reputation, and self-image. I believe in the First Amendment, too, Val—I really do—but we're not dealing solely with the abstract value of free expression here. We're dealing with people—very young people."

Sam had gotten so worked up while he was talking to Valerie, Morris, and David about the impact of pornography on the performers that tears welled up in his eyes. "I'll talk to you later," he said hurriedly to the three, to hide his embarrassment. "I've got to go see if Judge Reis needs me for anything during the lunch break."

As Sam was making his way back toward the front of the courtroom, he was startled by a voice out of nowhere.

"Where's that pretty girlfriend of yours?" he heard from behind. "I've been looking forward to seeing her all day."

Sam spun around and found Joey Mancini standing beside him, all alone.

"Wh—What are you talking about?" Sam said. He had never spoken to Mancini before.

"That girl you're dating. She's frickin' gorgeous. And what a body . . . I could make her a star."

"Fuck you, asshole," Sam said in a hushed, but angry voice. He could feel the hairs on the back of his neck standing on end. "I suggest you keep your fucking mouth shut, not only because of the affect stupid comments like that could have on your trial, but also because if you don't I'll bash your face in. You don't give a damn about anybody but yourself, do you?"

Mary had really gotten to Sam. He had never had an outburst like that before. He glanced down at his hands and noticed they were shaking. He tucked them into his pockets so Mancini couldn't tell.

Mancini said, "Hey. Mellow out, guy. I'm kidding." He laughed.

"You had better be." Sam walked away.

Sam's hands were still shaking when he inserted his key into the lock that guarded the entrance that separated Judge Reis's chambers from the courtroom. He took several deep breaths to bring his anger under control. He managed to open the door.

"What's wrong, Sam?" Carolyn asked, looking up from the blue and white sea of her computer screen.

"Nothing," Sam answered. "Just tired, that's all. Is the Judge in?"

"No, he's not. He left for lunch with Judge Sizemore about five minutes ago." Carolyn hit the SAVE key on her keyboard.

"Shit," Sam said. ". . . Sorry about that, C. I didn't mean to swear." He massaged the nape of his neck. It was as stiff as a new four iron. "He didn't say whether he needed me to do anything over the lunch break, did he?"

Carolyn smiled. She collected her purse and coat. "He specifically told me to tell you that he's all set. He thought you might prefer to spend your lunch hour with Mary. He wants you to take her someplace nice. He said it's on him. You know, for saving his life." Carolyn gave Sam a sisterly poke in the ribs. "I agree with the Judge. Women don't like to be neglected, you know. And as far as I can tell, you and Mary haven't been spending much time together lately. I think the last time I saw her was a couple of weeks ago when you two were in such a hurry to have lunch. Remember that, Sam? You almost knocked Jerry Cushing over on your way out the door."

Sam certainly did remember it. Judge Reis had "ordered" him to take Mary to lunch then, too.

Sam could never forget that day. He could never forget their first time together.

◆ ◆ ◆ ◆

"Boo!"

Mary jumped. "Stop that, Sam. You nearly scared me to death." She slapped him on the arm, but then flashed him a beautiful smile—*her* beautiful smile. She wasn't mad. She could never get mad at Sam. "What are you doing up here? You said you had some work to do for Judge Reis."

They were standing outside of Chief Judge Conigliero's chambers. Mary had just finished wishing her uncle a happy birthday and was about to head back to class. Portraits of federal judges from days gone by lined the long marble hallway. The light through the jalousie windows painted a kaleidoscope of colors on the dead men's faces.

Sam reached for Mary's hand. It was soft and warm, like a puppy stolen from a nap. "I do have work to do," he said, smiling. "Judge Reis ordered me to take you to lunch. What do you feel like eating? An order is an order. You don't want me to get in trouble, do you?"

"I guess not," Mary said, playfully. "But do we have to go to a restaurant?" She shot Sam a look that could have melted the chrome off a Buick.

They ended up having lunch at Mary's apartment. They forgot to eat, however. In fact, they had barely made it through the front door before they had ripped each other's clothes off.

Most new relationships had a lot of passion in them, but this one—Sam and Mary's—had more than any Sam had ever experienced. It wasn't the sex, either. It was what the sex represented: two people who had finally found what they were looking for, and who both knew it.

"Can I ask you something?" Mary said, wiggling into her jeans.

"Of course," Sam said, admiring the view.

"Why did you wait so long to ask me out? Frankly, I was wondering whether you were ever going to. And I was dropping about as many hints as I could at that party at the courthouse. You know, at the welcome party my uncle threw for you guys."

Sam looked away for a moment to think of what to say—or, more precisely, of *how* to say it. "The truth?" He put on his shoes.

"Yes."

"Well, to be perfectly honest, the combination of me not being Don Juan when it comes to women and you being so beautiful made it difficult. I'm not Chad, you know. Look at yourself. You're gorgeous. And I'm not just talking about on the outside."

Mary bent down and kissed Sam on the cheek. Her warm hand brushed against his bare leg. "No Don Juan, huh? That sounded pretty smooth to me. But don't you think you should wear pants to your meeting with Judge Reis?" She giggled.

"Probably." Sam's face was as red as the blouse Mary was wearing. "But only if you promise to have lunch with me more often."

"You've got yourself a deal, Mr. Juan." Mary kissed Sam on the cheek again.

And Sam couldn't have been happier about it.

CHAPTER TWENTY

Sam glanced at his watch. It read 12:58 P.M. Judge Reis was due back on the bench in two minutes.

Chad came scurrying through the crowd. He collapsed into his chair at the law clerks' table. "Did I miss anything?"

"No," Sam said. "The Judge isn't back from lunch yet." He studied his roommate's face. "Marone isn't going to show any videotapes, you know. Only Sutton will, and he's done for the day."

"A guy can always hope." Chad winked at his roommate and co-clerk.

Sam shook his head and smiled. His attention turned to the crowd. He knew Mary wouldn't be there—she always said hello when she was in the building to visit her uncle—but he looked anyway.

He glanced over at the prosecution table. Steve Sutton was organizing his pads and pens. A small stack of DVDs rested on top of his briefcase.

Next, Sam checked out the defense table. John Marone was pouring himself a glass of water. Joey Mancini was sitting stoically in his seat, his hands forming a small triangle over his thin mouth.

Sam could feel the blood rush to his brain like light through an open window as he considered Mancini's demeanor. He thought back to his confrontation with the defendant before the lunch break. How does that bastard know what Mary looks like? he asked himself. She wasn't in the courtroom during any of the preliminary proceedings in the case. Had Mancini run into her somewhere else in the building, perhaps in the hallway in front of Chief Judge Conigliero's chambers? There had to be some explanation like that. Nothing else seemed possible. Sam couldn't imagine any other way that Mancini could know Mary.

◆ ◆ ◆ ◆

John Marone stood before the jury like a matinee idol at a movie premiere. He looked as good as a man possibly could. Once again more than a few female members of the audience appeared mesmerized by his presence. Steve Sutton could only hope that the seven female members of the jury weren't similarly affected, Sam thought.

"Your Honor, if it please the Court," Marone said. He turned and faced the jury. He made eye contact with each and every juror. He lingered over the women. "Ladies and gentlemen of the jury, this is going to be an opportunity for me to speak with you like Mr. Sutton did this morning, and give you a brief outline of what I believe the evidence Mr. Sutton has in this case is going to show and what it's not going to show, and what I believe our evidence is going to show when we present our case."

Marone traced his fingertips through his thick black hair. He adjusted his Newbury Street tie. He smoothed the lapel of his hand-tailored Italian suit. Of course this was all for effect. He knew he was good-looking, and he wanted to call attention to his good looks. If you've got it, flaunt it, he seemed to be saying. He moved on to the substance of his remarks.

"The foundations for a free and open society are contained in the First Amendment." He removed a small copy of the Constitution from his suitcoat pocket and read the First Amendment aloud to the jury. James Earl Jones couldn't have sounded any better: "'Congress shall make no law respecting an establishment of religion, or prohibiting the free exercise thereof; or abridging the freedom of speech, or of the press; or the right of the people peaceably to assemble, and to petition the Government for a redress of grievances.'"

Marone waved his copy of the Constitution through the still air. "Through these words the Founding Fathers attempted to secure the freedom of conscience and the free communication of ideas. In the words of U.S. Supreme Court Justice Benjamin Cardozo, the freedom of thought and speech forms 'the matrix, the indispensable condition, of nearly every other form of freedom.'" Marone returned his copy of the Constitution to his pocket. "Justice Cardozo was one of our greatest Supreme Court justices because he understood, perhaps better than any other member of the high Court ever has, the significance of freedom of expression for the survival of liberty itself." He paused, waited precisely five beats, and then added with a poet's flourish, "Please keep Justice Cardozo's powerful message in mind throughout the course of this trial: his powerful message about the survival of liberty itself."

As Sam sat at the law clerks' table and listened to Marone's opening statement, he couldn't help but think that Marone wasn't just a famous name and a pretty face. There was both an eloquence and a weight to his remarks. He knew a lot more about the history—and the jurisprudence—of the First Amendment than Sam had expected he would.

Marone soldiered on, with the jury—with the entire courtroom—in the palm of his hand. "Only by tolerating different ideas and beliefs can democracy function and survive, especially in a culture as heterogeneous and heterodox as the United States. The history of America is largely the repudiation of orthodoxy by the spirit of individualism and nonconformism. Diversity is a value in and of itself. Mr. Sutton apparently believes otherwise."

Several of the jurors glanced over at the prosecution table.

Sutton did his best to maintain a poker face.

"Two things jumped out at me while I was listening to Mr. Sutton's opening argument," Marone said next. He moved closer to the jury box. "Two subtle yet crucial things. The first is that Mr. Sutton says he's, quote, 'prosecuting' Mr. Mancini. That's *almost* correct. Mr. Sutton is *persecuting* my client, no doubt because of who his father is."

"Objection, Your Honor!" Sutton cried out. He almost knocked over his chair in his haste to stand to his feet.

"Overruled, Mr. Sutton," Judge Reis said. "This is opening." The Judge shifted in his seat. "You may continue, Mr. Marone."

Sutton slumped back into his chair.

Meanwhile, in the rear of the courtroom, a slight smile crossed the weathered face of Iron Mike Mancini. John *did* know what he was doing, Iron Mike said to himself. Just like he said he did.

"Thank you, Your Honor. As I was saying," Marone repeated for emphasis, "Mr. Sutton certainly is *persecuting* my client. He had nothing on Mr. Michael Mancini, so he had to concoct something about his son. I'm a father myself. I know how painful this must be for Mr. Mancini, Senior."

Another slight smile captured Iron Mike's face. He was feeling so good watching Marone rip into the government's case against Joey that he almost forgot about his recent lung cancer diagnosis. Almost . . .

Marone strode back to the defense table. He reached for a legal pad. He flipped to a heavily highlighted page. "The second thing Mr. Sutton said that concerned me was his claim that, and I quote, 'the people have a right to live in a community free of moral depravity.'" Marone focused laser-like on the jury. F. Lee Bailey himself couldn't have looked more intense. "Now maybe the, quote, 'people' do. But I submit that it's up to *you*, ladies and gentlemen of the jury, and not to the *persecutor's* office, to decide whether the First Amendment means anything or not." He returned his legal pad to the defense table. He added, in an unexpectedly soft voice, "Please always remember that the First Amendment was designed to protect an *individual's* right of free expression. It should not be used as a moral code—as a tool for majoritarian tyranny—as Mr. Sutton would ask you to use it."

Marone marched back toward the jury box. He locked his hands behind his hips. "I need to turn for a moment, ladies and gentlemen, from the majesty of the First Amendment to the mundane of the RICO statute." He pointed at Sutton. This time Sutton flinched a bit. "Mr. Sutton has seen too many movies. And frankly, I resent the innuendo he's raising about my client: innuendo the *persecutor's* office has been raising about the Mancinis for years. The Mancinis are a hardworking, close-knit family who have overcome great obstacles to make something of their lives. Joseph Mancini is a working man and a loving parent, just like you good people are. He's married to a wonderful woman, and he's got two precious young daughters." Marone stopped, then spat, "To suggest that he's somehow involved with organized crime is more than absurd . . . It's—It's insulting."

Silvio Patrone placed a large hand on Iron Mike's slender shoulder, but the aging Don issued no response.

Marone stalked from one end of the jury box to the other. He was on a roll, and he was clearly enjoying himself. Trial lawyers lived for moments like these. "Mr. Mancini acknowledges that he's associated with Midnight Productions. However, the evidence will show that the videos the company produces and sells are *not* obscene. From what we've seen of the prosecutor's materials, some troubling tapes have surfaced. But those tapes were not produced and sold by Midnight Productions. They're fraudulent knockoffs that discredit the company's good name. Once again we see that the *persecution*, in its overzealous quest to finally *get* one of the Mancinis, has distorted the truth. On behalf of my client, Joseph P. Mancini, I thank you for your kind attention here this afternoon."

John Marone returned to his seat having clearly established that he intended to attack the prosecution at every turn. His use of controlled emotion to evince indignation undoubtedly had been designed to touch the viscera of the jurors by showing how wrong it was to have this charge leveled against Joey Mancini, "a hardworking man and a loving parent."

Marone's decision to accuse Sutton of going after Joey to get to Iron Mike had been particularly effective, at least to Sam. His substitution of the word "persecution" for "prosecution" was nothing short of brilliant.

Watching the jurors, Sam had sensed that they were quite willing to entertain Marone's accusation of governmental misconduct. That was good for the defense, because the videos were awfully smutty. In fact, Sam couldn't wait to see how Marone was going to try to characterize oral sex, gangbangs, and the like as "art." Sam's hunch was that Marone didn't think he could. That was why he was moving the ball and attacking Sutton.

◆ ◆ ◆

Silvio Patrone shut the door behind him. Don Mancini was settled in for the night. The Don hadn't had much to say on the drive back from the courthouse. That was surprising, Silvio thought. John Marone had done very well. Even Silvio knew that.

Silvio opened the drawer to his nightstand. He pulled out a bottle of Jack Daniel's and poured himself a drink. Silvio wasn't much of a drinker, but tonight he desperately needed a drink.

He removed his cell phone from his pocket. It had been too long, he said to himself. Months . . . Months since Vince had gone to work for Joey . . . Months since Silvio had spoken with his younger brother.

Don Mancini hadn't said anything about it yet, but Silvio knew it was only a matter of time. The Don didn't tolerate disloyalty. Almost everyone knew that. Silvio certainly did.

Did Vince?

CHAPTER TWENTY-ONE

"Would you gentlemen care for some champagne?" a tuxedo-clad waiter asked. He held out a sterling silver serving tray for the two newly arrived guests.

"Why not?" Sam Grimes answered.

It had been a long week—a *long* week—what with sitting through a mind-numbing number of X-rated videos and Mary's continuing status on the MIA list. Sam definitely needed some alcohol.

"I told you this place would be rockin'!" Chad Smith said. "I told you the Hewitts throw great Newport parties!"

Chad had already polished off glass number one of some of the finest bubbly Sam had ever tasted.

"Look," Chad added, pointing to his left. "There's Senator Chase standing next to the fireplace. I told you he'd be here. That's Governor Lombardi he's talking to. More importantly, look at how many gorgeous women are here."

Chad offered this last remark in a hushed voice. Obviously, he didn't want Suzanne to hear his comment about other "gorgeous women." He was right, though. The place was "rockin'," and gorgeous women did abound. Sam decided then and there that it was true what people said: Money and power equaled sex. Just ask Donald Trump and the three perfect tens he had married.

Sam and Chad began to make their way across the ornate ballroom. Sam had never seen so much marble and so many gilt-bronze trophies in his life. What looked to be an original Monet painting was hanging on the wall at the north end of the room. Sam would have recognized those out-of-focus water lilies anywhere.

Suzanne Hewitt seemed to spot the two roommates almost the moment they entered the ballroom. She rushed over to greet them. "Hi, guys!" she chirped. "I'm so glad you're here!" She reached for Chad's hand, and then turned her attention to Sam. "Where's Mary?"

"I don't know," Sam said, with more than a hint of discomfort in his voice. He stuffed his hands into his pockets and stared down at his shoes. He had forgotten to shine them. "I haven't heard from her in awhile."

"Why not?"

Suzanne was obviously oblivious to Sam's desire to talk about the weather—or about anything else, for that matter.

He said, "I guess she's been busy."

"Doing what?"

"*Come on*, hon'," Chad interrupted. He squeezed Suzanne's hand. "Let's give Sam a break about Mary. He's bummed enough as it is. Why don't you introduce him to Senator Chase? That's all he could talk about on the drive down after I told him the Senator would probably be here. You know how political science majors can be. They're worse than groupies when it comes to politicians."

Sam said, "I never got a chance to meet him at Chief Judge Conigliero's party for the new law clerks."

Sam's mood had brightened a bit. It wasn't a "groupie" thing, though. He wanted to sing Judge Reis's praises to the Senator. There had been another story in the morning's *Providence Journal*. Kaitlyn Ashmont had been able to confirm through an anonymous source at the White House that the choice to succeed Judge Sizemore on the First Circuit was definitely either Judge Reis or Chief Judge Conigliero.

However, before Suzanne got a chance to introduce Sam to Rhode Island's junior U.S. Senator, Raoul Hewitt called his daughter away.

"Okay," Chad said, smiling. "Now that Suzanne is gone, we can have some *real* fun. Billy and Alan want us to step into the billiard room for a minute. It's not to shoot a quick rack, either."

Sam felt a sudden push in the bottom of his back. "Oh, excuse me," he heard from behind. His champagne spilled to the floor. He spun around. He found himself face-to-face with the most beautiful woman he had ever seen. Her eyes were Elizabeth Taylor-like violet. Her hair was Farrah Fawcett-like blonde. Her body was Angelina Jolie-like dangerous. It was as if three generations of Hollywood beauty were standing eighteen inches in front of him. He was speechless. Literally . . .

"I'm *so* sorry," the beautiful woman said. She even talked sexy.

"It's—It's—It's okay."

All of a sudden Sam was stammering like Stuttering John on *The Howard Stern Show.*

"You're too nice. The least I can do is get you a refill." This beautiful woman—this human centerfold—caressed Sam's forearm as she took the empty champagne flute from his quivering hand. "And don't be so nervous."

"Hey, Sam, are you coming?" Chad bellowed from thirty feet away. He appeared surprised that Sam wasn't directly behind him. But the moment he saw the reason Sam had fallen back, he smiled. "Bring your friend," he said.

"My roommate and I are on our way to meet Billy and Alan Hewitt in the billiard room. You're welcome to join us if you'd like." Thankfully, Sam wasn't stammering anymore. His hands were no longer quivering.

"I'm not much of a pool player, but, hey, why not? A girl can always learn. I'm Jennifer, by the way."

"Nice to meet you, Jennifer." Sam extended his hand to make her formal introduction. "I'm Sam. Sam Grimes."

"Nice to meet you, Sam—Sam Grimes."

"Mary who?" Chad whispered into his roommate's ear. He watched the beautiful Jennifer lead the way. "Nice dress."

Chad was right, Sam said to himself. It was impossible to imagine Jennifer's dress being any tighter. Suddenly, he felt guilty as hell: Mary was probably sitting in the library at school studying for an upcoming midterm, while he was at a society party imagining what some upscale blonde looked like naked.

"Gentlemen," Alan Hewitt said when Sam, Chad, and Jennifer entered the billiard room. "I see you've met Jennifer."

The billiard room was chock-full of leisure apparatus. A big-screen Toshiba TV, a state-of-the-art NAD sound system, and a top-of-the-line Brunswick pool table were the most conspicuous of the Hewitts' many toys. Faux English pub signs lined the walls. The TV was tuned to the Mike Tyson-Lennox Lewis heavyweight championship bout (Tyson comeback number three; rematch number four). The announcer's wail struggled to compete with the Dave Matthews Band CD resounding from the quadraphone.

"I assume we're not *really* going to play pool," Jennifer purred. She traced her fingers across Alan's stomach.

"You know us too well, my beautiful friend," Alan said, reaching for her. His hands tracked the outline of her hips. He turned to his brother. "Will you do the honors, B?"

As Billy Hewitt was pulling a tinfoil pouch from his suit-coat pocket, something caught Sam Grimes's eye: a black Enzo Ferrari was parked beside a dormant rhododendron bush at the far end of the driveway.

Sam moved closer to the window to get a better look.

Billy did a line, and then passed the mirror to Jennifer. She leaned over the billiard table and prepared to inhale the generous portion that Billy had prepared for her. Chad and Alan appeared sufficiently preoccupied with Jennifer's low-cut dress for Sam to confront Billy with an obvious, though undoubtedly ill-advised, question.

"Is Joey Mancini here? . . . I know he's here. I can see his Ferrari parked in the driveway. He's got the only Enzo in the state."

Billy rolled a cue stick between his palms. "Who's to say it doesn't belong to one of Mom and Dad's out-of-town guests? My parents' parties are legendary, you know. People come from all over." He smiled.

"Come on, Billy. I'm not stupid. I can see the Rhode Island plates."

Billy sighed. "Okay, Sam. You got me. Yeah, he's here. At least I think he's still here. I haven't seen him in hours. He arrived about forty-five minutes before the party started. He came to see my father. My father's got a business venture going with Joey. Dad makes a good living as a lawyer, but it's certainly not enough in itself to allow the family to live in a place like this." Billy swept the cue stick through the expanse of the room.

Chad was taking his turn at the mirror.

Alan was flirting with Jennifer.

"What sort of business venture?" Sam was hoping it wasn't what he thought it was.

Billy smiled and shook his head. "Now, Sam. My good buddy, Sam. I've already said more than I should. Shit, Dad would kill me if he knew I had said anything at all. Let's talk about something else. Let's *do* some*one* else." He pointed the cue stick at Jennifer. "If we can get a few more lines into our beautiful friend over there, she can be a whole lotta fun, if you know what I mean."

"Of course I know what you mean, Billy. I think I'll pass, though. There's someone else I need to find."

Sam was almost to the door before Chad noticed he was leaving.

"Where are you off to?" Chad was sniffing repeatedly from the cocaine. He wiped his nose with the back of his hand. "It's your turn."

"There's something I've got to do first," Sam said. "Jennifer can take my turn. She looks like she could use an extra one."

"Don't go," Jennifer said. There was a surprising amount of tenderness in her voice. She quickly reverted to type, however. "The fun hasn't started yet." She winked at Sam.

As ready and willing as Jennifer appeared to be, and as horny and lonely as Sam knew he was, Sam was determined to find Joey Mancini. After all, Mancini must have known that Chad was dating Raoul Hewitt's daughter. At some point he had to show the system a little respect. Sam didn't care who his father was: Joey Mancini was on trial before the judge for whom two of the Hewitts' most frequent guests were employed. His business could wait. His goddamn business could fuckin' wait.

◆ ◆ ◆ ◆

The south wing of Chateau del Sol contained the previous owner's elaborate stables. The late Mrs. Jacqueline Ostenheimer Belmont had provided her horses with morning clothes, afternoon clothes, and evening clothes. In the salon above the stables there still stood to this day the stuffed and lifelike figures of two of her favorite horses. Seated upon them were figures of men in armor.

Adjacent to the stables in the far reaches of the wing was Raoul Hewitt's private study. There was indeed someone in there. Sam slowly—ever so slowly—turned the brass doorknob, hoping that whoever was inside wouldn't hear him. He was unsuccessful . . . It was Joey Mancini.

"Come on in, Mr. Grimes," Mancini said. "I was wondering whether I was going to see your smiling face tonight. It's quite a party, don't you think?"

"What are you doing here?" Sam's eyes swept quickly around the room. The activity transpiring on the television screen captured his attention. "From the looks of the TV, I think I've got a pretty good idea."

Mancini cackled. He sounded like a rooster crowing at dawn. "Pull up a chair. My partner and I are screening some of the latest releases from Midnight Productions. As my excellent lawyer John Marone would say, we're making the most out of the First Amendment." Mancini gestured to the screen. A teenaged girl—sixteen, tops—was performing fellatio on one guy while another guy entered her from behind. Both men looked old enough to be the girl's father. "Is this art, or what?"

"Yeah. Right. Some art," Sam spat. "Listen, man. You've got some nerve showing up here tonight when you knew that Chad Smith and I would be here. Don't you have any respect for the court?"

"Fuck the court!" Mancini thundered. The famous Mancini temper was now on full display. "I'm having to spend my valuable time and hard-earned money sitting in that goddamn courtroom defending myself against the trumped-up charges of the FBI. You're a smart guy, Grimes. You know what's going on. The FBI hasn't been able to get to my father, so it's trying to get to me. Fuck that." Mancini's face was as red as Chad's new Porsche. "And don't you dare take that high and mighty tone with me. I don't care how many goddamn degrees you've got. I'm *Joey Mancini,* and you'd best not forget it." He pounded his fist on Raoul Hewitt's desk, but then became remarkably composed. So composed, in fact, that Sam was beginning to think the guy was schizophrenic. "Speaking of the unforgettable," Mancini said next, "how's that beautiful girlfriend of yours? *Mary,* isn't it?"

"Fuck you!" Sam screamed. He bolted for the door . . . It was either the door or Mancini's throat. He slammed the door shut behind him as he exited the room. He heard a vase break. He hoped it was an expensive one.

CHAPTER TWENTY-TWO

Chad Smith navigated the twists and turns of Route 114 with the acumen of Dale Earnhardt Jr. His Porsche Boxster handled splendidly—even when traveling well in excess of the speed limit. He loved his car.

Sam Grimes could understand why. It was a fabulous automobile. It was fire engine red, with a black convertible top and whitewall tires capped in spoked chrome. The interior was a chic black glove-leather. The stereo system—a top-of-the-line Sony—sounded better than the one in their apartment did. The six-cylinder engine purred like a kitten and accelerated like a racehorse at the Kentucky Derby.

Of course Sam hadn't been able to figure out how Chad could afford the car. A Porsche Boxster cost about $48,000. As law clerks, Sam and Chad each made only $42,000 a year. Sam knew for a fact that Chad didn't come from money. His father was a high school math teacher and his mom worked part time in a doctor's office as a receptionist. Sam had decided long ago that the state of his roommate's finances was another one of life's mysteries. Maybe the Hewitts had bought Chad the car? Sam hoped that wasn't the explanation, but he was quickly learning that anything was possible when it came to the Hewitts.

"I found out what so-called business the Hewitts are doing during those awkward moments when they get so tight-lipped."

Those were the first words that Sam had uttered since he and Chad hit the road.

Chad turned his head and faced his roommate. The bright sunlight forced him to squint. "What is it?" He switched off the radio to better hear Sam's answer.

"They're pornographers."

"What?"

"They're pornographers. And guess who their business partner is."

"Who?"

"Joey Mancini . . . *Hey*, watch where you're driving!"

Chad jerked the Porsche back onto their side of the yellow line. An oncoming car honked as it sped by.

"How do you know that?" he asked. "More importantly, why would you want to know?"

"'How'? Because I saw Mancini's Ferrari parked outside the Hewitts' billiard room on Friday night. He's got the only Enzo in the state. You—Mr. *Car & Driver* himself—told me that. He was sitting in Raoul's study screening some new porn flicks. He told me that Raoul is his partner."

Sam's eyes were riveted to the road. Like it mattered if *he* watched where they were going . . .

"'Why'? Because I was pissed that he would show up at the party when he knew you and I would be there. My God, man, he's on trial before Judge Reis. He owes the system *some* respect. I don't think it's too much to ask that he find another day to conduct his goddamn business with Raoul. I think he showed up just to spite us. Or at least to spite *me*. We had quite a run-in the other day."

"What are you talking about? What run-in?" Chad shifted the Porsche into fifth gear and jetted past an SUV that was crawling down the highway. "Sunday drivers," he muttered.

"Mancini came up to me after Marone's opening statement and made a crack about how attractive Mary is," Sam said. "It wasn't complimentary, either. It was lewd. He even made reference to her potential as a porn actress. I didn't take him seriously, but it still pissed me off."

Chad whizzed past another car, then another, and then another. "I can understand why you'd be pissed." He paused, and smiled a bit. "I've got to admit, though, that I agree with Mancini's characterization of Mary's potential." He met Sam's eyes. He could see that his roommate wasn't amused. "Sorry about that, man," he said. "I was kidding. How did he know about you and Mary, anyway? She almost never visits you at work."

"I don't know," Sam said. "He definitely knows that we're a couple, though. At least I think we still are . . . I told him to shut the fuck up."

Chad whitened. His eyes grew as large as the reflectors dotting the winding road in front of them. "You didn't really tell him *that*—to 'shut the fuck up'—did you?"

Sam nodded yes.

"I can't believe you said that to Joey Mancini." Chad shook his head in disbelief. "Man, you're even crazier than I thought you were. Joey Mancini isn't some townie you got into a disagreement with at The Hot Club. He's the son of Iron Mike Mancini, the crime boss of New England. Shit, I've heard stories about people getting hurt—getting *killed*—because Iron Mike felt they had slighted him or his family."

Sam gazed out over Narragansett Bay as they crossed the Gallagher Memorial Bridge. The turbulent sea was a fitting metaphor for the current state of his life.

A half-hour passed in silence.

Finally, Chad said something. "I suppose that explains why you weren't around much yesterday and this morning. And to think that I thought you had discovered an exhibit at the Tennis Hall of Fame that you simply had to see, and see again. That's what I told Raoul, at any rate, when he asked where the heck you were all weekend."

"Sorry if I put you in the uncomfortable position of having to cover for me. I know how that feels . . ."

Sam and Chad both knew that Sam was talking about his covering for Chad at work. They laughed, but it was nervous laughter.

Sam wadded his hair into a short ponytail, as he often did when he was nervous. "You're right, you know," he said, in barely more than a whisper. "Joey Mancini does think I've shown him disrespect. And if there's any truth to Mario Puzo's novel, respect is the one thing that *La Cosa Nostra* insists upon. I can hear Don Corleone now . . ." He tightened the grip on his hair. "I'm not scared, though. Really, I'm not."

The incredulous look on Chad Smith's face suggested that he knew his roommate wasn't being honest with him—or with himself. No, Chad knew Sam was terrified.

◆◆◆◆

Silvio Patrone shut the door to his bedroom. It had been a long weekend. He had been on duty the entire time. He didn't mind that, though. He liked to work. No, what bothered him—what had him reaching for the Jack Daniel's in his cupboard again—was that Don Mancini had barely said a word to him in days. Silvio knew why, too: the Don wasn't pleased that Silvio had failed to take out Judge Reis.

Silvio poured himself a double Jack, neat, and then pulled his cell phone from his pocket. Last time, he couldn't bring himself to dial the number. Last time, he couldn't figure out what he was going to say. That was pretty sad, he said to himself as he activated the phone. Vince was his brother.

The number rang four times, and then switched into voice-mail mode. "Leave a message," it said.

It was Vince. Silvio would recognize that gruff voice anywhere. Even after ten months . . .

Silvio said, "Vince. It's me. Gimme a call. It's important. You know the number."

Silvio turned off his cell phone and returned it to his pocket.

Vince Patrone had heard his cell phone ring, but he was too busy to answer it. Sal was at the store buying supplies and he was due back any minute. More importantly, Joey had called about twenty minutes earlier to say that he was on his way, too. Joey had said that he had something important to talk to the girl about.

The girl wouldn't be difficult to find, that was for sure. She was lying under Vince at the moment.

What a job, Vince said to himself as he looked down into Tiffany's beautiful face. He would have never been allowed to have this kind of fun working for Don Mancini.

CHAPTER TWENTY-THREE

U.S. District Judge Artur Reis walked quickly down the corridor. He said, "Sorry I'm late." He slipped out of a pair of Isotoner gloves, and then reached into the pocket of his trench coat for his office key. "Eva is sick, so I had to take Marta to school. Like most six-year-olds, Marta is pretty difficult to get moving in the morning." The Judge glowed like the loving father he was. "She's worse than her brothers were at that age. And waking her brothers was like waking the dead."

It was before eight, and Carolyn hadn't arrived yet. Sam Grimes had come to discuss the most recent bench memo he had written for the Judge. He smiled and said, "No problem. I just got here myself."

"What's your excuse? Did Mary get the best of you last night?" The Judge winked at Sam. He held the door open for him.

Sam feigned affront. "Ha ha. It was a long weekend, that's all. Mary had nothing to do with it. She wasn't even there. Chad and I drove down to Newport to spend the weekend with the Hewitts. You should see the house they've got down there. It's unbelievable. It's like Tara in *Gone with the Wind*."

"I've seen pictures. It was featured in a photo-essay in the *Providence Journal Sunday Magazine* not too long ago. They gave it some French name, if I remember correctly."

The Judge placed a letter in Carolyn's in-box that he wanted her to type. He and Sam moved to his private office.

"'Chateau del Sol,'" Sam said. "It's actually a combination of French—the 'Chateau' part—and Spanish—the 'del Sol' part. It means 'house of the sun.'"

"I didn't know you were trilingual. Did you have a nice time?"

"I'm *not* trilingual. I barely know English, or so my father used to say after reading my high school term papers. Seriously, though, yes, I had a nice time. The food was great. You know me: if the food is good, I'm all set."

Sam had decided not to tell the Judge about his two recent encounters with Joey Mancini. He knew he probably should, but he just wanted to forget about them. Besides, he couldn't see how it would be good for the trial. He doubted that the Judge would be too keen about having one of his law clerks called to the witness stand to testify to an admission the defendant had made about being a pornographer. Sam had a hunch that Mancini would just deny it, anyway. Then everybody would look bad, including the Judge.

The Judge removed a hanger from the closet behind his desk and hung up his trench coat. He pressed the orange BREW button on the Mr. Coffee. The two men took their usual seats: the Judge on the overstuffed easy chair and Sam on the corduroy couch across from him.

Sam placed his briefcase on the coffee table. He sat on his hands to warm them.

"Thanks for your bench memo on Rule 403," the Judge said. "It looks like you owe Valerie lunch—and at someplace nice, too. *Anderson v. United States* is very helpful, obviously. A First Circuit precedent right on point: that's excellent work, Sam. I also benefited from *United States v. United Shoe Machinery Corporation*, and your analysis of, and analogy to, complex litigation was especially good. I'm still not sure how many of the videos I should allow Mr. Sutton to play, but I plan to adopt your suggestion of having him explain to me in advance which tapes he needs and why. After I get that information from him, I should be able to make a decision."

Sam couldn't help but feel proud of himself. Judge Reis always tried to compliment him and Chad when they did a good job, but, still, when the Judge—*any* judge—said he planned to adopt a law clerk's suggested plan of attack, well, that was about the highest compliment a law clerk could receive. Sam had even stopped thinking about Mary . . . for the moment.

"What's on tap for today?" he asked.

The Judge sank back into his easy chair. He pulled the handle on the side of the chair and popped up the footrest. "Mr. Sutton will most likely begin by eliciting testimony from the FBI agents assigned to the case about how and why they seized the videos in question. He obviously needs to tie the defendant to the tapes, but from what I've seen from the indictment that should be pretty easy for him to do."

Sam reached for his briefcase. "If it's okay with you, I'm going to grab a cup of hot chocolate from the snack bar before the morning session. The unseasonably cold weather has given me a real craving for it. Would you like some?"

The Mr. Coffee hissed to completion. The ten-cup decanter was filled to the brim. Judge Reis shook his head. "No thanks, Sam. My coffee here will do. But please ask Chad to come in for a minute. I'd like to see how he's progressing on the draft memorandum and order in Wagner versus Toyota."

Sam stood to his feet. "Yes, sir. Is there anything else you need?"

The Judge reached for his coffee cup. He wiped it clean with a paper towel. "There is. I'd like for you to get a jump on the jury instructions. I know the prosecution is only now about to start putting on its case, but this case is too important—too unusual—for me to rely on the form book."

"No problem," Sam said. "When would you like them by?"

"By the end of the week, if possible. I'd like to take them with me on the plane."

"The plane?"

"Yes. The White House has asked to meet with me about the upcoming First Circuit vacancy."

"That's terrific!" Sam almost dropped his briefcase from the excitement.

"Thanks. But nothing's been decided yet—by the President, or by me."

"Surely the President wouldn't ask you to fly to D.C. again if you aren't the choice. And why wouldn't you say yes if you are?"

"I probably will say yes, Sam. But to tell you the truth, it'll be tough to give up jury trials. As this case is almost certainly going to show, nothing beats the thrill of a good jury trial."

Well, Sam could think of at least one thing that did . . . But the task at hand was to track down Chad.

Much to Sam's relief, he found Chad hard at work in his office. The last thing Sam needed was to have to cover for Chad again. He had enough on his mind as it was. It was only 8:15 A.M. and he had been convinced he would have to come up with some kind of excuse for his roommate and co-clerk. He had been running through a few options on his way down the corridor. The "car trouble" excuse was out, given that their apartment was two blocks from the courthouse. He had been leaning toward "his alarm clock must've broken again."

He said, "Judge Reis wants to see you for a minute." He stepped over piles of books and papers. Half the law library seemed to be scattered around Chad Smith's cluttered office. "He wants a status report on *Wagner v. Toyota*."

Chad put down his pen. "No problem. I just finished proofing the memorandum and order." He was halfway out the door before he remembered the case file. He doubled back and retrieved it from the pile of papers closest to his desk. His eyes met Sam's. "Have you heard from Mary?"

Sam shook his head. "Not yet. But thanks for asking. I'm going to grab a cup of hot chocolate from the snack bar and get some air before heading up to the library for a bit. I've got a headache. Besides, the ball is in her court now. I've left at least three messages for her. If she wants me, she knows where to find me."

Chad pumped his fist in the air like Kobe Bryant after a spectacular slam-dunk. "There you go, buddy. Be strong, my man, be strong." Chad turned serious. "Sorry again for my comment yesterday about Mary. I know you know I was kidding, but I should've been more sensitive to how stressed you've been about her lately."

Sam forced a smile. "Yeah, I know you were kidding. But thanks for saying that. It means a lot." Sam hesitated for a moment, and then said, "We said it."

"Said what?" Chad's eyes were locked on Sam's.

"That we love each other."

"When?"

"During a, quote, 'lunchbreak' a couple of weeks ago."

"Man, you're crazy. You're f-in' crazy." Chad was smiling now. "You've been dating, what, for three or four weeks? It took me over *two years* to say it to Suzanne, and I only said it then because she was driving me nuts about it."

"Sometimes it's not about time," Sam said, softly. "Sometimes you just know."

CHAPTER TWENTY-FOUR

Sam hurdled up the marble stairs on his way to the law library.

Chief Judge Conigliero stopped him dead in his tracks.

The Chief Judge said, "Young man, this is a federal courthouse, not a gymnasium." Even sans robe and gavel, The Honorable Francis Conigliero cut an imposing figure.

Sam said, "Sorry, Your Honor. It's just that Judge Reis asked me to get started on the jury instructions for the Mancini trial, and I want to finish them as soon as I can in case he needs me for something else."

The Chief Judge studied Sam's eyes for what Sam felt like was a week. Sam couldn't tell whether the Chief was doing so because he had caught Sam running in the hallway again or because he suspected that Sam knew something about the First Circuit search that he—one of the leading candidates for the position—didn't know.

"Very well, Mr. Grimes," the Chief Judge finally said. "But please be careful. I don't want anyone getting hurt. There's a lot of traffic in this corridor."

"Yes, sir." Sam turned to leave, but a question came quickly to mind, a question he couldn't get *off* his mind. "You wouldn't happen to know where Mary Jackson is, would you?" He tried his best to appear only moderately interested in the answer.

"She called last week to say she's in New York. Her mother—my sister—has been sick. Why do you ask?" The Chief Judge studied Sam's eyes again.

Did he know? Sam asked himself. Did the Chief know that he was dating Mary? Aloud to the Chief Judge: "No reason, sir. Mary is a fr—friend of mine, and I haven't seen her around in awhile. Thanks for letting me know where she is. I hope her mom is all right."

"I'm sure she'll be fine." This time, it was the Chief Judge who turned to leave. "Give my best to Judge Reis," he said as he headed off in the direction of his chambers. "Tell him I'm pulling for him."

Sam knew that Chief Judge Conigliero didn't mean what he said about Judge Reis. He had no idea what to think about what the Chief had said about Mary.

◆ ◆ ◆ ◆

"We're planning to shoot three more installments in the *Naughty Nurses* series," Philmore Bottoms said to the middle-aged man with the cheap toupee and the custard-pie stomach. "We're scheduled to shoot them next week, in fact."

"Will Jennifer be starring in those, too?" the man asked. "Is—Is she here?" His bloodshot eyes darted around the convention hall like those of a junior high school boy hiding out in the girls' locker room hoping to sneak a peak.

"Yes to both," Bottoms said. He waved hello to a veteran male porn star who was sporting an expression of having evolved psychologically to the point where he was so incredibly cool and laidback that all of life was a yawn. Then, Midnight Productions's top director simply turned on his heel and left the middle-aged man standing alone in the cavernous room with his autograph book and disposable camera.

"Goddamn mooks," Bottoms said to Billy Hewitt.

Billy hustled to keep pace with the supercharged director. The guy had so much energy that he made Jim Carrey seem catatonic by comparison. "What's a 'mook'?"

This was Billy Hewitt's first Consumer Electronics Show. His father, Raoul, had wanted him to learn more about the family business in the hope that one day soon he could take over the reins from the aging workers' compensation lawyer. Billy's brother, Alan, had remained behind in Providence. Alan had wanted to come—he was *dying* to come—but their father had said he needed Alan's help on a workers' comp case that was about to go to trial. However, Billy knew the real reason their father hadn't wanted Alan to attend the convention: Raoul Hewitt feared that the sea of porn starlets in vinyl halter tops and six-inch stiletto heels, with buttocks less covered than shellacked, would be too difficult for his younger son to resist.

The CES was a major event. It was like a combination convention and talent show for the best and the brightest in the world of consumer technology. For example, Sun Microsystems was using the CES to launch its new version of Javascript, and at that very moment Bill Gates was delivering a packed-house speech about Microsoft's latest Windows program. Major players in TV, cable, and merchandising were hosting a panel discussion on the viability of HDTV. But far and away the most popular venue at the CES was what was called (with tongue firmly in cheek) the Adult "Software" Exhibition. A sign at the entrance to the exhibition hall decreed that people had to be twenty-one to get in. The median age inside was forty-five, almost all male. Every production company in the adult entertainment industry, from Anabolic to Zane, appeared to have a booth. This was Midnight Productions's first appearance at the convention, however.

"A 'mook' is a rube," Bottoms said. "You know, a fan." He smiled and shook his head. "I should be nicer to them, though. After all, without the mooks I couldn't make my movies. That's what your father keeps telling me, anyway."

They marched past the After-Hours Productions booth. A peroxide-blonde starlet in a black latex spaghetti-strap gown, chewing gum and blowing orange bubbles, was being videotaped by a disabled fan whose camera and parabolic mike were bolted to the arm of his wheelchair. The starlet was pointing to the tattoos on her right shoulder and explaining the origin and context of each one.

Next, was the Max-World booth. Producer/director/performer Max Hardcore had drawn an especially large crowd by having one of his girls squat on the countertop and pleasure herself with the butt of a riding crop. His promotional posters featured him carrying a girl in hot pants over his shoulder against the backdrop of innumerable big-city skylines. The pitches at the bottom of the posters read: SEE PRETTY GIRLS SODOMIZED IN MANNERS MOST FOUL! and SEE CUM-SPLATTERED GIRLS TOO STUPID TO KNOW BETTER!

Sigmund Freud would have had a field day with this shit, Billy said to himself. As for Billy, he took it all in as best he could. Frankly, he didn't quite know what to make of the feeling he had gazing at living human beings whom he had seen perform in porn movies—to shake the hand of a man whose precise erectile size, angle, and vasculature were familiar to him. As far as the women were concerned, a porn starlet entering any kind of room had a distinctive aura about her: Billy—like seemingly every male in the exhibition hall—would turn his head to look even if he didn't want to.

There were two major differences between the male and the female performers, though. One was that porn starlets were never alone. They were always accompanied by at least one flinty-eyed man, and sometimes as many as four. The general impression was that of a very expensive thoroughbred being led onto the track under a silk blanket. The male stars, in contrast, tended to stand off to the side glowering. The second difference, and one closely related to the first, was that the starlets took turns being interviewed by cable-TV reporters and writers from the sorts of magazines that sat shrink-wrapped behind the cash registers of America's convenience stores. The male stars avoided cameras like Mafiosi under investigation for money laundering.

"Where are we going?" Billy asked, his head spinning around the room like an overwound clock. He accidentally bumped into one of the starlets—or, more precisely, into one of her zeppelin-like breasts. It hurt—*him*. "Sorry," was all he could think of to say to her.

She simply adjusted her halter top and kept walking across the concrete floor while her fans shouted things like "How'd you get that dress on, baby?" and "Does your mother know where you're at right now?"

Bottoms said, "We've got to head up to the room for a while. "Some reporter from *The New Yorker* wants to interview me."

The New Yorker? Billy thought. Why on earth would a reporter for the nation's premier magazine want to interview a porn director? Maybe his father was right. Maybe pornography was a legitimate way to earn a buck.

CHAPTER TWENTY-FIVE

Special Agent Kevin Wright was twenty-nine years old. He had been with the FBI for five years. He had joined the nation's most elite law enforcement agency after receiving a master's degree in criminal justice studies from Northeastern University. He had received a bachelor's degree from the University of Rhode Island, graduating cum laude. Special Agent Wright was also built like a middle linebacker and this fact, coupled with his no-nonsense demeanor, suggested he wasn't someone to trifle with.

Wright testified that he was headquartered in Boston, that he was the junior agent assigned to the Mancini case, and that he had been working on the case for approximately two-and-a-half years. He, along with Special Agent William Mulkaski, had executed the original search warrant in Peterborough, New Hampshire, and he, also along with Special Agent Mulkaski, had seized most of the videos that formed the basis of the criminal complaint presently before the United States District Court for the District of Rhode Island. Special Agent Wright appeared to have a good rapport with the jury, which suggested to Sam Grimes that he had testified in court many times before.

Wright repeated much of what Mulkaski, the senior FBI agent assigned to the Mancini case, had testified to the day before. Given that Sam had spent most of yesterday's session working on the jury instructions, how the case against Joey Mancini had unfolded was still news to him. According to Wright, the FBI had been receiving complaints for a number of years from "citizens" (his word, not Sam's) all over New England who had grown increasingly concerned about the types of videocassettes and DVDs their local video stores were stocking. "From Portland, Maine, to Stamford, Connecticut, citizens were expressing outrage at the proliferation of pornography in their neighborhoods," Wright reported. "They were particularly concerned about what this was doing to the quality of life in their communities and to their ability to raise their children with good Christian values."

Steve Sutton cringed. Every good witness—especially a police witness—knew he needed to avoid sounding dogmatic to the jury. "Good Christian values" sounded dogmatic.

Maybe Agent Wright hadn't testified much in court before? Sam now thought.

Sutton endeavored to get his witness back on track. "I have here, Agent Wright, what has previously been marked for identification as the People's Exhibit Number 1. Do you recognize this?"

"Yes," Wright said.

"What do you recognize it to be?"

"Exhibit 1 is a DVD entitled *Anal All-Stars*. More to the point, it's one of the scores of videos we seized from video stores all across New England."

"Do you know which video store you seized *Anal All-Stars* from?"

Sutton let the video's title linger in the air. Clearly, he was trying to remind the jury that this case was about pandering "filth," as he had put it during his opening statement.

Wright twisted in his seat in order to face Judge Reis. "May I refer to my report?"

"Yes," the Judge said.

All was quiet in the courtroom while Agent Wright flipped through his thick report.

Sutton studied his own notes as well. He was undoubtedly reviewing the path he wanted his direct examination of Wright to take.

Sam turned his attention to less official business: he scanned the courtroom for Mary. He knew she wouldn't be there, but he looked anyway. He always looked . . .

"We seized *Anal All-Stars* from Video X-tra in Weymouth, Massachusetts," Wright finally said.

Sam's attention snapped back to the witness stand.

"We executed that particular search warrant on July 23rd."

"Can you identify for the jury, Agent Wright, who the producer of *Anal All-Stars* is?" Sutton asked next.

"Midnight Productions," Wright answered matter-of-factly. "It says so on the box."

The "box" to which Agent Wright referred was similar in both style and substance to the boxes Sam had found stashed in Chad's closet the day he had gone searching for his missing tennis racket. "The box cover sells the video," Chad had informed Sam at the time.

For the box cover of *Anal All-Stars*, Mancini had elected to go with a picture of an attractive young brunette bending over to expose her buttocks to a sleazy-looking guy leering at her like a predator about to devour a fresh kill. Sure enough, there was also printed in bold scripted letters the name "Midnight Productions." Sam glanced over at Joey Mancini. The defendant didn't reveal a hint of concern.

"Do you know who the owner and chief operating officer of Midnight Productions is?" Sutton asked, proceeding down his checklist of questions.

"Objection, Your Honor!" John Marone said, leaping to his feet. "There's been no foundation established for this line of questioning."

"Sustained," Judge Reis ruled.

Sutton was taken aback, which showed his inexperience in the courtroom. Having objections raised and sustained against you was part and parcel of the litigation game. A seasoned trial lawyer would have known that. Sutton recovered quickly, however. He retrieved a thin manila folder from the prosecution table. He removed an official-looking document from inside. He said, "I move to have admitted into evidence, Your Honor, this certified copy of the Articles of Incorporation of one 'Midnight Productions.'" He handed Marone the certificate.

Marone scanned it, and then returned it to Sutton.

"Any objection?" the Judge asked.

"No, Your Honor," Marone answered.

Marone had no choice. The Articles of Incorporation that Sutton was offering into evidence was an official public record, properly authenticated pursuant to Federal Rule of Evidence 902(4). FRE 902(4) provided for self-authentication of copies of official records or reports, or documents recorded or filed pursuant to law in a public office. The fact that a certified copy of a public record was self-authenticating didn't per se establish its admissibility. It also had to comply with other evidentiary requirements, including, in this case, the hearsay rule, because Sutton was offering the Articles to prove that Joey Mancini was the owner and chief operating officer of Midnight Productions. Importantly, however, the purpose for which Sutton desired to admit this record qualified for admission under the hearsay exception for public records and reports, which was governed by FRE 803(8).

To Sam, many of the Federal Rules of Evidence seemed circular. A public record, for instance, was self-authenticating, but it was still hearsay, but because it was a public record it was admissible under the public records exception to the hearsay rule. The reason for this was that public records and reports were considered trustworthy because of the duty that came with public service. In effect, it was presumed that public servants performed their tasks carefully and fairly. Sam's own experience with government bureaucrats suggested otherwise to him—he had encountered his fair share of red tape last summer when he applied for his clerkship, for example—but the long and short of it was that Steve Sutton had just proved that Joey Mancini was the owner and chief operating officer of Midnight Productions: the maker and distributor of *Anal All-Stars*. And he had done it with a simple piece of paper.

"With the Court's permission," Sutton announced from the prosecution table, "I would now like to play *Anal All-Stars* for the jury."

"May I see counsel at sidebar, please?" Judge Reis said as nonchalantly as he could so as not to make the jury think something was amiss.

The Judge was going to ask Sutton how many videos he intended to play.

◆ ◆ ◆ ◆

Philmore Bottoms answered the door of his hotel room wearing a large black cowboy hat and what had to be one of the very few long-sleeved Hawaiian shirts in existence.

Billy Hewitt was sitting on a vinyl couch between a couple of B-girls: second- or third-ranked porn actresses who were lower paid than a starlet and who were usually available for the more perverse, degrading, or painful sex scenes.

Jennifer—Midnight Productions's starlet-of-the-moment—was perched on a stool at the mini-bar. She, like the B-girls, was in her post-CES mufti: baggy jeans, oversized sweatshirt, big fuzzy slippers. Without her makeup and appurtenances, Jennifer looked even prettier than she did on the screen; the B-girls did not.

The television set was tuned to an *NYPD Blue* marathon on FX.

Billy could sense that *The New Yorker* reporter—a snappily dressed man of about forty-five who couldn't have looked more out of place if he tried— was caught up in a tense and convoluted brainstorm the moment he stepped over the threshold and onto the rust-brown carpet of the Midnight Productions suite on the seventh floor of the Mirage Hotel in Las Vegas, Nevada. Because porno movies' worlds were so sexualized, with everybody seemingly teetering on the edge of coitus all the time and it taking only the slightest nudge or excuse—a stalled elevator, an unlocked door, a cocked eyebrow, a firm handshake—to send everyone tumbling into a tangled mass of limbs and orifices, there was a strong vibe emanating from the reporter of expectation/dread/hope that this was what might happen at this very moment in Philmore Bottoms's hotel room.

Bottoms, of course, didn't appear to pick up on the reporter's vibe. Billy didn't know Bottoms well—the eldest of the Hewitt children had been formally involved in his father's side business for only a few months, and he had been asked to attend the CES at the last minute because Joey Mancini had to cancel on account of his trial—but he had already learned that Midnight Productions's number one director didn't pick up on any vibe that didn't relate directly and exclusively to him.

"Have a seat," Bottoms said.

The reporter sat on a metal folding chair that had the name of the hotel stenciled on the back.

Bottoms offered everybody disposable cups of cheap vodka before settling in to discuss what for him were the most pressing and relevant issues at this year's CES: the career, reputation, personal history, and overall life philosophy of one Philmore Bottoms.

"What's that?" the reporter asked between sips of vodka and awkward glances at the women in the room. He pointed to the statuette prominently situated in the center of the small wooden table at which Bottoms was sitting.

"It's my *AVN* Award," Bottoms answered proudly.

The reporter pulled a notepad from the pocket of his Brooks Brothers blazer and readied his pen with a quick click on the cap. "What's an *AVN* Award?"

"An *Adult Video News* Award," Bottoms said. "The Oscar of the adult film industry. The *AVN*s are always scheduled to coincide with the CES. The ceremony was last night."

"So that's what that was," the reporter said, scribbling away. "I tried to get in, but I couldn't get past the bouncers at the door."

Bottoms laughed. He refilled his plastic cup with another shot of vodka. "That sounds about right. The folks at *AVN* run a pretty closed shop. You gotta know somebody to get in. Too bad you didn't talk to me yesterday."

"Yeah. Too bad." The reporter flipped a page on his notepad. He glanced at the women again. "What did you win it for?"

"*Naughty Nurses IV*. For best DP, to be precise."

Bottoms was nothing if not precise, Billy knew. He swirled the vodka in his cup. This whole experience was surreal.

"What's a DP?" the reporter asked next, circling the acronym for emphasis.

"Double Penetration. You know, when one of the girls gets her nether orifices simultaneously accessed by two woodmen." Bottoms winked at the B-girls.

They giggled, and then returned their attention to the *NYPD Blue* marathon.

Clearly, the reporter didn't know the lingo. "What's a woodman?"

"A dependably potent male performer. Like Mickey Wad used to be." Bottoms shook his head in disgust. "There's too much waiting for wood nowadays. Shit, every guy with a ten-inch dick thinks he can do porn. Most of 'em can't take the pressure, though. Most of 'em can't deliver the money shot when I need it. That's why you see the same few guys in all the videos." Bottoms glanced over at Billy. "How long has Buck Steed been making pornos? . . . Fifteen years?"

Billy shrugged his shoulders. He still had a lot to learn about the history of X.

The reporter stood up from his chair and walked over to examine the trophy. It looked a bit like an Oscar/Emmy/Clio—except that the figurine's arms were up and out like Richard Nixon's at the climax of the 1968 Republican National Convention. It was also hollow and Little League-ish rather than heavy and solid, and it was manufactured from cubic zirconium, not gold or silver.

Bottoms said, "I also won for best director, but I haven't gotten that one yet."

"Why not?" The reporter placed the statuette back on the table.

"Because the dumb-asses didn't bring enough trophies." Bottoms let loose with a rumbling guffaw. "You'd think that with all the money this business makes every year, they'd bring enough trophies. But, no. They're as tight as the bark on a goddamn tree over there."

Billy expected that a reporter from *The New Yorker* would think to ask the obvious follow-up—namely, who were "they"?—but he didn't. Instead, the reporter started listening to Jennifer describe a stray dog she had found and had decided to keep. As she described the dog—its big floppy ears, its brown-and-white coat, and its eyes as wide as saucers—she seemed to be maybe fourteen.

The impression lasted only a second and it was heartbreaking.

CHAPTER TWENTY-SIX

It was 5:30 P.M. and Sam Grimes's day of watching dirty movies had come to an end. He had to admit that, at first, he had gotten a voyeuristic thrill from watching them. He was human. He was a guy. But after four or five in a row, the thrill was gone, to borrow from the great B.B. King.

Speaking of B.B. King, Sam and Mary were supposed to see him play at the Last Call Saloon on Saturday night. It was going to be the blues legend's fiftieth-anniversary concert. King had chosen the Last Call—which was over on South Water Street, about three blocks from the courthouse—for that auspicious occasion because it was an intimate venue. "It's the kinda joint I started out jammin' in a half-century ago," he had said in a radio interview when the concert was announced. "It'll be a trippin' gig . . . Y'all come on out. Me and Lucille will be waitin' for ya!"

Sam was really looking forward to the concert. He usually kept his passion for blues music to himself, but Mary had earned a special place in his heart. He wanted her to know everything there was to know about him. That was rare. He almost never let anyone inside. After Karen, he never thought he would again. Unfortunately, he was beginning to wonder whether he should start looking for another date. He knew that he and Mary weren't married or anything, but he thought that she would telephone to let him know how she was—or at least *where* she was . . . What does "I love you" mean?

Time passed quickly as Sam walked the streets of Providence. Brown, RISD, the Capitol: Providence was small enough that he had managed to make his way through all those neighborhoods in less than two hours.

Thankfully, Providence was also big enough, and had enough back streets, that he hadn't run into anybody he knew. He needed to be alone. He needed to think. He needed to figure stuff out. Maybe he wasn't good enough for Mary after all? She was smart, sweet, and beautiful. What could she possibly see in him?

He turned up the volume on his iPod. John Mayer's "Daughters" was playing:

"I know a girl.
She puts the color inside of my world.
But she's just like a maze where all of the walls all continually change.
And I've done all I can to stand on the steps with my heart in my hand.
Now I'm starting to see that maybe it's got nothing to do with me.
Fathers be good to your daughters.
Daughters will love like you do.
Girls become lovers who turn into mothers, so mothers be good to your daughters, too."

◆ ◆ ◆ ◆

"There's a message from Mary on the answering machine," Chad Smith announced from the kitchen of the third-floor apartment he shared with Sam.

Sam snapped shut the front door. He tossed his keys onto the cooking island. He clenched and unclenched his fists. His hands were cracked from the cold.

Chad had assumed his customary post-work posture: he was sitting at the kitchen table drinking a beer and reading a magazine. The beer was almost always the same—JW Dundee's—but the magazine was often different. This time it was *Sports Illustrated*. Barry Bonds, baseball's reigning homerun king, was featured on the cover. The caption read: Tainted Hero?

Sam and Chad's apartment was even more of a disaster area than usual. There were beer bottles, magazines, newspapers, and CDs strewn all over the living room. The kitchen was cluttered with an array of cereal boxes, soda cans, and potato chip bags. And the bathroom . . . Sam had seen more sanitary bathrooms at Fenway Park during a doubleheader.

"We need to clean up this rat trap one of these days," Sam said. "You never know when your mom might be stopping by."

"I was just thinking that." Chad lifted his eyes from the magazine. "Where have you been, anyway? It's almost 7:30. I was hoping we could run up to Mutts for dinner, but I was too hungry to wait. I thought about calling you on your cell phone, but then I remembered that you don't have a cell phone . . . Buy a cell phone, tight wad."

"Cell phone, schmell phone," Sam said. "My iPod here is all the modern technology I need." He pulled his iPod from his pocket.

"So where were you?" Chad snatched Sam's iPod and studied it.

Sam said, "Taking a walk. I needed to clear my head of all the impure thoughts I've been having lately. Some of us aren't used to watching what I spent five hours watching today."

The playful nature of Sam's give-and-take with Chad made Sam appreciate how much he cared about Mary. The realization that she thought enough of him to call from New York had lifted his spirits.

He punched the PLAY button on the answering machine. There was an unusual amount of background noise on the message.

"Hi, Sam. It's Mary. I just wanted to let you know that my mom is sick and that I had to rush home for a while. Sorry I haven't called until now, but it's been crazy around here. I don't know how much longer I'll be. You should probably find someone else to take to see B.B. King, though. Maybe Chad can go . . . Oh. Don't try to call me back. I'll be at the hospital most of the time . . . I—I miss you."

It was great to hear Mary's voice. It really was. But Sam couldn't understand why she wouldn't want him to at least *try* to call her back. He also didn't know what to make of the background noise. It sure sounded like there was a lot of commotion going on, although he had no idea what the commotion was. He did hear some other people's voices, though. He was certain of that.

"Did you hear that?" he asked. He walked back to the kitchen.

Chad was devouring a leftover slice of Mutts's legendary whole-wheat crust pizza. He wiped his mouth with a paper towel. He took a drink of beer. "What about it?" he said. "It was Mary. I've heard Mary's voice before."

"I know. But she sounded odd to me—what with all that commotion in the background and all."

"She was probably calling from the hospital. Those places are wall-to-wall commotion. Believe me, I know. When I was a paralegal for Raoul's law firm, I spent a lot of time in and around hospitals. 'There's money to be made there,' Raoul would always say." Chad smiled at the memory. Then, "You're making something out of nothing, Sam. You should be flattered that she called. She obviously thinks of you as her boyfriend. My God, man, are you forgetting that she told you she loves you? A million guys would kill to be in your shoes . . . I know I would."

"You're right. I just wish she had left a phone number, that's all. I can't help it if I'm worried about her." Sam started picking up the empty cereal boxes and potato chip bags. "By the way," he said, "do you want to go and hear B.B. King on Saturday night? It looks like I've got an extra ticket."

"You've got yourself a date, buddy." Chad flashed a mischievous smile. "You should know something up front, though."

"What?"

"That I don't put out on the first date."

Sam was smiling now. "I've heard otherwise."

He moved into the living room and started cleaning up in there. Two hours later, the apartment was clean. (Well, cleaner.) Two minutes after that, he started worrying about Mary again.

◆ ◆ ◆ ◆

"She's gorgeous, Joey," Philmore Bottoms said. "She's freakin' gorgeous. I love her legs. Legs are often overlooked in this business. Everyone is always obsessing about tits. 'Get me a girl with bigger tits' might as well be the motto over at Pussycat. But, me, I'll take a great pair of legs any day. We're often filming from behind, you know. The girl's legs are in almost every shot."

"Her tits ain't bad, either," Mancini said, grinning. He cupped his hands over Tiffany's breasts. Then, he signaled for Sal Chilleri. "Get her something to eat," he said to him. "She'll be needing her strength."

Sal did as he was told. He didn't appear happy about it, though. He still seemed pissed that Joey had changed his mind about sending him to Vegas with Bottoms.

Bottoms smiled. "Peter Boy will be delighted. He always gets up for someone new. Literally . . ." Bottoms offered Mancini a cigarette. "Where'd you find her?"

Mancini ignored the question. "How'd things go in Vegas?" He struck a match.

"Great," Bottoms said. "I won for best director again, and Jennifer won for best actress."

"How come business is in the toilet, then?"

"I don't know. But maybe the article in *The New Yorker* will help."

"*The New Yorker?* What the fuck are you talking about, Philmore? I thought that fell through."

"They pushed it back an issue, that's all. They interviewed me after the show. I think it's gonna be some sort of exposé on what the porn world is *really* like. 'Reality' entertainment is all the rage, you know. It went great, too. The reporter was practically taking a transcript of what I was telling him. At least when he wasn't staring bug-eyed at Jennifer . . ."

"Fuckin' mooks," Mancini said, shaking his head. "They try to call me Satan, but they can't get enough of the shit." He checked his watch. "Listen. I've gotta get back to Providence." He gestured with his cigarette toward the other room. "Don't forget to take plenty of still-shots during the shoot. I think we've finally turned the corner with this one."

Silvio Patrone was nursing his second cup of coffee. A half-eaten chocolate doughnut sat on a plate in front of him.

"Would you care for anything else?" the waitress asked. She pulled a pencil from her apron.

Silvio glanced at the clock above the counter. "No. Thanks. Just the check."

The waitress tore the check from her order pad and placed it on the counter in front of her only customer.

Silvio tossed a five-dollar bill onto the counter, and then reached for his jacket. He felt a strong hand on his thick shoulder. He spun around and saw his brother standing beside him. "You're late. I was about to leave."

Vince Patrone said, "So leave. You're the one who asked me to come."

He's as arrogant as ever, Silvio said to himself. Aloud to his brother: "Let's grab that booth in the corner." He signaled to the waitress for two more cups of coffee.

Vince barely managed to squeeze his massive frame into the tiny booth. "So what's this about? You said it was important."

The waitress served the coffee, and then returned to the front of the diner.

"It's about you," Silvio said.

"What about me?" Vince said.

"I'm worried about you, that's all."

Vince shifted in his seat. He poured two packets of sugar into his coffee. "Shit, Silvio. Why are you worried about me? Life is great. Livin' in Narragansett is great. Workin' for Joey is great. And the women . . . Shit, Silvio. The women are fuckin' *fantastic*."

"Don Mancini doesn't think it's so great, though. He never says much about it, but I can tell he's pissed that you left."

"Fuck Don Mancini!" Vince pounded his fist on the table. The pepper shaker crashed to the floor. "Don Mancini isn't my father!"

The waitress and the short-order cook were both staring at Vince and Silvio. Everyone in Rhode Island knew who Don Mancini was.

"But he is your *godfather*," Silvio said in a tone much less tonitruous than that of his brother. He retrieved the pepper shaker from the floor. He wiped it clean with a paper napkin. "I suggest you not forget it."

"Fuck that, Silvio." Vince's voice was still angry, but the volume of his reply had diminished considerably. "Don Mancini is an old man now. I hear he's sick, too—with lung cancer or something. The future of the family lies with Joey. Everybody knows that. Everybody but you and the Don."

Silvio smiled. It wasn't a happy smile, though. It was a smile of frustration. "You still don't get it, do you, Vince? You still don't understand how it works? There's a reason the Donetelli family is still standing after so many of the other families have been wiped out by the Feds. And there's a reason that Joey is the one who's fighting for his freedom in court at the moment. Power isn't about being young, and it's not about being healthy. It's about being smart. Shit, Don Mancini has got more brains in his little finger than Joey does in his entire head. And I'm here today—as your brother—to let you know that you better not forget it. Time is running out, Vince. And you're wrong if you think it's running out for the Don. It's running out for *you*. I can't be any more blunt about it than that."

CHAPTER TWENTY-SEVEN

"Did you sleep okay?" Chad Smith asked.

It was 8:15 A.M. and Chad was already dressed and ready for work.

"Yeah." Sam Grimes's voice was hoarse with sleep. "Thanks for asking, though. I must've slept like a log if you got up before I did." He checked the belt on his bathrobe. All secure.

"Would you like some coffee? It's that mocha stuff you like so much. You know, the stuff from the Boston Beanery."

"I'd love some. Thanks. But why are you being so nice to me all of a sudden? Do you need to borrow some money?" Sam took a seat at the kitchen table, forcing a smile as he did.

Chad shook his head. He poured the coffee. "No. I don't need to borrow any money. It's just that with Mary being away and now Mancini on your back, it seems like your circuits are overloading. Have you looked at yourself in the mirror lately? You're gray. Your skin is literally gray. You look like my grandfather did after his heart attack last spring. Maybe Judge Reis will let us take the day off to play some golf. We could head over to Montaup. That's a nice course, and it hasn't closed yet for the season. You could see if you can make another birdie on number twelve. You could use the break, buddy. You really could."

Sam took a sip from the ceramic mug he had purchased at a RISD crafts sale the weekend he had moved to Providence. The coffee was the mocha flavor he liked so much. He added three drops of cream, and then said, "I appreciate your concern, Chad. I really do. And you know how much I love to play golf. But we're in the middle of the biggest trial in New England. I can't bail on that now. Besides, I don't want Judge Reis to know anything about my run-ins with Mancini. *Please*, don't tell him. Promise me you won't."

Helen Keller would have picked up on the desperation in Sam's voice.

Chad certainly did. "Okay, I won't tell him. I promise. But what's the big deal?"

"I don't know," Sam said. "I guess I'm just afraid the Judge would take me off the case. Who knows, he might even recuse himself from it. You know what a Boy Scout he is. I don't want to put him in that position. I can handle Mancini. Frankly, I'm more concerned about Mary." He drained his coffee in two big gulps. "Now let's get to work."

"Don't you think you should get dressed first?"

Sam reddened. He checked his bathrobe again. "That's probably a good idea."

That made twice that Sam had almost left for work without putting on his pants: today and after his surprise "lunch" with Mary.

Boy, did he miss her.

◆ ◆ ◆ ◆

This was the day that Steve Sutton planned to play *A Girl and Her Dog* for the jury. John Marone intended to fight him every step of the way. Sam understood why: There was no way a jury would buy the argument that a girl having sex with a German shepherd was art. Needless to say, the courtroom was filled to the rafters. The jury wasn't present, though. Per Marone's request, Judge Reis was requiring Sutton to establish outside of the jury's presence that *A Girl and Her Dog*, as well as the other videos that depicted acts of bestiality, had in fact been produced and distributed by Midnight Productions. Joey Mancini—through Marone, of course—insisted they weren't. And even though Sam couldn't stand the guy, he believed him. Maybe it was that he *wanted* to believe him . . . Sam knew he would puke if the video was played.

"If you'd be so kind, Mr. Sutton, please remove the video player from in front of the bench," Judge Reis said. "I won't need to see the tape in order to assess whether you've established that Mr. Mancini's company is responsible for it."

The Judge was as reluctant as Sam was to view the video. He hadn't said anything about it, but it was pretty easy to tell that he wasn't exactly enjoying sitting through Steve Sutton's pornathon.

"With all due respect, Your Honor, I think you do," Sutton said, rising to his feet. "How else can you tell? By simply looking at the box cover?"

"For starters, Mr. Sutton, Mr. Marone has a witness who he claims will testify that the video is a knockoff. And given that this witness is the owner of the video store from which the tape was seized, I'm inclined to leave it at that." Judge Reis shot Sutton one of those hard looks that Sam had told Mary about on their first date. It was a look that invited no debate. The Judge added, peering over his half-glasses, "Unless, of course, you can provide the Court with an explanation about why this witness—a witness who's testifying against his own interests—should not be believed."

"I can't, Your Honor. But I've never heard of, let alone been given the opportunity to depose, this witness."

An awkward silence engulfed the courtroom. There was an edge to Sutton's voice, and no one—especially not Sutton—seemed comfortable with that. Judge Reis, the benchmark for judicial restraint, overlooked the young prosecutor's faux pas.

Sutton should be thanking his lucky stars that he wasn't trying this case before Chief Judge Conigliero, Sam thought. The Chief would have handed Sutton his head.

"Would you call your witness please, Mr. Marone." The Judge opened his bench book.

John Marone called Brian Newland to the stand.

Newland was dressed in black jeans, a plaid shirt, and a rumpled blue sports coat. A turquoise-and-silver bolo tie hung loosely around his pasty neck. He was forty-five, but he could have passed for sixty.

Holly Curran administered the oath.

Newland "affirmed"—rather than "swore"—to tell the truth, the whole truth, and nothing but the truth.

"Mr. Newland, would you please inform the Court as to your occupation?" Marone said.

"I own a video store. Video X-tra in Weymouth, Massachusetts."

Newland looked nervous, Sam thought. He should. If what Judge Reis had said was correct—and it almost always was—the witness was about to admit to renting and selling obscene—not simply sexually explicit—videos. The name of his store was a dead giveaway.

Marone gestured in his client's direction. "Do you know Joseph P. Mancini?"

"Yeah, I know Joey," Newland said. "I buy a lot of my merchandise from him."

"What do you mean by 'merchandise'?"

"You know, my videos. The videos I rent to my customers. I've been doing business with Joey for years."

Marone ambled over to Holly's table. He picked up *Anal All-Stars* and *Sisters*. He handed the videos to the witness. "Do you recognize these?"

"Yeah. They're a couple of the DVDs the FBI seized from my store this summer." The witness paused, scratched his whiskered chin, and then added, "They were two of my more popular rentals."

His attempt at humor fell flat.

"Where did you get them?"

"I bought 'em from Joey's company. You know, from Midnight Productions."

Marone returned the videos to Holly. He then borrowed *A Girl and Her Dog* from Sutton's table. He handed it to Newland. "Do you recognize this one?"

"Yeah. It's another one of the videos the FBI seized from my store."

"And where did you get this particular tape?"

The witness hesitated. He shifted in his chair, fidgeted a bit with his bolo tie, and then finally said, "From some Mexican distributor. I can't remember the name. I ordered it from a website."

"But Mr. Newland," Marone said, "if you'll take a look at the box it says 'Midnight Productions' on the cover, does it not?"

"Yeah. But that's not right. Midnight is an up-and-coming name in the adult video industry. It stands for quality. You know, high-class production values, good scripts, big name stars: the whole nine yards. Lots of companies in the industry wish they had Midnight's name. The Mexican outfit is undoubtedly one of them." Newland ran his hands through his thinning gray hair. "It's a knockoff tape. A rip-off. There are lots of those floatin' around."

Sam glanced over at the defense table. Joey Mancini sat stone-faced while one of his best customers tried to save his ass.

"Were you aware when you purchased the video that it wasn't a real Midnight production?" Marone asked next.

Newland hesitated again. He shifted in his chair again. "To be honest, I didn't pay too much attention to who was listed on the website as the producer. I do when I'm buying my mainstream videos. Like I said, it's a mark of quality—of artistic quality. But when I'm buying some of the more specialized tapes—you know, the fetish tapes—I don't. I only have a few customers who like those sorts of videos, so I don't pay much attention to 'em. A *Girl and Her Dog* and the other barnyard tapes on the list you showed me this morning fall into the fetish category."

"Thank you, Mr. Newland." Marone turned to the Judge. "I've got nothing further, Your Honor."

Marone returned to his seat. He looked pleased, Sam thought. He should. Newland had done well. His offhand remark about the Midnight Productions name standing for "artistic quality" was particularly helpful. So helpful, in fact, that Sam suspected that Marone wished the jury had heard it.

"Any cross-examination, Mr. Sutton?" Judge Reis made a notation in his bench book that Marone had finished with his direct examination of the witness.

"May I have a moment, Your Honor?" Sutton huddled with Jim Hodges. Then, he returned his attention to the Judge. "No questions, Your Honor. After hearing Mr. Newland's testimony, the People are willing to stipulate that *A Girl and Her Dog* and the other so-called barnyard videos are not Midnight productions. We withdraw our request to play for the jury any and all of the videotapes and DVDs on the list to which Mr. Newland referred."

Marone had won a big one. Sam suspected that Sutton had to believe that the government had enough ammunition for a conviction. Either that, or he felt that Newland was a compelling witness. Brian Newland may be a scumbag, but he was a persuasive scumbag. Moreover, given how gross *A Girl and Her Dog* undoubtedly was, Sam figured that Judge Reis would have bent over backward to avoid having to watch it. He was a great judge, but he was also a human being. Sutton clearly realized it and understood the consequences of it for his case.

"The Court will take a short recess," the Judge announced from the bench. "We'll welcome back the jury in fifteen minutes."

"All rise!" Holly Curran cried out.

◆ ◆ ◆ ◆

Pen and paper in hand, Sam dialed the access code to the answering machine at his apartment. There was a message. It was from Mary! It was great to hear her voice, although she sounded even more tired and stressed out this time than she had the last. There was still a lot of commotion in the background. It was a little more distinctive this time. Sam could hear what sounded like a young woman in pain. Maybe the woman was hurt? He also heard the deeper voice of a man. "Turn over," he thought he heard the man say. Maybe it was a doctor, or a paramedic, or perhaps a male nurse? Mary was speaking over the din. She said she was just checking in to say that her mom was doing better, but that she still needed to be with her.

Sam didn't understand why Mary hadn't tried to reach him at work. The answering machine reported that the message had been left at 10:20 A.M. Mary knew that Judge Reis almost always called a recess between 10:15 and

10:30. It was almost as if she hadn't wanted to speak with him—that she had only wanted to leave a message. That wasn't like her. Sam used to have a difficult time getting Mary to *stop* talking. Now, she didn't seem to want to *start*.

"What's going on?"

Sam jumped.

It was Chad.

"I was checking the answering machine," Sam said, regaining his composure.

"Anything?"

"Mary called. She sounded strange. Even stranger than last time. The background noise was there again, too."

Chad positioned himself on the edge of Sam's desk. He had an admiralty law hornbook in his hand. "I still say you're overreacting."

"Maybe. But I've got a funny feeling about things. Here, I'll show you." Sam redialed the access code and handed the receiver to Chad.

"Ten-twenty A.M.," the computer-generated voice reported. Mary's voice came on. "Hi, Sam. It's me. I wanted to let you know that my mom is doing better, but that she still needs me at home. I spoke to the dean of students at RISD a couple of minutes ago. She said I can take as long as I need. I hope everything is okay on your end. Say hi to Chad for me . . . I—I miss you."

Sam studied Chad's face.

"I have to admit," Chad said, replacing the handset, "she does sound a bit out-of-sorts. Mary is usually so bubbly. I've never heard her so down before. But, hey, her mom is in the hospital. I'm sure she's depressed about that. She can't be too far gone, though. She did tell you to say hi to me! Now, you'd better get going. Judge Reis is about ready to go back on the bench."

"You should've stuck around the other night. I would've given you a sneak preview of my upcoming releases. There's one you would've found particularly intriguing. It's about a group of law clerks who can't get enough of each another. It features a fresh-faced new girl who can't help but become a star. She's got a body that would launch a thousand ships."

This time, Sam knew whose voice it was: Joey Mancini's. He turned to confront his accuser.

Mancini was standing at the bottom of the stairs near the side entrance to the courthouse. He was smoking a cigarette. No one else was around.

Sam's reply was quick and to the point: "Save it for the witness stand, Mancini. If you've got the *guts* to take the stand."

Chad's admonition notwithstanding, Sam couldn't hide his disdain for the guy.

Mancini said, "How's Mary's mom doing?"

Sam lunged for Mancini's throat.

Mancini struggled to break free. He rammed Sam into the soda machine next to the stairs.

Sam countered with a left cross to the chin.

Mancini's head snapped back like a cattail in the wind. Then, he lowered his shoulder and rammed Sam into the soda machine again. The machine almost toppled over from the impact.

Sam put Mancini in a bear hug and started to squeeze the air out of him.

Jerry Cushing came barreling down the stairs. "Break it up!" he thundered. "Stop that, Sam!"

Jerry separated the two young men. Sam's shirt pocket was torn. Mancini had lost several buttons. Both men had blood seeping from their mouths and noses.

"You fucking asshole!" Mancini spat. He brushed dirt from his pants and shirt. He wiped a handkerchief across his nose. He applied pressure to stop the bleeding. "You'll regret this, you son of a bitch. You'll fuckin' regret this."

"Shut up, Mancini!" Jerry said. "Get your ass back into the courtroom. If you don't, I just might have to tell Judge Reis who I thought started the whole thing. And I won't be saying *Sam*, either."

Mancini glared at Jerry, and then at Sam. "You bastards are all the same. You're all corrupt." He walked away, muttering, "You'll see. You'll fuckin' see, Grimes."

Jerry turned to Sam. "What the hell got into you? Fighting with a defendant, and with a defendant named *Mancini* no less? Are you crazy?" Jerry handed Sam his handkerchief.

"Another McMurphy," Sam said, softly. *One Flew Over the Cuckoo's Nest* was one of Sam's all-time favorite novels. "Another goddamn McMurphy." He buttoned his suit jacket to hide the rip in his shirt pocket. He wiped his nose and his mouth with Jerry's handkerchief. "It's a long story, Jerry. I'll tell it to you later. But Judge Reis is probably reconvening as we speak. I can't be late." Sam wadded his hair into a ponytail. "Please," he added, "don't mention this to Judge Reis. I don't want to put him in an awkward position—especially with a First Circuit appointment on the line."

Jerry Cushing studied Sam Grimes's face like the friend Jerry had become to Sam. "All right," Jerry said to him. "I won't mention it to the Judge. I should, but I won't. I won't, because *you* asked me not to. But, please, do *me* a favor: Stay away from Joey Mancini. I told you at the outset that family is trouble."

"Thanks, Jerry. I owe you one. And I'll try to stay away."

Jerry shook his head. He placed a large hand on Sam's slender shoulder. "Do more than *try*, Sam. Stay away."

◆ ◆ ◆

Steve Sutton continued to play videos for the jury. Sam wasn't paying much attention, however. More than once his eyes wandered in Joey Mancini's direction, and more than once he wondered how Mancini had known about Mary's mom.

Judge Reis glanced over at his law clerk.

Sam wondered if the Judge could tell there was something wrong. Sam hoped not. The last thing he wanted to do was involve the Judge. Judge Reis had worked too hard to get to where he was—and to go to where he was about to go—for Sam to mess that up.

Sam could never forgive himself if he did.

CHAPTER TWENTY-EIGHT

Apparently, Sam was now a part of the Hewitts' inner circle. Billy and Alan had grown fond of him, and Suzanne viewed him benevolently as well.

At first, Sam didn't think Suzanne liked him very much. Chad had told him that she thought he was too single-minded about work. But now that he was—or at least he *thought* he still was—dating Mary, Chad said that Suzanne thought he was more balanced about life. Chad also said that Suzanne's brothers had spoken highly of Sam to her. They thought he was "interesting," albeit difficult to understand. Sam knew they were talking about women. And if they had found it difficult to understand why he would pass on an evening of trolling for women at Venus de Milo, his walking out on a sure thing with Jennifer at Chateau del Sol must have seemed like pure lunacy to them.

Sam's newfound place in the Hewitts' hearts and minds had gotten him invited to dinner again at their home. This time it was at their house in Providence, the one on Congdon Street, where John Brown used to live. According to Chad, Suzanne was worried about Sam being lonely now that Mary was away. (Talk about doing a one-eighty in your feelings about someone.) Sam appreciated that. He really did. But he was more interested in having another free meal. As a bachelor, he never—and he meant *never*—turned down a free meal. The fact that the food at the Hewitts' was always fabulous made it all the better. Cybill, the Hewitts' longtime housekeeper, was a marvelous cook. She was also incredibly nice. Sam had never left a dinner at the Hewitts' house without a doggie bag big enough to carry him through the week.

Sam didn't see Chad's Porsche out front when he arrived at the Hewitts' house at 7:10 P.M. He was feeling brave, not to mention hungry, so he decided to go in without him.

Mrs. Hewitt answered the front door wearing an eye-catching satin pantsuit. The door—a massive oak structure with wrought iron trimming—must have weighed close to two hundred pounds and she always seemed to struggle with it.

Sam said, "Sorry I'm late." He helped Mrs. Hewitt crack the door open wide enough for him to squeeze through. "I had to stay behind for a few minutes and talk to Judge Reis about a case. I also wanted to stop and pick up some wine. I know it's not as fancy as what you're used to drinking, but my parents seem to enjoy it."

"That's very thoughtful of you, Sam," Mrs. Hewitt said, beaming like the summer sun. She took the bottle of Mont Binoche Chablis from Sam's outstretched hand. She read the label. "I'll ask Cybill to put it on ice. It'll be lovely with the Chicken Cordon Bleu. But about being late, you're not. Suzanne and Chad haven't returned from the bakery yet. They drove up to Federal Hill to pick up some of Mr. Pancino's wonderful chocolate cheesecake. You like cheesecake, don't you Sam?"

"Yes, ma'am. I love it. And Chad goes on and on about Mr. Pancino's. I can't wait to try it."

Mrs. Hewitt gave Sam a motherly smile and stroke on the arm. "Good. I think you'll enjoy it." She adjusted the diamond tennis bracelet that adorned her thin wrist. "Now, why don't you go and say hello to the boys. They're so looking forward to your visit. I think they're downstairs playing billiards. *Again*. I swear, sometimes I think that's all those boys know how to do. Not like you and Chad. Your mothers must be so proud of the fact that you're clerking for a federal judge. My husband tells me how difficult it is to get a job like that. He says you have to be at the top of your law school class—the very top."

Sam deflected Mrs. Hewitt's compliment—just like his mother had taught him to do—excused himself from the room, and went to find Billy and Alan.

They weren't in the billiard room. Sam had never been downstairs in the Hewitts' house before, so as he stumbled around in search of his new friends he found himself visiting rooms he had never imagined to exist.

There were six fully furnished rooms in the basement: a billiard room, two guest bedrooms, an exercise room, a laundry room, and the room in which Sam currently found himself—what looked to be someone's study. From the newspaper clippings, bar certificates, and professional service awards hanging on the walls it had to be Mr. Hewitt's.

Much of what Sam saw came as news to him. For example, he hadn't known that Mr. Hewitt was a member of the U.S. Supreme Court bar. He also hadn't known that Mr. Hewitt had been named "lawyer of the year" by the Rhode Island Bar Association on three separate occasions. Commingled with Mr. Hewitt's law materials were family photos and mementos. Sadly, though, what most caught Sam's eye was a series of porn videos on top of the television. They were from Midnight Productions. That confirmed it: Raoul Hewitt *was* in business with Joey Mancini.

There were six videos in all—all apparently forthcoming releases. Mr. Hewitt, too, must have been previewing the new tapes. There was *Sylvia's Secret*, *Ginger Jones Rides Again*, *Big Top*, *Sorority House Party*, and *Anal All-Stars 2*. However, what stood out most was *Law Clerks in Love*. Given what Mancini had said about it in the hallway the day before, this was a video that curiosity required Sam to see.

Sam switched on the TV and the DVD player. He adjusted the volume so that only he—and barely he—could hear it. He removed the DVD from the box. This was *definitely* a new release—so new, in fact, that Mr. Hewitt and Mancini hadn't had a chance yet to plaster the cartoonishly suggestive photographs on the box cover. Why was he spending so much time with the Hewitts? Sam asked himself as the phone sex ads assaulted him from the screen. He needed to start thinking more about *that*.

The feature presentation was set in what was described by a gravelly voiced narrator as "a federal courthouse in a prominent New England city." The camera panned a makeshift courtroom. It stopped momentarily on a "judge" sitting at his "bench" listening to an "attorney" make a wooden "argument" to four "jurors." At least Sam assumed they were supposed to be jurors. Given that four was an unconstitutionally small number, and that the four were in various stages of undress, he couldn't be certain.

After remaining for several minutes on the jurors, the camera returned to the judge. This time, it panned underneath the bench to where an attractive young woman in ridiculously tight and revealing clothes was in the process of giving His Honor a blow job.

The next scene found two male "law clerks" discussing how they planned to, quote, "fuck Chief Judge Calliperi's hot young niece. She's got a body that would launch a thousand ships."

The connection brought to Sam's life by Joey Mancini's use of a phrase in a conversation with him the day before that a couple of human genitals were now using in a porn video made his skin crawl. However, what happened next did more than that: it made his heart stop . . . The Chief Judge's "hot young niece" was Mary.

Sam felt as if he was going to be sick.

Mary entered the law clerks' office wearing the standard garb of a porn actress: high heels, miniskirt, and a blouse that was about three sizes too small. She also was wearing way too much makeup. But the fact that Mary was wearing too much makeup was the least of Sam's concerns. It was what she *wasn't* wearing as the scene progressed—namely, clothes—that had him sick to his stomach.

The two male law clerks pounced on Mary like wild dogs on raw meat. One sucked her breasts while the other lapped at her vagina. Rarely did the camera show Mary's face—it was too preoccupied with her voluptuous body—

but when it did she looked terrified. There was no way in hell that Mary was making the video voluntarily, Sam said to himself. There *couldn't* be . . .

Sam leaned closer to the screen. He was only inches away. He couldn't believe his eyes. This couldn't be happening, he repeated over and over in his head. It just *couldn't* be . . .

"What's going on?" Chad asked.

Sam was so transfixed by the video that he hadn't heard his roommate enter the room.

Chad said, "Oh my God! That's *Mary!*"

"No shit, it's *Mary!* Now where the fuck is *Raoul!*" Sam shot up from his seat with such force that he knocked the chair into the bookcase, dislodging more than a few of Mr. Hewitt's precious legal treatises in the process.

Billy came running. "What's all the racket about?"

Sam shoved the box cover to *Law Clerks in Love* in Billy's face. "*This* is what the racket's about! Have you seen *this*?! Did you know about *this*?!"

Sam was trembling—and on the verge of hyperventilating.

Billy was flabbergasted—and obviously uncertain of how to respond.

Chad said, "Calm down, buddy." He was plainly trying his best to restrain Sam from going after Billy—and any other Hewitt his roommate might happen to see.

"What the hell are you talking about? It's a porno tape. So what?" There was real fear in Billy's voice.

"'*So what*'?! '*So what*'?! I'll tell you, '*So what*'! *Mary* is in this video! That's *what!*" Sam threw the box cover onto Raoul Hewitt's desk with the same velocity he used to have on his serve before his arm went out from playing too much tennis. The brass lamp that dominated the desk crashed to the floor.

"Mary? Who's Mary?" Billy eyed the lamp—an antique—that was lying shattered at his feet. "You mean *your girlfriend* Mary?"

"Correct, Einstein! Now where the fuck is *your father*?!"

Billy stammered, "Dad's down in Kingston on—on business." He struggled to gather his thoughts. "You—You've got to believe me, Sam. My dad couldn't have known about Mary. *I've* never seen Mary before. I'm—I'm sure Dad has no idea who she is. I mean, that she's your girlfriend."

Sam and Billy stared at each other for what seemed like forever.

Sam finally said, in a far more composed tone of voice, "I want to believe you, Billy. Really, I do. I've got to talk to your father, though. Maybe he knows where Mary is." Sam glanced down at the shattered lamp, and then back up at Billy. "I promise you this, though: If I find out that your father knows who Mary is, I'll kill him. I'll fuckin' kill him. There's no way in hell that Mary would make a porn video of her own free will. Something fishy is going on here, and Joey Mancini is at the bottom of it. I know it. I just know it."

"We'll take one of my father's cars," Billy said, his eyes riveted on Sam's. "Where we're going, we'll need to be as familiar as possible." Billy turned to Chad. "Are you coming?"

Chad didn't hesitate. "Damn right, I'm coming. I can't let Sam deal with this by himself. And let me be clear about something, too: If I find out that your father knows who Mary is, my roommate here and I will be drawing straws over who gets the first crack at him."

Billy led the way out of his father's study.

Sam pulled Chad off to the side. He was still trembling. "I appreciate your comment just now, Chad. I really do." Sam stopped and looked his co-clerk, roommate, and *friend* straight in the eyes. "But you didn't know anything about this, did you? You didn't know anything about Mary making that video?"

Eyes unblinking—eyes locked on Sam's—Chad told his roommate what he wanted to hear. "No. Of course I didn't know anything about Mary being involved in a porn video. I'd suspected for a while now that the Hewitts were in the skin business. I'd been to a few places with Billy and Alan that had made me suspicious. And Suzanne was also unusually knowledgeable about pornography. At first, I just thought she was kinky. But when she started talking about financial twists and turns—about how much money the industry made—I knew there was probably more to it than that. But, I swear, the first time I heard straight out that the Hewitts are pornographers was on Sunday, when *you* told me on the drive home from Chateau del Sol."

"Thanks for telling me that, Chad." Sam took a deep breath. He couldn't seem to get enough air. "Let's go find Mary," he said, voice cracking. "We've got to find her. We've just *got* to."

CHAPTER TWENTY-NINE

The drive to Kingston passed with nary a word shared among Sam, Billy, and Chad. The hour's journey felt like eternity in the fires of hell as Sam replayed over and over in his mind the image of Mary being ravaged by two faceless men.

Finally, they arrived.

Billy pulled his father's Silver Seraph into the parking lot of a nondescript two-story brick building. He turned off the engine, and then the lights. There were no other cars around. The building was dark.

Billy said, "This is it—the headquarters of Midnight Productions."

Only someone who had been to it before would have known this to be the case. There was no company sign on the building, or anywhere else the eye could see.

"Where is everybody?" Sam asked, exiting the Rolls. "Don't tell me we came all this way for nothing?" He slammed shut the car door.

Billy kicked at a wooden stile that marked the parking space. "They're probably on a location shoot. They go on a lot of those." He gestured toward the building. "There are a number of sets in the building, but they often shoot on location—in old mansions, for example. I noticed a list on Dad's desk at home that says they're shooting a period piece titled *The Ovulator*." Billy paused for a reaction—for a chuckle at the title, perhaps. None was forthcoming. "Think what you want to think about what Joey and my father do for a living, but they have high production values. They don't produce gonzos. You know, a string of sex scenes with no story to them."

"So I've heard," Sam snapped. "Some guy named Brian Newland testified yesterday that Midnight Productions is, quote, 'the mark of artistic excellence.' Or some such bullshit . . . What do you suggest we do?"

Billy glowered at Sam's crack about "artistic excellence," but otherwise let it pass. He raked his hands through his wind-swept hair. "Let's go inside," he said. "We might find something that says where they are."

"How many people work here?" Chad asked, breaking an uncharacteristically long silence on his part. His eyes searched the darkness.

Billy flipped one switch, and then another. Two rows of fluorescent lights flickered on like fireflies in the night. "One or two people are here every day keeping the place going. Cataloging the orders, shipping the orders, answering the phone, paying the light bills—things like that."

Billy easily could have been describing the day-to-day workings of the local hardware store. Instead, he was describing the most sophisticated pornography operation on the East Coast.

"What about the actors and actresses, the cameramen—those sorts of folks?" Chad asked next.

Sam interrupted. "What about *Mancini* and *your father?*"

"Joey hangs around a fair bit." Billy fidgeted with his keys, and then added, defensively, "My father is rarely here, though. He puts up some of the money and helps Joey with some of the big decisions—like what videos to shoot. He *is* a lawyer, though. He does *practice* law. Midnight Productions is an investment for him. It's—It's nothing more than an investment." Billy looked at Sam. Sam didn't look convinced. "As far as the cast and crew go, they're independents. They're here only if there's a shoot. And it's rarely the same people. Sure, they'll usually shoot a couple of videos back-to-back, but that only takes about a week. When they're done, they're gone. They're off to shoot for other companies—like Vivid or Sin City. Most of them live in Los Angeles. That's where most of the industry is located—in the San Fernando Valley. Frankly, I don't see how Midnight stays in business way out here."

Sam said, "I'm sure it doesn't hurt to toss the Mancini name around. If what I've heard is true, it's probably not too smart to say no to a Mancini."

Billy no longer looked defensive. He looked angry. "You can say what you want to say about a lot of things, Sam. But be careful with *that*." He jabbed his keys in Sam's direction. "There's never been any proof that the Mancinis are involved with organized crime. My father has certainly never said anything about it, and he certainly isn't involved himself."

"The government has never been able to obtain a *conviction* against a Mancini. At least not yet . . . There's been *plenty* of proof. There's a difference, and you know it. And as far as your father is concerned, anyone who's in business with a Mancini is involved with organized crime. It's as simple as that." Sam shot Billy a glare that could have burned a hole in the side of a barn.

"*Come on*, guys," Chad interrupted. "We're here to find Mary. We can talk about this other stuff later."

"You're right, Chad," Sam said, quietly. "You're right."

Chad motioned for Billy to lead the way.

Billy led them through a carpeted corridor and down a well-worn flight of stairs. Most of the sets were in the basement. Billy said it was for lighting purposes, but Sam suspected it was because the basement was the part of the building most immune from public view.

There were three sets in the basement. One was of a living room. The most prominent feature of this particular living room was a deep-cushioned couch. An Ethan Allen end table, a well-pruned floor plant, a shiny brass wall clock: they all framed the couch. The next two sets were of bedrooms. Two smartly furnished bedrooms. Both were equipped with king-sized beds.

"I don't see any sign down here of where they might have gone," Billy said. "Let's go upstairs and check the second floor."

Billy was walking around like he knew the place.

Sam was waiting for the right moment to ask how well.

Sam got an eerie feeling when they arrived at the second floor. He knew why: This was where they had shot Mary's sex scene for *Law Clerks in Love*. The cluttered office set in which two sex-starved men had ravaged her was directly in front of them. It looked almost quaint sitting there in the dark, illuminated by only the safety light in the hallway.

"This is it," Sam said.

"This is what?" Chad said.

"This is where they raped Mary."

CHAPTER THIRTY

"Now what do you suggest, Billy?" Chad said, breaching the silence. "You've given us the grand tour, but we've discovered absolutely nothing about where Mary might be."

Billy fidgeted again with his keys. He said, "I'm sorry about that, guys. I really am. I guess we'll just have to wait until they come back. They could be anywhere—literally anywhere—in the southern part of the state."

Silence returned to the headquarters of Midnight Productions.

The rumblings of Billy's stomach interrupted it. "We never did get a chance to eat." He was clearly trying to sound upbeat. "Let's grab a bite. We might have a long wait in store. We'll have to drive over to Narragansett, though. There aren't any restaurants in Kingston Village."

"How can a college town survive without restaurants?" Chad asked.

"I don't know," Billy answered. "That's just the way it is at URI. I guess everyone eats at the cafeteria."

Sam said, "Maybe your father should've opened up a Burger King instead of a porn studio."

This time it was Sam who waited for a reaction. And it wasn't for a chuckle, either.

They piled into the Silver Seraph and headed for Narragansett, which locals referred to as "the Pier," after a now-demolished amusement wharf.

In the early twentieth century Narragansett had been a posh resort. It was linked by rail with New York and Boston, and it also was a major stop on the New York-Newark steamboat line. The rich and famous would travel in to gamble at the opulent Narragansett Pier Casino. President Teddy Roosevelt was a frequent visitor, as was oil tycoon John D. Rockefeller. However, like many once-glamorous New England cities and towns, today Narragansett was in rough shape.

It took Sam, Billy, and Chad less than ten minutes to reach Narragansett—Rhode Island was a tiny state—but fifteen minutes more to find a restaurant that was still open. They found Peppers, an all-night diner renowned for its twenty-four hour breakfast menu.

It was almost 10:00 P.M. by the time they ordered. Billy ordered the Hungry Man Special: four pancakes, four eggs, four strips of bacon, a tall glass of orange juice, and a bottomless cup of coffee. Chad ordered waffles, a breakfast steak, two sides of hash browns, grapefruit juice, and coffee. Sam had just coffee.

"I hope you boys are hungry," the waitress said, smiling like it was morning rather than night. She unloaded a series of plates balancing precariously on her arm, placing them on the dingy Formica table at which Sam, Billy, and Chad were sitting.

She had a point, Sam thought. It was one thing to visualize a meal from a menu, it was quite another to see it sitting in front of you. They could have split Billy's order and still had plenty left for tomorrow.

"Are you sure you don't want anything, darlin'?" the waitress asked Sam. She reached into her apron for her order pad.

Sam said, "Coffee's fine."

"Well, you just let me know if you change your mind. Cal can scramble up some eggs in nothin' flat." She smiled again, and then headed back to the kitchen.

"Can I ask you something, Billy?" Sam said.

"Of course." Billy reached for the pepper.

"Why do Mancini and your father do it? Why do they make porno movies?" Sam reached for the cream. He added a teaspoon to his coffee.

Chad was on the edge of his seat for this one. Why, indeed, would someone want to be a pornographer?

"My father's in it for the money," Billy said, without a moment's hesitation. He placed a fried egg and two strips of bacon between two pancakes in what appeared to be a makeshift Egg McMuffin. "There's a lot of money to be made in the adult film industry. The costs are low—you can make a decent X-rated flick for about ten thousand bucks—and the demand is great. People get all high and mighty about pornography, but the stuff sells. It freakin' sells."

"The Attorney General's report says that pornography is a five-billion-dollar-a-year business in the United States," Chad interjected. He had obviously read the copy of Sam's bench memo to Judge Reis that Sam had left on his desk in September.

"I don't know the exact numbers," Billy said, "but yours don't surprise me. My dad may be a successful lawyer—and believe me, he is—but we couldn't live like we do on his law-firm income alone. You've been to our houses in Providence and Beacon Hill, not to mention to Chateau del Sol, so you know what I'm talking about. And if you think those places are impressive, you should get a load of my folks' house in Beverly Hills."

"I didn't know your parents had a house in Beverly Hills," Chad said. He looked genuinely surprised. He washed down a huge bite of breakfast steak with a big swig of grapefruit juice.

"They do. That's how my dad makes most of his industry contacts. Like I said earlier, most of the industry is located in L.A. . . . . How do you think he met Jennifer?"

Sam and Chad both dropped their utensils.

"You mean to tell me that Jennifer is a porn actress?" Sam said. He was stunned.

"Damn right, she is. She's one of my father's more recent discoveries. Some West Coast porn actor brought her to one of Dad's Beverly Hills parties last summer. One thing led to another, and now she's an up-and-coming porn starlet."

Sam studied Chad's face. He looked as stunned as Sam was. Sam took a long drink of ice water, and then a deep breath. "What about Mancini? Why is Joey Mancini into pornography?"

"I'm gonna take the Fifth on that one, Sam."

"Come on, Billy," Chad said. "We won't say anything. Besides, Sam's got a right to know—given what's happened to Mary and all."

Billy massaged his temples with his fingertips. He cracked his neck to the left, and then to the right. "Okay," he finally said. "I guess I do owe it to Sam to tell him everything I know. This is gonna be pure dime-store psychology, though. So take whatever I say with a grain of salt."

Chad could be awfully persuasive when he wanted to be, Sam knew. What had just transpired between him and Billy was another example of that fact.

"Please proceed, Dr. Hewitt," Chad said.

The waitress refilled their cups. It was 10:30 at night and they were chugging coffee like it was water. None of them was going to sleep tonight. Sam wouldn't have anyway. He was too keyed up about Mary.

Billy began. "Well, if you've ever seen Joey with his father, he doesn't seem to like him much. I'm talking real resentment here."

Sam asked, "Why does he resent him?" He could barely wait for Billy to finish a sentence.

Billy took a sip of coffee. "I think it's because Joey wants his father to name him as his successor, but his father won't do it. Apparently, Iron Mike doesn't think Joey is tough enough to run the family when he's gone. He's also resisted Joey's push to involve the family in the porn business. Iron Mike thinks pornography is disgusting, and Joey knows that. So, as a sign of rebelliousness at his father, Joey has embraced pornography wholeheartedly. He's even acted in some of his movies. And his only friends—if you can call them 'friends'—are his porn contacts. You mentioned one earlier, Sam. Brian Newland. Frankly, I'm not surprised that Newland gave testimony that was helpful to Joey. They're friends. There are a few others as well. You already know about Jennifer. Shit, who do you think brought her to the party the other night? . . . Joey, that's who."

Billy stuffed a piece of bacon into his mouth and drained his orange juice. He wiped his face and hands with the remnants of a paper napkin. Then, he continued with his explanation of what made Joey Mancini tick. It was an explanation that was both sophisticated and persuasive. In fact, it was so well stated that Sam was finding it difficult to believe that Billy had flunked out of law school a couple of years earlier.

"Joey enjoys presenting himself as being attached to no one and needing no one," Billy said next. "His rebellion against his father isn't in his appearance or demeanor but in his work, which is his only interest, day and night."

Chad interrupted. "You mentioned the other day, Sam, that you caught Mancini previewing videotapes at Chateau del Sol. Think about it: there's a fancy party going on, with lots of good food, good champagne, and interesting people. And what's Mancini doing? Previewing porn tapes."

"There's something else, too," Sam said. "Mancini's *on trial* for a crime involving pornography. And what does he do? He accosts me about pornography. The guy is obviously oblivious to anything else that's going on around him . . . It's sad."

"It *is* sad," Billy said. "And I'm pretty sure that Joey thinks it's sad, too."

"What do you mean?"

"What I mean is, I don't think Joey is happy. In fact, I think he hates his life—perhaps even more than he hates his father. He talked to me about it once, albeit briefly and in extremely veiled terms. But my sense is that he hates what he does for a living—that it makes him feel like a pervert. He used that word—'pervert'—when he was talking to me about it. Shit, I think I even heard him mutter something about suicide. I pressed him on that one, but he ignored me. He ignores most people most of the time."

Sam Grimes stared into the bottom of his now-empty coffee cup and tried to assess what Billy Hewitt had just relayed to him about Joey Mancini's self-doubts. Sam never could have imagined that a person as openly aggressive and hostile as Mancini was could ever doubt himself about anything.

Chad said, "I hate to bring this up, Sam, but tomorrow is a workday."

Chad's observation about the coming morn snapped Sam back from the twilight zone this conversation—this entire day—had put him in. Three cups of strong coffee notwithstanding, Chad and Billy looked exhausted. Sam suspected that he did, too.

He said, "I don't know what to do. I need to find Mary. I can't leave until I find her." His head was pounding. He rubbed his temples for relief. He wasn't getting any.

"I know you do, buddy," Chad said. "But it's like looking for a needle in a haystack. None of us is Sherlock Holmes. I think the best thing we can do is head back to Providence, notify the police, and let them take it from here."

Billy started. His face turned as white as the paper napkin crumpled in his hand. "You—You *can't* do that. That—That would lead to my father. My father didn't have anything to do with Mary's disappearance. I know he didn't. I just know it. Can't—Can't we figure out some other way? My father'll be at his law office tomorrow. Let me find out from him where the shoot is. Then, I'll help you get her back. I promise I will. I promise."

Sam was torn. He now considered Billy a friend, and he believed him when he said that Mr. Hewitt couldn't have known about Mary. But his number one consideration had to be *for* Mary. Perhaps because he wasn't thinking straight, or perhaps because of the anguished look on Billy's face, Sam resisted his better judgment.

"All right," he said, after an awkward silence. "I'll give you until noon tomorrow. Be clear about this, though. Be crystal clear about this: If I don't hear from you by noon, I'm going to the police. Now let's go. We've got a long drive ahead of us."

CHAPTER THIRTY-ONE

Sam's alarm clock startled him out of bed, which showed how much the stress of the last few weeks—and especially of yesterday—had gotten to him. Yesterday had taken a heavy toll on Chad as well: Sam had to bang more loudly on Chad's door than usual before there was a hint he was stirring.

"Are you as zonked as I am?" Chad asked as he marched unevenly into the kitchen. His thick blond hair was matted to his head like muddy straw to a farmer's boot. He was still wearing the sweat pants he slept in.

"Yeah. My alarm beat me up this morning. And you know how much I hate that frickin' sound." Sam was still in his sweats, too. He grabbed a couple of coffee cups from the plastic dish rack next to the sink. He filled them. "Here. Maybe this'll help. I made it extra strong this morning." He handed Chad a cup of coffee that looked an awful lot like an oil slick.

"What are you going to do?" Chad blew on his coffee to cool it. "Are you going to talk to Judge Reis?"

Sam hesitated, and then said, "I don't know what I'm going to do. I've got to find Mary. That's all I know. But as far as talking to the Judge is concerned, I don't think so. I don't want to get him involved . . . At least not yet."

"He should know, Sam. You are talking about going after a guy who's currently on trial in his courtroom."

Sam gazed uncertainly through the skylight. A soft-yellow sun was struggling to break through a pack of hard-gray storm clouds.

"You're probably right," he finally said. "But let me get the cobwebs out of my head before I decide. You promised you wouldn't say anything. Please keep your word. *Please.*"

Chad couldn't help but be affected by his roommate's plea. He looked Sam squarely in the eyes. He looked more serious than Sam had ever seen.

He said, "I will. I promise, I will. But *you* have got to promise *me* something."

"What?"

"That you'll let me know what you decide to do before you decide to do it. I don't want you doing something stupid."

Sam said, "I promise."

◆ ◆ ◆ ◆

"Sam . . . Sam . . . Sam!"

"Sorry, Judge. I guess my mind was elsewhere there for a minute."

Sam tried his best to appear as if everything was okay. He wasn't successful, though.

"I'll say it was," the Judge said. "You look like your dog got hit by a car. What's wrong?"

"Another long night with the Hewitts, that's all."

It had been. So at least he wasn't lying.

Carolyn buzzed Sam and the Judge into chambers. They exchanged good mornings. She was her typically pleasant self. Sam obviously wasn't: Carolyn asked him what was wrong, too.

Sam gave her the same explanation he had given to the Judge, and then followed the Judge into his office.

"Here, Sam. Maybe this'll get your motor started." The Judge handed his law clerk a cup of coffee. Sam was almost too distracted to notice. "And try one of these. Eva made them."

"Thanks, Judge. I can use both of these." Sam took a long sip from a UVA Law mug, and then a large bite from a homemade cinnamon bun. Judge Reis's coffee was certainly a lot better than the oil slick Sam had made. That stuff was so bad that he couldn't drink it. Mrs. Reis's cinnamon bun hit the spot as well. It was the first thing Sam had eaten since yesterday morning. "This is great," he said, popping coils of homemade pastry into his mouth. "Chad and I were running late this morning and we didn't have a chance to eat. Is it okay if I grab one for him?"

"Of course." The Judge wiped his mouth with the clean side of his handkerchief. "Eva will be pleased to know that her baking is a hit. She doesn't bake as much as she did when the boys were little, but she can still keep up with the best of them." He passed Sam the foil tray on which the cinnamon buns were piled high. He added, mouth full, "Believe it or not, Mr. Sutton is about finished with his X-rated film festival. Mr. Marone should be beginning his cross-examination of Agent Wright by late morning. That should be interesting. People can say what they want to say about John Marone, but they also have to give the man his due. He's an excellent courtroom lawyer. I rank him right at the top in the Rhode Island bar."

"So I've heard." Sam quickly changed the subject. He had been doing a lot of that lately. "Will you be needing me for anything this afternoon?"

He asked because he knew he would be leaving early to drive back down to Kingston to search for Mary.

The Judge said, "I don't think so. Why?"

"I've got some errands to run, if that's okay."

"That's fine. You can head out after lunch." The Judge brushed some crumbs from his pants leg. He tossed them into the wastebasket next to his desk. "But try to take it easy tonight," he added, smiling. "A man needs his sleep, even a young man. From what I hear from Chad about you law clerks' extracurricular activities, you must never get any rest."

"I'll do my best, Judge. But you know what they say: 'No rest for the wicked.'" Sam tried to sound funny, but he was too tired to pull it off.

Judge Reis turned serious. "How's Mary's mom doing? Chief Judge Conigliero mentioned to me at lunch yesterday that she's in the hospital."

"I don't really know, to be honest with you. I've only heard from Mary twice since she left town."

Again, at least he wasn't lying. He wasn't sure whether Mary's mom was sick or not. He wasn't even sure where Mary was. He wasn't sure about anything anymore.

"No wonder you've been looking so sad lately. The love of your life is away." The Judge winked and squeezed Sam's shoulder. He reached for his robe and they headed for the courtroom.

The usual cast of characters was at the bar when Sam and Judge Reis entered the courtroom: Holly Curran, Judy Bloom, Steve Sutton, Jim Hodges, John Marone, and, yes, Joey Mancini himself.

Sam glared in Mancini's direction.

The mobster's son offered no response.

Sam scanned the rest of the courtroom. Jerry Cushing was in the back directing spectators to their seats, but not one of Sam's fellow law clerks was present. They must have grown tired of Sutton's pornathon, Sam thought. He certainly had. Porn flicks might have been titillating at first, but after five days of them—six, counting opening statements—they had gotten old. Sam didn't even get aroused by them anymore. He was numb to them, in fact. He had tried approaching them as comedy, but that hadn't worked either. There were too many tragedies behind them, too many lost or stolen souls. He was living through that right now with Mary.

"Mr. Marone will begin his cross-examination when we return at 10:40," Judge Reis said.

"All rise!" Holly Curran cried out.

Sam was so far out of it that he had missed the entirety of Steve Sutton's final session with Agent Wright. After the break, it would be John Marone's turn to question Wright on cross. In other words, it would be Marone's turn to perform before the jury.

"Hello, Philmore?" Joey Mancini whispered into his cell phone. "It's me. Listen. I've only got a minute. We're on a break up here. How are things down in Watch Hill? Is Tiffany giving you any more trouble?"

"Not really," Philmore Bottoms said. "She does what I tell her to do. Apparently, the little chat you had with her this morning had the desired effect. Pretty much so, anyway."

"What do you mean, 'pretty much so'?"

"Let's go, Joey!" John Marone called out from the far end of the corridor. "The Judge is about to reconvene."

Mancini signaled to his attorney that he was on his way, and then said, "Listen, Philmore. I've gotta go. I'll call you later. Oh. One more thing: Don't forget that I've set aside the 21st for editing. My trial should be over by then."

CHAPTER THIRTY-TWO

The courtroom returned to order at 10:40 A.M., precisely as the Judge had decreed it should.

"Your witness, Mr. Marone."

"Thank you, Your Honor." John Marone swaggered toward the witness stand like John Wayne in an old Saturday afternoon western. He asked, mid-stride, "Agent Wright, have you ever heard of a man by the name of Michael Mancini? Or, better yet, 'Iron Mike' Mancini?"

Wow! Marone didn't believe in much of a warm-up! Sam thought.

"Yeah."

Wright, showing either that he was no dummy or that he disdained criminal defense lawyers, said only as much as he was required to say.

"Who, if I may ask, do you know Iron Mike Mancini to be?"

"Objection, Your Honor! Mr. Marone's question is irrelevant!" Steve Sutton thundered as he jumped to his feet.

Judge Reis said, "Overruled, Mr. Sutton. Mr. Marone outlined during his opening statement why this question is relevant for the defense." The Judge switched his attention from the prosecutor to the witness. "Please answer the question, Agent Wright."

Sutton had lost again. More importantly, he had looked foolish again in front of the jury.

Agent Wright said, "Iron Mike Mancini is the head of the Donetelli crime family, the richest and most powerful organized crime family in New England. The Donetelli crime family is closely linked to the Varisco crime family in

New York, the richest and most powerful organized crime family in the United States." Wright leaned forward and reached for his water glass.

Marone interrupted him. "When you say 'organized crime family,' Agent Wright, what do you mean by that?"

"I mean that the Donetelli crime family is engaged in illegal activities. Specifically, in airport cargo hijacking, labor racketeering, extortion, loan-sharking, bookmaking, illegal restraint of trade, counterfeiting, car theft, and murder."

Wright looked proud of his ability to recount from memory the ins and outs of the life and times of Iron Mike Mancini, Sam thought. However, by the look on Marone's face it seemed that Wright's bubble was about to be burst.

Marone said, "You're making some rather grand accusations there, Agent Wright. Isn't it true, though, that no law enforcement agency, federal or state, has ever proved any of what you're alleging—despite devoting countless time and resources to seeing my client's father brought to, quote, 'justice'?"

There wasn't a sound in the courtroom, as everyone awaited Agent Wright's response. Sam noticed that even Judge Reis was on the edge of his seat, albeit with gavel at the ready.

"That's true," Wright said. "We've never secured a conviction against Michael Mancini."

"And isn't it true, Agent Wright, that the FBI's number one priority in New England for the past ten years has been to secure precisely such a conviction against Michael Mancini?"

"That's true."

"And isn't it true, Agent Wright, that the decision was made to pursue my client, Joseph Mancini, because of the FBI's inability to secure a conviction against his father, said same Michael Mancini?"

Agent Wright shifted in his chair. He said, in a voice verging on anger, "The decision was made to devote considerable resources to the arrest and conviction of Joseph Mancini. I don't think it's fair to say, however, that

that decision was based on any so-called 'inability' to obtain a conviction against Michael Mancini."

Marone moved in for the kill. "So, Agent Wright, what you're asking the ladies and gentlemen of the jury to believe is that it's merely a *coincidence* that my client happens to be the son of someone whom the FBI has been pursuing with the obsession of a jilted lover?"

Wright said nothing.

"Your silence speaks volumes, Agent Wright," Marone said.

Sutton rocketed to his feet again. "Objection, Your Honor! Mr. Marone is making an argument, not asking a question! Objection!"

"Sustained," Judge Reis ruled. He turned and faced the jury. "The jury will please disregard Mr. Marone's last remark." He returned his attention to Marone. "Please ask your next question, counselor. And please make it a question, not an argument."

It was difficult for Sam to know who had won the skirmish that had just transpired. No trial lawyer liked having an objection sustained against him, and certainly not when it was coupled with the sort of shot at the lawyer that Judge Reis had delivered to Marone. This said, anyone who thought that jurors disregarded "inadmissible" matters they had seen and heard in the courtroom—especially provocative matters such as Marone's retort to Wright—failed to distinguish between law in books and law in action. Sam's hunch was that Marone had known that Sutton would object to his remark and that Judge Reis would sustain the objection, but that he had thought his line of questioning with Wright leading up to the remark would make the remark memorable enough to stick in the jurors' minds. No matter what Judge Reis said to them afterward . . .

After listening patiently to Judge Reis's admonition, Marone returned to the defense table, where he lingered over notes written on a legal pad. Sam was close enough to make out that the notes were an outline of the issues Marone wanted to cover with Agent Wright, but he was too far away to read what the issues were. Technically, he shouldn't have been trying to figure it out, given that Marone's notes were protected by the work-product privilege—a close cousin to the sacred attorney-client privilege.

Marone then demonstrated what a magnificent courtroom performer he was, and Sam was using "performer" as a synonym for "actor." By taking a few moments to review his notes, Marone was conveying to the jury that he was serious about the case and that he was well prepared. By returning his notes to counsel table before he resumed his questioning of Wright, Marone was conveying to them that he only needed to refresh his recollection—that, in other words, he knew the case inside and out. It was a subtle image Marone wished to place in the jurors' minds. He appeared to have succeeded, though: throughout his entire performance at counsel table none of the jurors seemed to waiver in the undivided attention they were affording to him.

"Agent Wright," Marone continued, now back near the witness stand, "a few days ago, at the very beginning of Mr. Sutton's direct examination, if I recall correctly, you said something to the effect that 'the people have a right to live in a community free of moral depravity.' Am I quoting you accurately, Agent Wright?"

"Yeah."

"Good. I wouldn't want to misquote you." Marone smiled as he prepared to deliver another body blow. "*What*, may I ask, could you possibly have meant by *that?*"

Wright finally lost it. He unleashed a flurry of sounds that were so intense he actually fell back in his chair upon speaking them. "What I meant by that, Mr. Marone, is that I've come to learn during my time investigating this case that pornography is evil. The crime rate rises everywhere pornography rears its ugly head. It decimates the lives of the young people who have somehow been lured into selling their bodies—and *souls*—for money, and in many cases, for drugs. And to respond directly to your question, Mr. Marone, pornography destroys the moral fabric of the communities in which it's allowed to exist. As we've seen by watching the countless videotapes and DVDs that Mr. Sutton has introduced into evidence during this trial, pornography appeals to the base urges of a public that has already gone too far down the path of moral degradation." Wright stopped, took one quick breath, and then spat, "You've asked me a lot of questions here this morning, Mr. Marone. Now I'd like to ask you one: What possible good can this *filth* contribute to society?"

Judge Reis sounded his gavel.

All eyes turned to the bench.

The Judge said, "I'm sure Mr. Marone would be delighted to answer your question, Agent Wright, but the rules of trial procedure don't permit him to do so. I believe that now would be a convenient time to take our lunch recess. The Court will reconvene at 1:15. Enjoy your lunch, ladies and gentlemen."

CHAPTER THIRTY-THREE

Like apparently everyone else in the courtroom, Sam Grimes had gotten caught up in the drama of John Marone's cross-examination of Agent Wright; so caught up, in fact, that he had almost forgotten that Billy Hewitt was going to be leaving a message for him about where he might be able to find Mary. However, now that Judge Reis had announced the lunch recess, Sam's single-mindedness of purpose had returned.

It took Sam less than a minute to travel from the majesty of the courtroom to the mundane of his office, and then only a few seconds more after that to dial the access code to the answering machine in his apartment. Fortunately, the access code was easy to remember: REDSOX. Sam could barely remember his name at this point. He couldn't imagine having to dig much deeper in his memory bank than something to do with his favorite baseball team.

There were three messages on the machine. The first was from Sam's mother. She wanted to know on what day he would be coming home for Thanksgiving. Sam's life had been so wild and crazy lately that he had forgotten that Thanksgiving was just around the corner. (When you were dealing with Sam's mother, five weeks *was* just around the corner.) "Are you planning to bring that nice girl I've heard so much about?" his mom asked as only a mother could. The second message was for Chad. *His* mother wanted to know when *he* was coming home for Thanksgiving. "Are you bringing Suzanne?" Mrs. Smith asked. Moms were all alike, Sam said to himself. God bless 'em for it. The third message was the one for which he had been waiting. "The shoot is at an old mansion on Bluff Avenue in

Watch Hill," Billy said. "I'm not sure whether Mary is there or not, but it's worth a look. Meet me at my folks' house at lunchtime, and I'll show you where the place is. Dad's used it before."

The hushed tone of Billy's voice suggested that he was calling from work: The Law Offices of Raoul Hewitt, P.C.

Sam slammed down the phone and rushed for the door. He felt like what Professor Alan Dershowitz had said O.J. Simpson felt like filming a Hertz commercial—but *not* running from the crime scene at Bundy Avenue—as he bobbed and weaved his way through the mix of people that crowded the corridor. (Sam had taken a criminal law seminar from Dershowitz that focused on the famous clients the professor had defended over the years.) Sam even hurdled over a chair, just like the professor had said O.J. used to do.

Jerry Cushing called to him, but this time Sam simply waved and kept running.

Sam arrived at the Hewitts' Congdon Street palace—and it really did seem like a palace to him—and suddenly realized that he had forgotten to tell Chad what he had decided to do. Sam always tried to keep his word, so the moment Billy answered the door he asked if he could use the telephone.

"Use the one in my mom's sitting room," Billy said. "It's private in there. I'll meet you in the car. We'll take the Silver Seraph again."

Billy grabbed his favorite bombardier jacket from the hall closet and headed for the garage to get the car.

Sam ducked into Mrs. Hewitt's private sanctuary to call Chad.

He tried to reach Chad at the office. There was no answer. He next tried the apartment. Again, no answer. Finally, he tried Chad's cell phone. The voice mail picked up. Sam said, "Chad. It's me. I'm about to head down to Watch Hill with Billy. He says that's where the shoot is. It's 12:35. I promised I'd let you know, so that's what I'm doing. Please don't tell Judge Reis anything. *You* promised *me*. I told him I had some errands to run. That is technically true. I'll talk to you later."

Billy had already pulled the Silver Seraph around front in the less than two minutes it had taken Sam to leave a message for Chad. He said, "It should take us about an hour to get to Watch Hill."

Sam assumed his seat on the passenger's side of Raoul Hewitt's favorite car. The glove-leather interior contrasted sharply with the cloth mesh that covered the seats in Sam's pre-owned Honda.

All the fancy houses were nice, but Sam sensed that Mr. Hewitt loved his Silver Seraph more than anything else. He loved it, he had once told Sam over a snifter of cognac and an imported Cuban cigar, because of the symbolic value it held as marking his arrival in high society. "Someday you'll own one, too," he had assured Sam.

Little did Raoul Hewitt—lawyer/pornographer extraordinaire—realize how unappealing the thought of a materialistic lifestyle was to Sam Grimes. Sam would much rather live simply and maintain his perspective on what was truly important in life: having good friends and loving someone special. Someone like Mary . . .

It wasn't until they were past East Greenwich before either Sam or Billy had anything else to say.

Sam was the one who broke the silence. "Do you think we'll find her?" The concern in his voice was palpable.

"I hope so. I mean, I hope she's not making another porn movie, but I hope we find her." Billy was clearly struggling for the right thing to say. "You know what I mean, Sam. I hope we find her and I hope she's okay. I've never met Mary before, but she must be pretty great for you to be as worked up about her as you are."

Billy had somehow managed to say exactly the right thing.

"She is great. Thanks." Sam's eyes were transfixed on the side of the road. This brought him to the sudden realization that almost all the leaves had fallen from the trees.

One of Sam's first memories as a child was the time when he was about six and he told his mother how spooky it was when the leaves were off the trees. "It's like all the trees are dead," he could remember saying to her. His mother had said that he was worrying about nothing—that the trees were just sleeping—but deciduous trees still made him feel like there was death in the air.

Sam's mind skipped ahead some twenty years to the present. He asked, "How much longer until we get there?"

Billy turned down the volume on the car radio.

Sam was so out of it that he hadn't noticed the radio was on.

Billy answered, "About forty-five minutes, give or take a few. There'll be plenty of daylight left, so we shouldn't have a problem finding things like we did last night."

They made it in thirty.

Billy swung a hard right onto a long gravel driveway. The sign at the entrance read OCEAN HOUSE. At the end of the driveway, tucked behind an assortment of evergreen trees and bushes, sat a yellow-clapboard Victorian mansion whose immensity nearly took Sam's breath away.

Billy clearly picked up on how taken Sam was with the house. "Ocean House was built in 1868 by George Nash, a famous New York architect," he said, exiting the Silver Seraph. "It was one of the grand mansions that helped earn Watch Hill its reputation as a nineteenth-century place to be. It looks a bit rough on the outside these days, but the inside is well kept and it still offers unparalleled views of the Atlantic."

Sam slid out of the leather car seat and stepped onto the dirt sidewalk. "That's great, Billy. But let's find Mary first. Then we can take a tour." He sounded pissed off, and he felt guilty about it. Billy was trying to help. "Sorry about that, man. I'm just anxious to find Mary, that's all. And it looks like we're close. *Very* close . . ."

"Don't worry about it. I know you're freaking out." Billy zipped his jacket. "Let's go inside and see if we can find her. We've got to be quiet, though."

"Does anyone live here?" Sam asked when they reached the front porch. His question was prompted in part by his interest in discerning how Billy knew so much about the place.

Billy answered almost immediately. "Not anymore. It's owned by the town historical trust."

"By the town historical trust? Why on earth would a town historical trust permit a porn movie to be filmed on one of its properties?"

The absurdity of this scenario wasn't lost on Billy. "Because Joey Mancini requested it, that's why. People aren't dumb, even people who get off on history. They know who Joey is. Or at least who he's reputed to be."

It was the first time Billy had acknowledged Mancini's mob ties.

He opened the heavy black door that marked the entrance to Ocean House. The foyer was adorned with implements of the sea—a barometer, a spyglass, a compass—that bespoke the location and activity of the manor. In the parlor, a giant mounted cod kept watch over the stone fireplace that rested quietly beneath it. Sam and Billy stumbled around the ground floor, then the second floor, and then the third. Nothing. Not a clue about whether Midnight Productions was here, let alone about whether Mary was with them.

"Where the HELL is everyone?!" Sam's anger had returned with a vengeance. "You SAID there was a SHOOT here!"

"There is. Or—Or at least there's supposed to be," Billy stammered.

"And WHO, pray tell, told you THAT?!"

"Monica." Billy had quickly regained his composure, although Sam had not. Billy was used to being around people who flew off the handle. People like Joey . . . "She's one of the staffers over in Kingston. She's the office manager, so she should know. She keeps a log of what movies are being shot, and where."

Sam exhaled two long breaths to try to calm himself. It worked. A little. "Well, it strikes me that Monica doesn't know shit. What the fuck is the number over there? I'll ask her myself."

"I wouldn't do that, Sam. It was awkward enough when I asked her. Dad and Joey don't like her giving out much information, for reasons that are too obvious to mention. I'll call her again."

"You do that. And try to get some useful information from her this time."

Sam and Billy returned to the ground floor, where Billy proceeded to call Monica from the telephone in the kitchen. While he was doing that, Sam had another look around. Finally, he stumbled across something that might lead him to Mary. Sitting haphazardly next to a *Farmers' Almanac* on the coffee table in the parlor was a single white sheet of paper on which was typed the day's itinerary. The paper had several creases in it, and it was stained by a series of coffee rings, but it was legible.

Sam read it.

The Ovulator

Shoot Schedule

Wednesday, October 16

7:00 a.m.–12:30 p.m., interiors at Ocean House

   —Performers: Tiffany, Jennifer, Vivianna, Stacy, Peter, Tom, Randy

   —Crew: Zed (camera), Jay (photos), me

12:30-1:30 p.m., travel (lunch in the van)

1:30-4:00 p.m., exteriors at Narragansett Pier

   —Performers: Tiffany, Vivianna, Stacy, Peter, Tom

   —Crew: Zed (camera), Jay (photos), me

4:00–5:00 p.m., exteriors at The Flying Horse Carousel

   —Performers: Jennifer, Stacy

   —Crew: Zed (camera), Jay (photos), me

5:00–10:00 p.m., interiors at Ocean House (dinner on the set)

   —Performers: Tiffany, Jennifer, Vivianna, Stacy, Peter, Tom, Randy

   —Crew: Zed (camera), Jay (photos), me

Thursday, October 17

9:00 a.m.–3:00 p.m., interiors at Ocean House (lunch on the set)

—Performers: Tiffany, Jennifer, Vivianna, Stacy, Peter, Tom, Randy

—Crew: Zed (camera), Jay (photos), me

3:00–8:00 p.m., editing at the studio

—Crew: me

8:00–11:00 p.m., story board for *Co-ed Fever*

—Crew: me

P.B.

What was most striking about the shoot schedule was how rigorous it was. The performers were slated to shoot sex scenes for fourteen hours the first day and for six hours the second day. Sam didn't see how that was physically possible.

Billy hung up the phone and strode into the parlor. He had a disappointed look on his face. "Monica says we just missed them. They left for Narragansett at 12:30."

Sam said, "I know. I found an itinerary while you were on the phone. They'll be at some place called 'The Flying Horse Carousel' at four, and then back here from five to ten."

"That's what Monica says, too. What should we do? Do you wanna drive over to Narragansett, or do you wanna wait here? It's your call, Sam."

"How closely do they follow the shoot schedule? I mean, are they definitely coming back here this evening?"

"It depends. Let me see the itinerary."

Sam had refolded the sheet of paper on which the itinerary was typed and placed it in his pocket. He unfolded it and handed it to Billy.

Billy studied it. "P.B.," he said. He bit down on his lower lip. "Philmore Bottoms. Philmore Bottoms is directing the video. Philmore flies by the seat of his pants. Dad's an organization freak. If anything isn't the way it's supposed to be, he has a shit fit. Philmore drives Dad nuts because he's always changing things in midstream. 'For the art,' he always says. To Philmore, these aren't videos about people fucking. They're 'post-modern cinema.'"

Billy had learned this about Bottoms during their recent trip to Las Vegas.

"So you're saying that the director isn't going to stick to the shoot schedule?" Sam asked, confused. "And what's up with that name: 'Philmore Bottoms'?"

Billy shrugged his shoulders. "It's not his real name, obviously. Porn people are always coming up with crazy pseudonyms for themselves. 'Philmore Bottoms' is a play on *fill more asses*. Philmore's specialty is anal sex. With respect to the shoot schedule, though, he probably won't stick to it, but there's really no way of knowing. It all depends on what kind of mood he's in. For all I know he could be back here at 5:00 P.M., sharp. But he also could decide to shoot everything else in Narragansett and not come back here at all. He's the most unpredictable director that Midnight uses, but he's also the most profitable. His videos sell far better than anyone else's do. It's not even close."

Billy had learned this, too, in Las Vegas.

Sam stared off into the dormant fireplace and tried to figure out what to do—how best to find Mary. His fancy education wasn't worth a damn at this particular moment in his life—the most important moment *of* his life. He had to go by his gut.

"Given that scenario, we should split up," he finally said, with far more certainty in his voice than he actually felt. "Why don't you take the Silver Seraph and drive up to Narragansett to see if you can find them. I'll wait here. My gut tells me they'll come back. I want to be here when they do."

"Fair enough," Billy said. "But let me write down the phone number to this place before I go. I'll call you from Narragansett if I find them."

Billy knew that Sam was still one of the few people in the United States who didn't own a cell phone. He headed back to the kitchen.

Sam followed closely behind him.

Billy wrote down the phone number on a discarded envelope.

"You do that," Sam said. "I'll steal a car to get there if I have to. Good luck."

"To you too, man. And be careful. Philmore's got a few screws loose. I'll tell you about our trip to Las Vegas sometime."

"Okay." Sam then apologized to Billy—again—for flying off the handle a few minutes back.

Billy said—again—not to worry about it: that Sam's reaction was perfectly understandable. He said he would be more concerned if Sam wasn't flying off the handle.

They shook hands—a guy thing—and split up.

CHAPTER THIRTY-FOUR

Watch Hill, Rhode Island, with three and a half hours to kill. Sam Grimes had never been in this situation before. Shit, he had never been in any of the crazy situations in which he had found himself during the last several weeks: snorting cocaine in the backroom of a Mafia-controlled café in the North End of Boston; partying with the rich and famous in Newport; getting into a fight with a criminal defendant on trial before his boss; being exposed to the world of adult filmmaking; and last but far from least, falling in love with an art student—an art student who happened to be the sweetest, most beautiful woman he had ever met in his life. One thing *was* for sure, though. He couldn't just sit around a big empty house and wait for something to happen. He would go nuts if he did. He might as well try to find a place to eat. He needed to keep up his strength. It might be another long night.

He found the Olympia Tea Room.

Billy had mentioned during the drive down that everyone in Rhode Island ate at the Olympia at one time or another. The list now included Sam.

The Olympia Tea Room was an authentic early-twentieth-century seaside-resort soda-fountain café, with black-and-white checkerboard floor tiles, well-used wooden booths, sidewalk tables, and waitresses in black dresses with white aprons. It was the end of the lunch hour, so Sam had no trouble finding a seat. Actually, he was the only customer in the place. He grabbed a vacant booth near the front window and watched the local world go by. A waitress who looked an awful lot like his Aunt Sharon—Shirley

Temple hairstyle, rosy cheeks, heavyset, always smiling—offered him a "good afternoon, young man" as she handed him a menu. She said her name was Cathy.

Sam scanned the menu.

Cathy chimed in, "You look like a daring sort, hon'. The Olympia is famous for its gutsy garlic-laced clam stew. I had some for lunch myself. Maurice—he's the cook—outdid himself today."

"Sounds good to me," Sam said. "I'll take a Pepsi, too, please." He closed the menu and handed it back to Cathy.

"Comin' right up, hon'." Cathy shuffled off to get Sam's lunch.

Sam stared into space, alone again with his thoughts. He tried to figure out how Mary could have ended up in a porno movie. It didn't make any sense. She was a straight-A student at one of the best art colleges in the United States—the prestigious Rhode Island School of Design—for Christ's sake. He balled up a paper napkin and pitched it at the wastebasket next to the counter. He missed by a mile. Cathy brought him another one with his lunch.

Sam was halfway through a clam stew that would have put hair on the chest of a newborn baby when he got a jolt as if he had been struck by lightning. Whom did he see strolling into the Olympia Tea Room in Watch Hill, Rhode Island, during the middle of a fall afternoon? It was none other than Jennifer, the drop-dead gorgeous girl from the Hewitts' party at Chateau del Sol. Sam could never forget that face. Apparently, she remembered his face as well.

She walked over—if you could call what she did *walking*—and said, "Well, well. Fancy meeting you here, Sam. You took off so quickly from the party the other night that I never thought I would see you again. What are you doing here? I thought you worked in Providence."

Jennifer looked as stunning standing before Sam now in a stressed-leather jacket, yellow cardigan sweater, and stonewashed blue jeans as she had at the Hewitts' party when she had been wearing a low-cut evening gown.

Sam said, "I'm taking the afternoon off. I've heard a lot of good things about Watch Hill. 'A sort of Newport-in-miniature,' a friend told me. I thought I'd have a look. How about you?"

He motioned for Jennifer to take a seat. She removed her leather jacket, hung it neatly on the wooden peg attached to the booth, and took the seat directly across the table from him. Her Elizabeth Taylor eyes, her Farrah Fawcett hair, her Angelina Jolie body: there was nothing about this girl—or at least about how she looked—that wasn't perfect.

"I'm here on business." Jennifer took a sip of Sam's Pepsi.

"What kind of business?" Sam tried his best to pretend like he didn't already know.

"Do you really want to know?"

"Sure. Why not?"

"I don't want to shock you."

Cathy returned to the booth.

Jennifer ordered a Caesar salad—light on the dressing—and a cup of hot tea.

Sam ordered a slice of apple pie—heavy on the whipped cream—and a cup of coffee.

Cathy headed back to the kitchen.

Sam said, "I'm tough to shock. What business? Come on, Jen. You can tell me."

Jennifer fidgeted with her bracelet, took another sip of Sam's Pepsi, and then looked him straight in the eyes.

Boy, did she have beautiful eyes, Sam thought again. Violet and the size of half dollars.

"I'm making an adult video." She paused, clearly awaiting Sam's reaction. He had none. "I warned you," she said. "I shocked you, didn't I?"

"Not at all." Sam shrugged his shoulders. "My dad is an egghead at Yale who still gets high before he teaches. My mom is a plant nut from Hickville who talks to trees. To each his own—or *her* own, as the case may be."

Jennifer smiled a smile that revealed more than she intended. It was a smile of relief.

"Thanks," she said. "Most people don't understand. They think I'm a whore or something. To be honest, I don't tell many people. I'm tired of being judged."

Sam wanted desperately to ask Jennifer whether she had seen Mary, but given how secretive Billy had said people involved in the adult film industry were, he decided it was best to try to win her confidence first.

He said, "Can I ask you something?"

She said, "Of course."

"Why do you do it? I mean, why do you make adult videos? I've never met a porn actress before, and I've always wanted to know why people do it. I don't know why I want to know, I just do. Maybe it's my psychology minor talking."

Jennifer smiled a different kind of smile this time. It was the smile of someone who liked to laugh. It was an infectious smile, and Sam couldn't help but return it in kind.

"I do it because I want to do it," she said. "I've got a teacher's certificate. I can make a decent living teaching school. For the longest time I felt sorry for women—women like my mother—who had to wear makeup, with their beauty-parlor hair, their high heels, and their pretty clothes, who always needed a man's approval for their self-worth. *I* didn't need that. *I* didn't need to be my mother."

Jennifer waited while Cathy placed her Caesar salad and hot tea in front of her and Sam's apple pie and coffee in front of him.

"Do you need anything else, hon'?" Cathy asked, looking only at Sam.

"We're all set," Sam answered, looking at Cathy and Jennifer both.

Cathy moved out of earshot.

Jennifer continued with her story about why she made porn movies. "I had exhibitionistic fantasies. I just did it in different places than my mother and those other women did. So-called feminists don't understand sexual exhibitionism: a self-respecting woman enjoying being naked and pretty.

'Man is the enemy, and we're the victim,' they always say. I grew up believing that most men, if they could rape you, probably would. Catharine MacKinnon—I bet you didn't think I knew who she was—is on a personal vendetta. She's a prime example of a woman out for revenge because no one asked her to the prom."

Sam and Jennifer laughed. However, Sam had to admit—to himself, at least—that Jennifer was right: given the way she looked, not to mention her chosen profession, he had thought she was just another dumb blonde. But she had obviously thought long and hard about the sort of question he had asked, even before he had asked it.

"That's interesting," he said. "I've always thought differently. I mean, after reading the *Miles Commission Report* and all. So everyone involved in the adult film industry has thought a lot about it and wants to be involved?"

Jennifer added a sprinkle of ground pepper to her salad, and then took a sip of her tea. "No, not everyone. In the shoot I'm on now, there's this eighteen-year-old girl who shouldn't be there. I'm talking great tits, great ass, pretty face. But she's not mentally there. Whatever the reason, she's finding the realities of porno movies aren't something that suit her. And she's having a mild freak-out: 'I need to maintain control of the situation for my sanity,' I can hear her saying to herself. I don't blame her for that. I don't. I do blame her for being here in the first place. It's like, 'You obviously don't want to do this: Why are you here? What agenda do you have?' The girls don't talk about that. But these are the girls who later hate the business, leave the business, and complain about being used and abused, even though no one ever said, 'You must suck this dick.'

"She came to the set and worked and didn't like it. I don't know who is, quote, 'to blame for this.' If you're going to think in terms of Piaget—in terms of emotional development—eighteen years old is when you should be focusing on intimate contact with a single person and trying to figure out who you are in your relationships. Public sex isn't what you need to be doing at eighteen. I was twenty-one before I started having sex on camera—after two years of practicing having sex on stage. I realized, 'Okay, I've got permanent records that will affect my life, ten to fifteen years from now. Okay, I can handle it. Okay.'

"So, many of these young girls *are* different. It looks so glamorous. They get contracts with companies, and contracts mean getting picked up in limousines, being driven to the set. They take care of your airfare. They take care of your hotel. They take care of everything for you. You get to the set, they take care of your hair, they do your nails, they do your makeup, they have someone telling you what your lines are, they have someone to dress you. You wear these fancy clothes, and you go to parties, and you're on movie sets with movie people. It seems so glamorous, but it's not. So it's easy for them. Easy to get sucked in. Easy for them to handle a situation they're not handling. People are handling it for them. The problem is, these young girls are eighteen, and the company does everything for them without making sure they understand that porn will affect the rest of their lives. It all comes down to one simple fact: There's a big difference between being a girl and being a woman. We have an alcohol law that says you can't drink until you're twenty-one, but you can make a porno movie. That's just wrong.

"So I thought about it. You're right. These girls come to it for a variety of reasons. Not only the money and sex, but wanting to get back at Daddy for being a prick. Like, for sure, 'Mom and Dad will really freak out if I come home with a black boyfriend.' She came off the set saying, 'God, I hate . . . I'll never do two guys again. I can't stand it.' I just said, 'That's just youth talking. You have two of the best guys in the business.'"

Jennifer reached over and drained the rest of Sam's Pepsi. She glanced at him and blushed. "I told you I'd shock you. You're white as a ghost."

Sam smiled a nervous smile. "I'm not shocked. Really I'm not, although I have to admit that your candor caught me a bit off guard . . . Would you like to try some of my pie? It's apple."

Jennifer giggled at Sam's lame attempt at nonchalance. "You're sweet, Sam." She turned somber. "I don't expect you to understand where I'm coming from. I appreciate you listening, though. It feels good to talk about this stuff with someone who isn't judging me. And I do know you're not judging me."

Jennifer flashed her violet eyes. She studied Sam's face. She did seem convinced that he wasn't judging her.

And he wasn't.

He said, "If you don't mind me asking, what do your parents think about what you do for a living?"

"I can hear my mother now: 'Jennifer, you were such a good little girl. Always so respectful and polite. Why are you doing this? Where did I go wrong?' I never told my father. My mother did that. My father won't even speak to me now. I'm 'Daddy's little girl' no longer. It's sad, really. I miss being able to go home. It's especially tough during the holidays, like now, what with Thanksgiving and Christmas being just around the corner."

Jennifer's eyes welled up with tears. She wasn't so tough, after all.

"Here . . ." Sam handed her his handkerchief.

"Thank you." She wiped her eyes and blew her nose.

"You can keep that," Sam said.

Jennifer now smiled the smile of a scared and lonely young woman. It was a smile that broke Sam's heart. Exhibitionistic fantasies my ass, he said to himself. Jennifer regretted the life she had chosen.

CHAPTER THIRTY-FIVE

Cathy brought the check.

Sam said, "I'll get that." He snatched the check from the center of the table.

Jennifer said, "Are you sure?"

"Yeah. It's my pleasure. I enjoyed the company. I can think of a lot worse things than buying lunch for an intelligent, vibrant, young woman."

Sam purposely avoided including "beautiful," or any other comment about Jennifer's looks, in his description of her virtues. That she was beautiful went without saying. More importantly, she needed to know that people could see her as something more than just a pretty package.

"I enjoyed the company, too," she said.

Their eyes met as a romantic moment passed between them: between Jennifer, the beautiful (yes, beautiful) young porn actress; and Sam, the confused (yes, confused) young law clerk.

Sam was ashamed to admit it, but he had forgotten about Mary while he and Jennifer were talking. Now, however, he remembered why he was in Watch Hill. It was because of Mary. He had to find Mary. He *had* to.

He left fifteen dollars on the table, and then helped Jennifer with her jacket. He held the door for her. He asked, "Where are you off to now?"

She answered, "We've got a 4:00 P.M. shoot at The Flying Horse Carousel. It's 3:30 now. I've got to get back to work."

"Can I watch?" Sam's face reddened at the crassness of his remark. "I mean, can I come and see how an X-rated movie is made? I'm not trying to cop a cheap thrill or anything. Really, I'm not. It would be interesting, that's all."

He was actually trying to find a way to reach Mary, and he was thinking that Jennifer might be his best shot—perhaps his *only* shot—to do so.

Jennifer stopped in the middle of the street. She caressed the contours of Sam's face. Her touch was soft and sensual. Sam shuddered with excitement. Suddenly, the fact that it was only forty degrees outside was lost on him. It felt like a hundred. They could have been in the Bahamas, for all Sam knew.

"I wish you wouldn't come." The sadness had returned to Jennifer's voice. "I don't want you to see me like that—in a way you might think is slutty and cheap. Besides, Philmore—he's the director—doesn't like strangers on the set. He's paranoid about it. He'd freak if I showed up with you. No offense."

They continued to stand in the middle of the street. A white BMW swerved to avoid them. A salesclerk from the flower shop next door to the Olympia Tea Room shouted for them to watch out. Sam and Jennifer laughed again. People could say what they wanted to say about the two of them, but they were able to laugh together, even in the midst of trauma.

Sam stated the obvious. "We should probably get out of the street. Why are we standing here, anyway?" He took Jennifer's arm and led her to the safety of the sidewalk.

"I have no idea," she said. "We must have gotten lost in the moment." She appeared pleased that Sam was still holding onto her arm. "I've got to go," she said next. "Philmore will kill me if I'm late."

The fact that the porn industry was controlled by the likes of Joey Mancini made Jennifer's last remark potentially more than a figure of speech.

"Okay," Sam said.

Jennifer kissed him on the cheek. "Maybe I'll see you at another party sometime. I—I hope so."

"I hope so, too." Sam stepped away from her. A pregnant pause passed between them like a warm breeze through the branches of a willow tree. "Be careful" was all he could think of to say to her. Then he thought of Mary. "Wait a minute, Jennifer. At least let me walk you back. I won't go in. I promise. The director will never know."

Several minutes elapsed in contented silence as Sam and Jennifer strolled along Bay Street. They could have been any young couple out window-shopping for the afternoon. Unfortunately, their lives were more complicated than that. *Much* more complicated.

Sam broke the silence. "You know when you asked me in the restaurant about why I'm in Watch Hill today?"

"Yes." Jennifer brushed a loose strand of hair from her angelic face.

"I lied. I'm not here because I've heard so many good things about the place. I mean, I have heard good things about Watch Hill, but that's not why I'm here. At least that's not why I'm here today."

"Why are you here, then?" Jennifer looked puzzled, and perhaps a little hurt.

"I'm here to find my girlfriend."

"Your *girlfriend?*" Now Jennifer looked stunned.

"Her name is Mary. I met her at a party at work. She disappeared a couple of weeks ago. At first, I thought she went home to take care of her sick mother. She left a couple of messages on my answering machine that said that was where she was. I had no reason to suspect otherwise, although I have to admit I found it a bit odd that she left town without first coming to say goodbye. After all, we had been seeing quite a lot of each other. We weren't talking marriage, but it was obvious there was something special between us. I also found the messages themselves odd. They didn't sound like Mary. She sounded distant, and there was a lot of commotion in the background. Chad, my roommate—you know Chad Smith—said not to worry about it. He said it was natural to sound different—distant, or whatever—if your mom was sick, and commotion was par for the course at a hospital. So I felt a little better about it, after talking to Chad, I mean. Until . . ."

Sam's eyes clouded.

Jennifer reached for his hand.

"Until what?" she said. "Until *what?*"

"Until I was at the Hewitts' house and I stumbled across an X-rated video called *Law Clerks in Love*. It was a preview copy that Mr. Hewitt had in his office at the house. *Mary* was in it."

"Your girlfriend was in a porn video?"

"Yeah."

"I'm sorry, Sam. I'm surprised she didn't tell you about it, though. When I meet a guy I really like, I tell him what I do for a living. I don't at first, but after we've spent some time together and it's obvious that we care about each other, I tell him. More often than not, the relationship ends shortly thereafter. 'Something has come up,' he always says. Then I never hear from him again. It's sad, but I don't want to be with a guy who's uncomfortable with who I am—with what I do. Maybe Mary was afraid of losing you. Maybe that's why she didn't tell you."

The white BMW sped past again.

"I don't think that's it," Sam said. "I don't think she's here of her own free will. Mary's an art student at one of the premier art colleges in the United States, for God's sake."

"You mean she's too good to be a whore." Jennifer began to cry. The tears flowed like waterfalls.

Sam panicked. He never had been good with tears. "I didn't mean *that*. I didn't. I just meant that her career path was already set. She seemed to love art, especially interior design. The colors, the creativity—the whole nine yards. This porn-actress thing is too different—too much of a departure. Besides, I've read where many of the women in these movies—present company excluded—are coerced into them. And the way Joey Mancini was razzing me about the way Mary looks and how he could, quote, 'make her a star' makes me think that she's not here because she wants to be."

"How do you know she's here, anyway?"

Thankfully, Jennifer had stopped crying. She dabbed her eyes with the handkerchief that Sam had given to her at the restaurant.

Sam said, "Billy Hewitt checked into it for me. He's not sure, but he didn't recognize the name of one of the actresses."

"Which one?"

"Tiffany."

Jennifer started. She grabbed Sam's arm. "Is Mary about five-four, with a gorgeous wall of brown hair, brown eyes, fabulous legs, curves in all the right places, and a birthmark on her left shoulder?"

"Yeah."

"So is Tiffany." Jennifer paused, thinking. "Come to think of it," she finally said, "I haven't been able to get a peep out of her. No one has. She keeps to herself. Most of the new girls like to make their presence known. You know, so they'll be remembered and get invited back for another shoot. Tiffany is different, though. She does her scenes when Philmore tells her to, but then she goes off by herself." Jennifer's eyes danced with fright. She pulled on Sam's arm. "Come on," she said to him. "We've got to hurry."

CHAPTER THIRTY-SIX

They had just about reached The Flying Horse Carousel when Jennifer decided it would be best if she tried to figure out what was going on with Mary without Sam around. "You don't want to get on the wrong side of these people," she had said. "Joey Mancini's got some pretty scary friends. He calls them 'production assistants.' They're both around six-five, weigh about two hundred and fifty pounds, and don't smile much. They're the ones who had a chat with Stacy after she freaked out about doing two guys. It's remarkable how cooperative she's become since then."

Sam had tried to convince Jennifer that he should accompany her to the set, but he was unsuccessful. She was probably right, though. He was a law clerk, after all, not a private detective, and he was certainly in no position to take on a couple of thugs by himself. He seriously doubted they would be intimidated by his quoting the *Yale Law Journal* at them. They spoke a different language: the language of violence.

So, there Sam sat in the Olympia Tea Room once again. He stared across the street at a small park and into a police kiosk next to an old oak tree. His better judgment told him that he should report what was going on, but he decided against it from fear that something would happen to Mary—and to Jennifer—if he did.

Cathy—Sam's new friend and personal waitress—asked if he had had a fight with his girlfriend. She meant Jennifer. He said yes in order to forestall a conversation about matters he wanted to keep under his hat. He had been at the Olympia for so long—it was already 6:15 P.M.—he was about to order dinner. He needed something to keep him busy . . . something to occupy his mind.

Just as he decided on the clams and sausages on linguine, Billy Hewitt walked through the door. "I had about given up on you," Sam said.

"I know." Billy sat without removing his jacket. The billows of lambskin that adorned his collar made him look like one of the star-nosed moles that had been wreaking havoc on the gardens of southern New England that year. "Sorry about that. I had to be really careful snooping around in Narragansett."

Cathy rushed over. There was still no one else in the restaurant, and it was pretty obvious that she was happy to have the business, as well as the company.

"I'll have what he's having," Billy said to her. "And a coffee, too." He took off his gloves and tossed them onto the table. He rubbed his hands together to warm them. "A rush on the coffee, if it's not too much trouble."

Billy's coffee came quickly, and he couldn't have been more grateful. "You're a lifesaver," he said to Cathy.

Cathy smiled, and then dashed off to ask the cook how dinner was coming along.

"Man, it's cold out there." Billy let the coffee's steam engulf his wind-burned face.

"Yeah, I know," Sam said. "But what did you find out?"

"Not a lot, I'm afraid. I managed to speak to Philmore during a break. He knows me from a couple of things—including a recent trip to Vegas. Still, he wasn't too comfortable about having me around. I suppose it's because these guys know they're breaking all kinds of laws with their movies—Joey's innocent plea in your courtroom notwithstanding. He kept asking me if my father had sent me—about whether my father was getting anxious about the progress of the shoot. I said I was looking for a friend—for a new girl named Mary. He said he didn't know what I was talking about. 'There's no Mary on this shoot,' he said. 'There are a couple of new girls—a Stacy and a Tiffany—but,' he said, 'there are always new girls.' I kept pressing him, but he wouldn't let me on the set. He said the word has got to come directly from my father, or from Joey, before anyone not on the production list is allowed on the set. By then, Vince and Sal—these two huge guys who work for Joey—started looking at me funny, so I hauled ass out of there." Billy glanced away. He traced his warming fingers around the lip of the sugar bowl. He added, quietly, "Sorry I let you down again."

Sam flew off the handle again. "I know you're sorry, Billy! And I appreciate you trying! But sorry doesn't cut it! Sorry doesn't find Mary!" He paused and took a gulp from a cup of coffee—the remnants of cup number seven—that was the flip side of Billy's steaming cup. "I'll tell you what," he said, in a more reasonable tone, "why don't you call your father and finagle a way onto the set. I'll keep working my end."

"What's your end?" Billy asked. He looked surprised.

"Jennifer," Sam answered.

"You talked to Jennifer?" Now Billy looked excited. He had fucked her.

"Yeah. She said there's this new girl in the video named Tiffany who matches Mary's physical description."

"What are you sitting here for, then?"

"For the same reason you are: because you've got to play it close to the vest when you're dealing with the Mancinis and the Hewitts—no offense—of this world. Jennifer said she was afraid for her safety—and for Mary's—if she brought me on the set. I promised I'd let her see what she can find out on her own before I went crashing in like a bull in a china shop."

"Fair enough. But I still say you're showing remarkable restraint. I don't see how you can stand the waiting."

"It's not easy. In the words of Tom Petty and the Heartbreakers, 'the waiting is the hardest part.'"

Sam listened to a lot of oldies radio.

Cathy arrived with two heaping plates of clams and sausages on linguine.

Sam had almost forgotten that they had ordered dinner. Not that the service had been slow—quite the contrary. It was just that he was so preoccupied with trying to figure out a way to find Mary.

"That was fantastic!" Billy said. He looked like he was going to burst. He wiped his mouth and hands with a paper napkin. "I haven't had clams and sausages in ages. And never like that."

"Cathy will be pleased," Sam said. He pushed aside his plate. He had barely touched his dinner. "Don't let me forget to leave her a big tip. I've been here for over four hours. I should be paying rent."

"Don't worry. I won't let you forget. But now what? Are we gonna sit here all night?"

"Frankly, I don't know what to do. I can't lose sight of the fact that I've got a trial to get back to tomorrow. I am a law clerk. I do have responsibilities. Judge Reis thinks I'm out running errands, for God's sake." Sam's fingers snagged as he raked them through his hair. He wadded his hair into a ponytail. "According to the shoot schedule, Jennifer is tied up—perhaps literally—at Ocean House until at least 10:00 P.M. I need to be here when she's finished. I—I told her I'd be here. I'm open to suggestions, though."

The frustration in Sam's voice clearly wasn't lost on Billy.

"No pressure, huh!" Billy snatched a sausage from Sam's plate. He devoured it in two big bites. "Seriously, though: I think you—uh, we—have got to stay and wait for Jennifer. In the meantime, I'll put that call into my father and see if I can get him to tell Philmore to let us on the set. You, on the other hand, might want to call Chad and let him know what's up. He might need to cover for you tomorrow. It might be another long night."

"Those are all good ideas."

Imagine, Sam thought, Chad covering for *me*. What a switch that would be. Come to think of it, that would make twice that Chad had covered for him recently: once with Mr. Hewitt at Chateau del Sol and now with Judge Reis at the courthouse.

He signaled for Cathy.

"Yes, hon'," she said, short of breath. She reeked of cigarettes.

"Is there a pay phone we can use?"

"In the back. Near the restrooms." Cathy pointed to a small hallway behind the cash register.

Billy placed the first call. He gave his father some bullshit story about wanting to show a friend around the set. Obviously, he didn't tell him that the friend was Sam. In fact, he said it was some guy from the Midwest who had expressed an interest in distributing some of the product in America's heartland. He said he had met the guy at the Consumer Electronics Show in Las Vegas.

Although Raoul Hewitt didn't know that Sam had flipped out at his house yesterday—it was only *yesterday*, wasn't it?—when he had seen the preview copy of *Law Clerks in Love*, the senior Hewitt did know that his partner in Midnight Productions was presently on trial before Sam's boss. Consequently, Sam knew that he was probably second behind Judge Reis on the list of the last people on earth Mr. Hewitt would want snooping around the set of one of his porno movies.

"We're in," Billy said, replacing the handset. "Dad's gonna put a call into Philmore right now to get us on the set. He even said that he was proud of me for looking out for the family business. What a joke . . ."

Billy looked upset.

Sam could understand why: no one liked to lie to his father, even if that father was a pornographer.

"That's great news, Billy. I appreciate your sticking your neck out like that. I know it's not easy." Sam patted Billy on the shoulder.

Billy nodded.

Sam said, "Now it's my turn." He reached for the telephone. "Where's my stupid phone card?" He fumbled through his wallet. "Credit card, credit card, credit card, bank card . . . Got it." He dialed what seemed like a thousand numbers: the area code for Providence, the phone number for the apartment, the personal identification number for his phone card.

The phone rang seven or eight times.

"Hello," Chad finally said.

"It's me."

"Where the fuck are you, man? I've been worried sick. And Judge Reis must've asked me ten times today, 'What's going on with Sam?' Jerry Cushing did, too."

"What did you say?"

"I said you were bumming about your girlfriend. That is, as you're so fond of saying lately, 'technically true.' So, where the fuck are you?"

"I'm still in Watch Hill. Right now, I'm at the Olympia Tea Room with Billy. We're waiting for Jennifer. We're on our way to the set of *The Ovulator*."

Sam was apparently talking a million miles an hour.

Chad said, "Slow down there, partner. What do you mean, 'you're waiting for Jennifer'? And what do you mean, 'you're on your way to the set of *The Ovulator*'?"

The anxiety in Chad's voice crackled through the phone line like an electric shock in an unsuccessful high school science experiment.

"Before I explain about that," Sam said, "what's going on with the trial? I should know. I need to know. It is my case."

"Well, since you were away for most of the day, Judge Reis asked me to sit in. I'll tell you something, man: You missed quite a show. Marone was fantastic. First, he got Agent Wright to admit that the Attorney General— that asshole Miles—urged the FBI and the various U.S. Attorneys' offices around the country to conduct a 'moral crusade' against not only obscenity, but also non-obscene sexually explicit materials. 'Moral crusade.' Can you believe it? Marone actually got Wright to say the words 'moral crusade.' He also got him to say that Miles directed that the forfeiture provision of RICO be used to drive the producers and distributors out of business. Marone then got Wright to state the obvious: that the forfeiture provision is 'draconian'—that's another quote—given that someone convicted of selling as few as two obscene items over a ten-year span can lose everything. And I don't just mean all of his porno tapes. I mean *everything*: his Walt Disney tapes, his *Star Wars* tapes—shit, his entire store and everything in it. And that wasn't all."

Now Chad was talking a million miles an hour.

"What happened next?" Sam asked, as if *he* was conducting a courtroom examination. Some habits died hard . . .

"Well, after Marone got finished with Agent Wright, he put on his own case. One goddamn witness. That was it. Can you believe it? But, boy, what a witness it was. It was Timothy Collins. You know about Collins. He's the big-time First Amendment scholar from Yale Law School we talked about during the motion to dismiss. He brought a copy of his prize-winning book with him: *When RICO Seizure Is Used to Fight Obscenity, We End Up Forfeiting the First Amendment*. Needless to say, the jurors were impressed by a witness who had written a book about the law in question. At least they seemed impressed to me. Professor Collins's testimony was brief, and he made only two points. But they were powerful points."

"What were they?" Sam asked next, still in trial lawyer's mode.

"The first point was that the RICO forfeiture provision leads to an increase in self-censorship—a 'chilling effect' on the First Amendment, Collins called it—because a simple miscalculation between protected and unprotected speech can result in the forfeiture of an individual's entire inventory. Consequently, fewer people will want to get close to the line, so the First Amendment loses its vitality. The second point was that there's greater government censorship of sexually explicit expression. Agent Wright's description of Attorney General Miles's directive was right on target in this regard. In essence, Professor Collins predicted in his book that what has happened under the Miles regime—Collins's book was published before the President named Miles Attorney General—would happen: that a Justice Department official ideologically opposed to erotic but non-obscene materials would use a few obscene books and videos to drive an adult-product supplier completely out of business." Chad searched for breath, and then added, "I can't wait for Marone's closing argument. You said that Marone didn't have a prayer of convincing the jury that Mancini wasn't guilty, but I think you would feel differently if you saw what I saw today."

"It sounds like it," Sam whispered. The thought of Joey Mancini going free had brought Sam down. And he didn't think he could get any more down.

"What about on your end?" Chad asked.

"You remember Jennifer," Sam answered. "She was the knockout from the Hewitts' party at Chateau del Sol who followed me into the billiard room. You know, the one who you, Billy, and Alan did while I was off looking for Mancini."

"Of course I remember Jennifer. As I recall, she wasn't a very good fuck. Beautiful, yes. But not a very good fuck."

Chad laughed at what he obviously thought was a funny line. Before, Sam might have laughed along with him. But now, given what Jennifer had shared with Sam earlier in the afternoon, he didn't find it funny.

Chad continued with his questions. "But what does Jennifer have to do with the price of beans, or with whatever that stupid expression is?"

"Jennifer's got a lot to do with, as you put it, 'the price of beans.' For one thing, she's performing, as we speak, in a porn shoot that Billy and I suspect Mary is in."

Chad was evidently so stunned by what Sam had just said that he was at a loss for words.

Sam continued, "Jennifer and I had a long talk over lunch. I described Mary to her, and she said there's a girl on the shoot who goes by the name of 'Tiffany' who matches Mary's physical description—including the sexy birthmark I told you about and, of course, those legs to die for. Porn actress or not, Jennifer is a wonderful person. She's just had some tough breaks along the way, although she won't admit it. She's trying to find out if Tiffany is Mary. She promised to come back to the restaurant with the word after the shoot."

Chad said, "I can be there in an hour."

Sam said, "I know you can. But I think it's best that you stay in Providence. You know, in case you have to cover for me again tomorrow with Judge Reis. Actually, that's Billy's idea, but I think it's a good one."

"What do you mean, in case I have to cover for you again tomorrow?"

"Who knows how long this will take? Billy says that sometimes, when they're running behind schedule, these porn shoots can run into the wee hours of the morning. The producers typically put up ten thousand dollars a day, and to them sometimes a day is a day. You know, twenty-four hours. I'm too close to pack it in now. I know Mary's here. I just know it . . ."

There was silence from Chad's end of the line. He clearly knew how worked up Sam was about this whole mess. However, before Chad got a chance to respond, Billy chimed in. "We should get rolling, Sam. I'm sure my dad has given the word to Philmore by now." He grabbed the phone from Sam's hand. "Chad. This is Billy. Listen. Stay there and cover Sam's ass. I think that's the best way to go."

More silence from Chad. Then, "All right. But you had better make sure that you cover his ass on your end. I'm worried that he's in over his head. He's not thinking clearly. He never does when Mary's concerned. You know that world a whole lot better than he does. Watch his back. And keep me posted."

"I will. I promise, I will. Now we've got to head over to the set. Philmore is expecting us."

Billy hung up the phone and they left—Sam *finally* left—the Olympia Tea Room.

CHAPTER THIRTY-SEVEN

Sam and Billy entered Ocean House like they owned the place.

Philmore Bottoms was none too happy they were there. He did try to be civil, however. "Welcome to *The Ovulator*, gentlemen. Billy, I know. But who might you be, sir?"

This guy was a cliché, Sam thought. He *looked* like a dirty old man. He had stringy gray hair, a three-day beard, and he appeared to have slept in his clothes. Deodorant was unfamiliar to him.

Joey Mancini's production assistants stared suspiciously in Sam's direction. Jennifer was right: these guys were *huge*. They made Lennox Lewis look wimpy. Their boss was nowhere to be found, though.

Sam said, "I'm a businessman from Bloomington, Indiana—home of the Hoosiers."

Billy had advised Sam on the drive over how Sam should play this thing. "Be matter-of-fact," Billy had said. "And for God's sake, don't act shocked by what you see. Philmore's gotta think that you're making the rounds on the porn circuit. You know, to see who makes the best quality product."

"What brings you to Rhode Island?" Bottoms asked, continuing with his interrogation. He swept strings of oily hair from his pasty face. His eyes were vacant and the color of burnt charcoal.

Mancini's production assistants still appeared suspicious. Sam was convinced they were *paid* to be suspicious. They inched closer in his direction. One was never more than a couple of feet from the other.

"In a nutshell," Sam answered, "I own a chain of video stores in the Midwest—from Wisconsin to Missouri. I've got about a hundred and fifty stores in all. You've probably heard of them: All American Video. I'm thinking about stocking some adult tapes. I read the newspapers. I know adult videos are a five-billion-dollar-a-year business that accounts for more than a quarter of all rentals and sales at the average general video store."

Sam paused to give his performance—not Academy-Award caliber, but not half bad—dramatic effect.

He added, "I'm no fool. I know I can help my business if I supplement *Harry Potter* with *The Ovulator*. I'm not saying I approve of what you do. Not by any means. But I am a businessman. This is business."

"Yes, it is." Bottoms seemed offended by the judgmental quality of Sam's answer. "And *my* business is making movies. If you'll excuse me . . ." He reached for a Rhode Island Rams baseball cap sitting on a chair next to him. He pushed his hair behind his ears, and then plopped the cap on his head. He turned and walked away. "Places, people!" He tugged on the bill of his cap. "Woodman! Where's my woodman?!"

There was obvious tension on the set, and it wasn't merely because Sam and Billy were there. The guy who was supposed to perform in the scene that Philmore Bottoms was trying to shoot had disappeared.

"Where the fuck is Randy?!" the director shouted.

"I think he's upstairs doing a line," a mousy-looking cameraman said. He was munching on a cinnamon bear claw. "He said he needed a little something to make sure he can keep it up."

Even Sam knew that "keep it up" meant keep *it* up. Literally.

Finally, after ten minutes of Philmore Bottoms's shouting, Randy North showed up on the set.

"Where the fuck have you been?" Bottoms snarled at the stud of the moment.

"Getting ready," Randy replied sheepishly.

Ready indeed, Sam thought. The guy looked high as a kite.

"You had *better* be ready. If there are any more of those performance problems that plagued you on *The Midnight Rides of Paula Revere*, you'll never work on one of my films again. Do you understand me?"

The crew laughed at Philmore Bottoms's cruel remark about Randy North's "performance problems."

Randy stumbled over to his place on the couch.

"Do you understand me?!" Bottoms repeated, adding considerable volume to his question. "And where the fuck is your script?!"

"Hey, I can remember one goddamn line." There was newfound resolve in Randy's voice. The cocaine must have kicked in. "Bring out the girl I'm supposed to fuck."

Sam's heart raced like that of a teenager hopped up on Ecstasy while he waited to see who the girl was whom Randy North was supposed to fuck.

"Randy reflects the new direction in male porn performers," Billy whispered to Sam. "In the early days of porn—I'm talking the 1970s, here—the actors were legitimately trained in the theater. They made porn films partly to make a living and partly because they were products of a politically and sexually rebellious time. Some of their films, most notably *Deep Throat* and *Behind the Green Door*, achieved mainstream success. The second generation was a product of the 1980s boom in porn and they viewed porn as a low-rent version of that decade's 'greed is good' ethic. In other words, they saw porn as a quick and undercapitalized way to make a lot of money. The current generation of male performers, epitomized by our friend Randy North here, sees porn as a way to achieve celebrity. They care, perhaps too much. Randy's aggressive 'bring-me-the-girl-I'm-supposed-to-fuck' demeanor is just an act. But it's an effective act. He throws the girl around. He pile drives her until she protests. Then he cums on her face. He's pure aggression. It sells, though. Guys love to watch that shit."

Billy's description of Randy North's "acting" technique made Sam even more nervous than he already was about whom Randy's partner was going to be. Then, he saw who it was . . . It was Jennifer. She was dressed in a white see-through fishnet tank top, a black miniskirt, and red high heels.

Billy leered at her. "Check that out."

Unfortunately, Sam couldn't share Billy's testosterone-powered enthusiasm. After having spent a wonderful—troubled, but wonderful—afternoon with Jennifer, it broke Sam's heart to see her dressed like a whore. He moved behind a light standard so she couldn't see him. She had asked him not to come—not to watch her like this. He had come only because he had to come in order to find Mary.

"Quiet on the set!" Bottoms thundered.

A hush came over the room. The camera lights blared. The action began.

"Did you have a nice visit with Stacy?" Randy asked Jennifer. His eyes made a slow pass over her voluptuous body. He clearly liked what he saw. Any man would.

"I did, but I missed your cock," Jennifer purred. It was the same purr she had used with Sam, Billy, Alan, and Chad in the billiard room at Chateau del Sol.

Jennifer dropped to her knees and unzipped Randy's fly.

There was definitely no performance problem this time: Randy's flag was flying at full mast.

Jennifer ran her tongue along the shaft of Randy's erect penis, and then proceeded to perform deep throat.

"Close in tight on this, Zed," Bottoms said to the mousy-looking cameraman. "This is great stuff . . . Beautiful, Jennifer. Beautiful . . . Look at me."

Jennifer opened her violet eyes and gazed directly at the camera, all the while continuing to perform fellatio on Randy North.

Randy placed his hands on Jennifer's head and guided her to the appropriate tempo.

Sam felt sick to his stomach. He couldn't bear to watch anymore.

"Billy. *Psst.* Hey, Billy."

Sam finally got Billy's attention.

"What's up?" Billy said. "Besides my dick, that is. Jennifer is really going to town on this guy. She was nothing like that at the party the other night. She's like an animal with him. I feel so cheated . . ."

"It's an act, man. She's acting. She's playing to the camera. That *is* what your father pays her to do."

An uncomfortable moment passed between Sam and Billy.

Sam continued, "I'm going to see if I can find Mary. She's obviously not in this scene."

"Do you want me to come with you?" Camera flashes flickered from over Billy's shoulder. "Still-shots," he said. "You know, for the box cover."

"It's probably best if you don't come," Sam said. "You can keep an eye on Bottoms. If he asks where I am, tell him I went to have a look around. That is technically true."

CHAPTER THIRTY-EIGHT

Sam stumbled through the house in search of Mary. He checked in one room, then another, and then another. Nothing. Not a clue about where she might be.

He kept looking . . . searching . . . hoping. Still nothing. The house seemed bigger now than it had in the morning: emptier, even though there were more people in it now than there had been then.

"Hey, buddy," Sam heard from behind. "What are you doing here? This is supposed to be a *closed* set. I told my agent I only work on *closed* sets."

Sam turned and faced his accuser: a young guy—about Sam's age—who looked as if he spent half his life in the gym. He reminded Sam of the guys he used to see posing on the Venice Beach boardwalk during the summer he had interned at a Beverly Hills law firm: all muscle and hair spray. It was during that summer when Sam had first discovered how unappealing the lifestyles of the rich and famous truly were.

"No worries, mate, no worries," Sam said, borrowing a line from the *Crocodile Dundee* video that Mary had given to him as a joke. "I'm here at the invitation of Midnight Productions."

"Here to do what?" muscle boy asked. He had dropped his guard slightly.

Sam answered, "I own a chain of video stores in the Midwest. All American Video, they're called. I'm interested in expanding into the adult market. I own a lot of stores, so I'm talking about a lot of money. I work hard for my money, so I want quality product, not that endless display of facial cum shots, gangbangs, and pounding anal sex that passes for a movie. I want pretty porn: a good story, realistic sets, and actors who can actually act."

Sam sounded so convincing that even *he* was beginning to believe his own bullshit. He appeared to have convinced muscle boy as well.

"This is the place to be, then. This is top-of-the-line product. My name's Peter Boy." Muscle boy extended his hand in welcome.

"Nice to meet you, Peter. I'm Jason Nixon."

Obviously, Sam wasn't going to use his real name. He chose a name that combined the names of his two favorite Red Sox players: Jason Varitek and Trot Nixon.

"I mean it," Peter Boy continued. "Midnight makes quality product. And I'm not just saying that. I've done more than my fair share of down-and-nasty videos. I'm talkin' in-the-toilet, up-against-the-wall stuff. We call them 'one-day wonders,' because they're shot in one day. *The Ovulator* is different. Sure, it might have a goofy name—a lot of porn videos are satires of mainstream movies: *The Aviator* in this case—but it's very well done."

Peter Boy shot Sam a sidewise glance, apparently to see if Sam—Jason—was taking him seriously.

He was.

"How's it different?" Sam asked.

"It's different in a lot of ways. But mostly because the director's got enough money to do the video right. I'm not talking the millions of dollars they've got to spend on movies like *War of the Worlds* or *The Da Vinci Code*, but Joey and Raoul get us good locations—like this house, for instance—and they give us a couple of days to shoot. Shit, I shot three videos in one day for Pussycat last week . . . I thought my goddamn dick was gonna fall off."

Peter Boy laughed at his characterization of the recent trials and tribu-lations of his penis.

Sam, however, had something more serious to worry about. He decided the time was now to see whether Peter Boy knew anything about Mary.

"I should let you get back to work," he said, knowing he had to be care-ful about how he broached the subject. "I appreciate your time, and I'm grateful for your insight. It's very helpful . . . You know what, though?"

"What?" Peter Boy said.

"I wouldn't mind talking to one of the actresses to see what her take on things is. You know, to get the feminine perspective on Midnight Productions. It would help me come to closure on this deal. Is anyone around? One of the camera guys told me there's a girl named Tiffany who might be of some use."

Sam was trying his best to appear as if finding this girl—*his* girl—was no big deal.

Peter Boy looked amused. "The camera guys don't know shit. You wouldn't find Tiffany of much use. I did a scene with her this morning and it was like fucking my pillow. I mean, the girls are usually into it, but Tiffany was just going through the motions. She would do what Philmore told her to do, but she didn't seem to enjoy it." Peter Boy paused, checked his hair in the mirror, and then said, "I don't know what it is with these new girls. There's this other girl—Stacy—who's been a real pain in the ass, too. All she does is bitch and moan. Tiffany doesn't do that—she doesn't say anything, actually—but she's no Jennifer. She's no pro, like Jennifer. Nah, you don't wanna talk to Tiffany. Besides, we've got a scene to shoot in a few minutes. She's gotta be on the set. I sure hope there's more life in her this time. She's got such a great body. She should enjoy it—or at least let *me* enjoy it."

Peter Boy checked himself in the mirror again. This time the focus was on his butt. He obviously liked what he saw. How, indeed, could Tiffany not be into him? he seemed to be asking himself.

Before Sam could think of anything to say, or perhaps do, in response—such as punch Peter Boy in the nose—he heard Philmore Bottoms's voice reverberating through the house.

"Peter! Tiffany! I need you on the set! You're up! Let's make it hot this time!"

Peter Boy made his way downstairs to get laid for money.

Sam Grimes found the nearest wastebasket and threw up for love.

The set was in chaos as everyone searched for Mary: still Tiffany to everyone but Sam.

"Where is that bitch!" Bottoms shouted. "I knew I shouldn't have used her again after *Law Clerks in Love*! She was bad news then, and she's worse news now! This is the last time that Joey Mancini is gonna tell me who to cast! I don't care who his goddamn father is!"

Bottoms wasn't directing his diatribe at anyone in particular. He was too out of control for that kind of focus.

Then it happened.

"Oh my God!" Peter Boy screamed from the third floor.

He didn't need to say anything else. They all knew what it meant. The entire cast and crew rushed to the site of Peter Boy's distress.

Even Philmore Bottoms looked sad when he saw the scantily clad body lying motionless in the pool of blood. She had jammed a pair of scissors into her heart. And, yes, Tiffany was Mary, although Sam was still the only one who knew it. To everyone else, Tiffany was Tiffany: just another young woman who had lost her way.

Sam said nothing, because he couldn't. He did nothing, because he couldn't. Billy tried to console him, but he couldn't. He led Sam to the car—to Raoul Hewitt's beloved Silver Seraph—and drove him back to Providence.

Peter Boy had promised to notify the police. Sam should have been the one to do it, but he couldn't. Bottoms had said he was calling off the shoot. "The fuck with *The Ovulator*," he had said. "The fuck with Joey Mancini's money."

CHAPTER THIRTY-NINE

"Madam foreman, have you reached a verdict?" Judge Reis asked juror number five.

A forty-nine-year-old high school civics teacher from Cranston rose to her feet. "Yes, Your Honor."

She looked more than a little nervous, Sam thought. He certainly was.

"Very well." There wasn't a hint of emotion in the Judge's strong voice. "Please hand the verdict to Ms. Curran."

Holly walked deliberately to the jury box and received the verdict form from the forewoman's quivering hand. The form was folded in half, so not even Holly could see what it said.

It took what seemed like forever for Holly to walk the five short steps from the jury box to the Judge's bench. She handed the Judge the form the instant she arrived. He unfolded it, studied its short paragraph, refolded it, and returned it to Holly. His face revealed nothing as to the outcome of the trial.

Holly returned to her post at the courtroom clerk's desk, verdict form in hand. All eyes were upon her—including Sam's, perhaps especially Sam's.

"Will the defendant please rise," Judge Reis said.

Joey Mancini stood to his feet. John Marone followed suit. Steve Sutton and Jim Hodges did as well.

An eerie silence engulfed the courtroom. It was difficult for Sam to believe that two hundred and fifty people could be so quiet. Chad leaned over and whispered something—"good luck," Sam thought he heard—into Sam's right ear. Sam tried to say something in reply, but couldn't.

All eyes remained on Holly as she prepared to read the verdict. At this particular moment in time only thirteen people had the information that everyone else in the courtroom—including Sam, perhaps especially Sam—was waiting with bated breath to hear. Those thirteen people were Judge Reis and the twelve members of the jury. Sam turned and faced Mancini. Like everyone else in the courtroom, Mancini, too, was staring straight at Holly.

Holly unfolded the verdict form and cleared her throat. She scanned the form—now fourteen people knew the outcome of the trial—and then read, "As to the charge of violating the Racketeer Influenced and Corrupt Organizations Act, we the jury find Joseph Paul Mancini not guilty."

"Yes!" Mancini exclaimed in a muffled cheer.

Marone placed his left hand on Mancini's right shoulder to hold his client in place. They turned to each other and smiled. They shook hands. This time it was a lawyer-client thing.

The two hundred and fifty people in the courtroom were no longer able to maintain their silence. Judge Reis gaveled them to order. Most of them complied. Sam said nothing, because he couldn't. Sam did nothing, because he couldn't. Time seemed to stand still as he replayed the verdict over and over in his head. He thought of Mary. He wiped a tear from his eye as he did. Chad placed his hand on Sam's. He whispered something into Sam's ear again. "I'm sorry," Sam thought Chad said this time. Sam tried to say something in reply, but couldn't.

◆ ◆ ◆

Sam figured that the Legal Realists had been right: the "artful lawyer" had carried the day again. John Marone's closing argument had been a sight to behold. His reference to Jesse Helms—the U.S. senator who had been voted most likely to be a reactionary—being the sponsor of the original amendment that had added obscenity as a predicate offense to the RICO statute had been an inspired tactical choice. His assault on Attorney General Miles's "moral crusade" against sexually explicit materials had been equally effective. "Just remember the title of Professor Collins's prize-winning book," Marone had urged the jurors. "*When RICO Seizure Is Used to Fight Obscenity, We End Up Forfeiting the First Amendment.*"

Or maybe Mark Twain had been right: jurors didn't know their asses from their elbows. How could a jury not have found a video of young women getting fucked in the ass obscene? Of big-breasted women having sex with myriad men? Of guys sucking each other off? The system didn't work. It was as simple as that, Sam thought. The government had seized five hundred videos. *Five hundred!* It didn't make any sense.

Nothing made sense anymore.

PART III
Post-Judgment Relief

CHAPTER FORTY

"Come in," Sam Grimes mumbled from underneath the covers.

He glanced up at the digital clock sitting on the windowsill above his bed. The display read 1:17 P.M.

Judge Reis had insisted that Sam take the day off. The Judge had said that it looked as if the trial had taken a lot out of his law clerk. Sam had said that the Judge was right. They both had known they were talking about Mary.

Chad Smith gently opened the door to Sam's bedroom. He walked toward Sam's bed. It smelled like he brought food with him.

"I thought you might like something to eat," Chad said. "I'm sorry it's not breakfast, but, hey, when we're out drinking you always say it's never too late for a Zero's meatball sub. Maybe it's never too early, either . . . *Early?* Who am I kidding? It's lunchtime already!"

Chad was obviously trying his best to cheer up Sam, but nothing could at this moment in time. Chad clearly knew that, but felt compelled to try anyway. Sam was grateful for Chad's efforts. He truly was. Chad had turned out to be a wonderful friend. Sam had been wrong to ever have doubted him.

Sam propped himself up on his elbows, and said in a voice barely loud enough to hear, "I appreciate you thinking of me. I really do. I'm not hungry, though. Maybe later."

Chad placed the meatball sub on the card table that Sam used for a desk, moved Sam's clothes from the only chair in the room, and sat down. "The mail came," he said. "There's quite a bit of it, too." He removed the rubber band that bound the sizeable stack. He separated his mail from

Sam's, and then asked, "What's up with all these letters from law schools? There must be ten of them here."

"Nothing much," Sam answered. "Judge Reis and I were meeting about Marone's motion to dismiss Mancini's indictment awhile back—man, it feels like centuries ago—and we got to talking about law teaching. I'm thinking about becoming a law professor, if you can imagine such a thing." A slight smile crossed Sam's face, but it quickly disappeared. "I don't think I want to practice law. I didn't much like the idea of it when I was in law school, and I certainly don't think much of lawyers now—what with the verdict in the Mancini case and all." He pulled the cord that opened the Venetian blinds. A sudden blast of sunlight forced him to squint. "I've always liked school, and I've always liked to write. So maybe I'll like being a law professor. Maybe that'll help take my mind off things. I've got to try something. I can't sleep the rest of my life away, no matter how much I might want to try."

Chad didn't say much. There wasn't much he could say. He stood from the chair and mentioned that there was Pepsi in the refrigerator, for when Sam was ready for the meatball sub. He was almost to the door when he seemed to notice something in his stack of mail. "Here's another one of yours," he said. "It was stuck to the bottom of the water bill."

He handed Sam a plain white envelope on which Sam's name and address were typed. There was no return address, but the post office seal read KINGSTON.

"Who's it from?" Chad asked.

"I'm not sure," Sam answered. "It was sent from Kingston, though."

Sam opened the envelope. The letter was typed, too. It wasn't a long letter, but it didn't need to be.

Sam read it.

Tuesday, October 15

Dear Sam,

I'm sorry I've only been able to leave messages on your answering machine, but that's all he would let me do. He was even listening in when I called. He would kill me if he knew I was writing this letter, but I wanted you to know that I love you and that's why I'm here. I hope you don't think I would make these kinds of movies unless I had to. Joey Mancini made me do it. He confronted me a couple of weeks ago and said he had a movie in mind—*Law Clerks in Love*, I think he finally called it—that yours and my relationship had inspired him to make and that only I could bring to life. I said forget it—that he was disgusting me—but he wouldn't take no for an answer. He said he would have you killed if I didn't make the movie. He said he wasn't kidding—that he'd had people killed for a lot less. He reminded me of who he is—of who his father is. Well, one movie has turned into two . . . I don't know how much more of this I can stand. Whatever happens, please always remember that I love you.

Mary

"Well, who's it from?" Chad asked. His eyes were riveted on Sam's.

"It's from Mary," Sam answered, again in a voice barely loud enough to hear. "I knew she wouldn't have made those movies unless she had to."

"What do you mean, 'unless she had to'?"

Sam tried to say something more, but he couldn't.

Chad took the letter from Sam's hand and read it.

Several minutes passed in silence.

"You've got quite a view of the Roger Williams church from your room," Chad finally said. "I've never noticed that before."

Sam knew that Chad was trying his best to say something that would ease Sam's pain. It didn't work, though. As if anything could . . . Mary had wanted to see the view of the Roger Williams church for herself some morning. Sam had never gotten the chance to show it to her.

Now, he never would.

CHAPTER FORTY-ONE

In the eighteenth century, Kingston, Rhode Island, had been a quaint little community of black-shuttered white-clapboard houses. It had been known as "Little Rest." Two stories surrounded the nickname. The first was that in the eighteenth century, Kingston had been one of the seats of the Rhode Island General Assembly, which, when it was in session, had been a place of "little rest." The second story was that as troops from the Massachusetts Bay and Plymouth colonies and Connecticut had worked their way to the Great Swamp in 1675 to fight the Narragansett Indians, the Colonial soldiers had stopped in Kingston to catch their breath. They had gotten, in other words, a "little rest."

Today, Kingston was home to the University of Rhode Island, a notorious party school. Despite this fact, it remained a quiet, restful place, rich in historic and architectural highlights; its only known business establishments were a gas station and a general store. And this was precisely why Joey Mancini had selected Kingston to serve as the headquarters of Midnight Productions—this, and the fact that Kingston was far enough away from both Pawtucket and Providence to avoid the prying eyes of his father.

Vince Patrone was standing in the parking lot enjoying a cigarette when he spotted a familiar car turning into the driveway.

It was Silvio's.

"What are you doing here?" Vince said to his brother. He blew a cloud of smoke into the thick night air. "I've got nothing else to say to you."

Silvio strode across the parking lot. He stopped five feet in front of Vince. He looked his brother squarely in the eyes. A lifetime of memories flooded over him. He reached inside his jacket and pulled out his pistol. He shot two bullets directly into his brother's brain.

Vince crumbled to the ground. Blood splattered the pavement like paint on an artist's palette.

Silvio got back into his car and headed to The Players' Club to tell Don Mancini that the deed had been done.

He had never said a word to his brother.

◆ ◆ ◆ ◆

"I didn't think you were gonna show, Philmore," Joey Mancini said, opening the door to the editing bay. "I saw what you said in the newspaper." He pointed to a copy of the morning's *Providence Journal*. It was lying face up on an empty wooden chair next to the video projector. The headline blared: **MANCINI ACQUITTED, BUT SAGA CONTINUES**. He peeked at his director. "Are you really gonna quit? Are you serious about getting out?"

"I think so," Philmore Bottoms said. "The girl was the last straw." He glanced down at the newspaper, and then back up at Mancini. "Did you read that B.B. King dedicated last night's concert to her? Apparently, the Judge's law clerks got a message through to him and asked if he would do it."

"I saw that. That was nice of him to do." Mancini searched his pockets for his Marlboros. He struck a match. "I'm not an animal, Philmore. I feel bad about the girl's death, too. But it was an accident, a tragic accident. Some of these girls are in over their heads. You know that. Tiffany was one who was. Stay with Midnight, Philmore. You're the best director in the business."

Bottoms paced around the room, thinking. "Where did you find the girl, anyway? This Tiffany . . . This Mary."

"No offense, Philmore, but my lawyer doesn't want me to say anything about that. Not even to you." Mancini stubbed out his cigarette and flicked it into the overflowing wastebasket in the south corner of the room. He had taken only a couple of puffs. He was trying to quit. He didn't want to end up like his father . . . "You saw how hard the government came at me about my movies—about *our* movies. There's no telling what they'll do about the girl."

"So she didn't come to you voluntarily?"

Mancini lit another cigarette. He *was* weak. His father had been right . . . "She came to me, Philmore. She wanted in. You know how much these pretty girls like to strut their stuff." He smiled.

Bottoms reached for the newspaper. He read the cover story one more time. "I'll give it some more thought," he finally said. "This is what I do." His arm swept through the room. "I make movies." He left.

Mancini slowly turned the hand crank on the video projector. He liked to edit the old-fashioned way. *The Ovulator* advanced frame-by-frame before him. "There's gotta be a way to salvage this thing," he muttered to himself. "Maybe I've got my own *Savannah's Last Dance* here. Videos featuring recently deceased porn starlets are gold mines." He fumbled for his editing shears. The door swung open. "Back already, Philmore?" he said, eyes transfixed on the video monitor in front of him. "I knew you were too much of a pro to let one minor setback keep you from your life's work. Why don't you see what you can do with this thing. You're a much better editor than I am." Mancini swiveled in his chair. "Hey! How did you get in here?! What are you—"

The editing shears were jammed into Mancini's heart in one powerful thrust. He slumped to the floor. His body lay motionless in a pool of blood.

THE END flashed across the video screen.

CHAPTER FORTY-TWO

Cheers erupted from the TV set in the west corner of the hotel room. The Boston Red Sox's ace reliever Keith Foulke had just gotten the St. Louis Cardinals's powerful slugger Albert Pujols to ground into a game-ending out. The Red Sox were now the World Series champions for the first time in eighty-six years! The Curse of the Bambino was officially vanquished. Car horns pealed on the street below like synthesized trumpets in a modern jazz quartet as word quickly spread through the historic neighborhoods of Boston.

Dr. Edward Jackson was a lifelong New York Yankees fan and was therefore unable to share in the Boston fans' jubilation. He flipped through the hotel's pay-per-view movie selections. He quickly skipped over the mainstream choices to focus on the adult options. He selected *Daddy's Little Girl*. He watched the opening sex scene between a middle-aged man and a porn starlet dressed to look like the man's teenaged daughter, and he was ready to rock. He punched the mute button on the TV's remote control. He placed his ear against the wall to hear if his own daughter had returned from the hotel's indoor swimming pool.

Mary Jackson had begged her mother to come on the trip to visit Boston University—one of the colleges Mary was considering most seriously for her undergraduate studies—but her mom had said that her father insisted on taking her.

"Can't you both come?" Mary had said. "Please, Mom. *Please.*"

But Mary's mother wouldn't come. She never came when Mary needed her.

Mary had stayed at the pool as long as she could. She would have stayed longer if the lifeguard hadn't shut it for the night.

She heard a knock on her door. She had the radio playing so that she could pretend she didn't. Unfortunately, her father had asked for two keys to her room. "My daughter's always locking herself out," Dr. Jackson had told the clerk at the hotel's check-in desk.

He pushed open the door to his daughter's room.

She closed her bathrobe. "What's that?" She pointed to the black case in her father's strong surgeon's hand.

Dr. Jackson said, "While you were at the pool relaxing I did a bit of shopping. We are staying in the Back Bay. I ducked into Filene's and bought myself a new toy." He placed the case on his daughter's bed and popped open the lid. He smiled like a little boy at Christmas.

However, Mary wasn't a little girl anymore, and her father clearly knew it. She said, "A video camera?"

He said, "Yeah. I thought it might be fun." His eyes danced through the room. His expression changed from that of a little boy at Christmas to a middle-aged lecher after one too many bourbons. "Why don't I film you, sweetheart?" He pawed at his daughter's bathrobe. "Like I did when you were little."

"Please, Daddy. Don't."

Mary had never told her father no before. She had always wanted to, but she also wanted to be a good girl.

"Come on, sweetheart. It'll be fun. Besides, you've still got your bathing suit on."

Seventeen-year-old Mary Jackson quickly became five years old again: doing what her father asked her to do because he had asked her to do it. She untied the belt on her bathrobe and let the robe slip from her shoulders.

Her father switched on the video camera. "You look great, Mary. The camera really loves you . . . So do I." Dr. Jackson pulled the tripod from the camera case and attached the video camera to it. "Sit on the bed."

Mary did as she was told.

Her father joined her.

◆◆◆◆

Sam Grimes couldn't sleep. It was two o'clock in the morning, dark as coal outside, and quiet as a courtroom during jury deliberations inside, but he couldn't sleep.

He slid out of bed. He picked his pants off the floor, pulled them on with a weary tug, and then slipped into the New York Yankees sweatshirt that Mary had given to him on their last date. "We'll get you this year!" she had teased the newly confident Red Sox fan when she had handed him the gift. Sam had vowed never to wear it—"George Steinbrenner is the devil!" he had told her with a grateful smile—but now he knew he *had* to wear it.

He exited the apartment as quietly as he could so as not to wake Chad. He hiked up Thomas Street, made a quick right onto Benefit, and then a left onto Angell. Four blocks later he reached 137 Olney Street. He placed the key in the lock and pushed open the door to apartment 3-A: Mary's apartment.

The apartment was just as Sam remembered it from the last time he saw Mary, with the exception of the fact that the air smelled stale from two weeks of inactivity. He cracked the living room window to let in some fresh air, and then did the same for the bathroom and the bedroom. He returned to the living room and began to clean. He was certain the police wouldn't appreciate it, but he felt compelled to clean. Mary had always liked things neat, and he wanted to give her what she wanted. One last time . . .

He began by dusting the coffee table with a rag he had retrieved from the kitchen. Next, he swept the floor. After he had finished, he decided to organize Mary's desk. He was surprised by how many bills she had received: Visa, American Express, Bloomingdale's, Ann Taylor, and on and on. Apparently, if you could charge it, Mary did.

Sam was tickled by what he saw next: a package of videotapes from EDWARD JACKSON, 663 OAK BROOK LANE, BRIDGEHAMPTON, NY 11932.

The tapes were from Mary's father. There were three tapes in all, and each tape was labeled MARY. Sam smiled at the thought of seeing Mary again, perhaps riding one of her beloved horses at her parents' house in The Hamptons or playing tennis with her dad at the country club. The package was already open, so Sam saw no harm in taking a look. He *needed* to look. He *needed* to see Mary again. One last time . . .

Sam switched on the TV and the VCR and popped in the first tape. It was of a young Mary taking a bath. She appeared to be about five or six. She was as cute as a speckled pup: the wall of brown hair, the coffee-brown eyes, the birthmark on her left shoulder. It was Mary all right. "Wave to Daddy," Sam could hear Mary's father say from behind the video camera. But she wouldn't do it. She wouldn't look at her father.

Sam stopped videotape number one and popped in videotape number two. An older Mary appeared on the screen. She looked about twelve or thirteen in this tape. She was still a child, but she was on the verge of blossoming into the beautiful young woman whom Sam would come to know and love some six or seven years later. After about five minutes of Mary riding her horse, the scene shifted to Mary in the bathroom again. Videotaping a five-year-old in the tub might be regarded as cute by many, but filming a twelve-year-old taking a shower had to be considered problematic by anyone who wasn't an indicted pop singer or a defrocked Catholic priest. "Look at me," Sam could hear Mary's father say. Mary wouldn't look at her father this time, either.

Sam moved on to videotape number three. In this tape, Mary was all grown up, albeit two or three years younger than she was when she died. She appeared to be in a hotel room. She was kneeling on a bed. She said, "Should I take my bathing suit off?" Her father said, "Yes." Sam couldn't watch what happened next: Mary having sex on camera with her father, and seeming to enjoy it.

Sam fast-forwarded through the rest of the tape. Scene after scene of Mary having sex with her father assaulted him from the screen. When the tape had finished—when the nightmare had ended—Sam buried his face in his hands and cried.

EPILOGUE

(Ten Months Later)

The sun was shining straight into his eyes. No matter how much he adjusted his cap, or how hard he tried to shield his eyes with his glove, he couldn't see a thing. It was, as they said in the big leagues, a high sky. If the ball was hit to centerfield, he was a dead man. It didn't really matter, though. They were already losing 15 to 2. This was one lousy softball team. It just went to show that these people had spent too much time with their noses in law books.

If you had told Sam Grimes a year earlier that he would be standing in a softball field in Charlottesville, Virginia, on a Wednesday evening in September, he would have said that you were nuts. It happened, however. Judge Reis was obviously being serious when he had said that he thought Sam would make a good law professor and that he would do everything in his power to help his law clerk get a good job. And a good job Sam got. He taught at the University of Virginia School of Law, Judge Reis's alma mater. Classes had started two weeks ago. In this, Sam's first semester as a law professor, he was teaching Introduction to Criminal Procedure and a special seminar on Pornography and the Law. Initially, Dean Gibbs—Sam's new boss—hadn't been too keen on the pornography class. The Dean hadn't thought that a first-year law professor was ready to teach an upper-level seminar. But Sam's persistence had prevailed—that, and a separate letter from Judge Reis explaining Sam's interest in the subject. (Judge Reis had turned down the promotion to the court of appeals. He had said that trying cases was "in his blood." Chief Judge Conigliero had been named to the seat.)

As far as the rest of Sam's clerkship went, he didn't remember much about it. Sure, he recalled writing more bench memos and more jury instructions and stuff like that, but he couldn't say *what* they had been about. It was all a blur, really. He had received a letter from Chad yesterday, though. Chad had gone to work for Goodwin, Sullivan, and Peabody after their clerkships had ended in July. He had called it quits with Suzanne. He asked if Sam still thought about Mary. Sam did. *A lot.* He also asked if Sam had heard the latest news about the Mancini case: the police *still* hadn't figured out whether Joey Mancini's death had been murder or suicide. At first, they had suspected that the person who had killed Mancini's bodyguard had also killed Mancini. But the forensics evidence had conclusively rebutted that theory. Chad said that he had saved the newspaper clippings for Sam to read during Sam's trip over fall break. Sam had planned to visit Chad in Providence after a short stop in The Hamptons to see Mary's father.

Sam heard the crack of the bat. He watched the ball fly toward him. He tried to catch it, but he couldn't.

Acknowledgments

I would like to thank my father, Stan Gerber; my stepfather, Ken McDonald; my stepmother, Linda McShann; my sister, Margot Gerber; my sister-in-law, Margaret McDonald; and my friends Joe Badal, David Keenan, Eddie Kritzer, Doug Litowitz, Melissa Moore Sale, Lynn Sametz, and Holly Rachel Smith for reading drafts of this novel. I also would like to thank my mother, Sandra McDonald; and my friends Stephen Billias, Peg Cain, Ron Collins, Julie Hilden, Merrill Kinstler, and Leslie O'Kane for their advice and encouragement.

Jennifer's explanation in the scene at the Olympia Tea Room of why she became a porn actress is drawn from the work of the late psychiatrist Robert J. Stoller in Robert J. Stoller and I.S. Levine, *Coming Attractions: The Making of an X-Rated Video* (Yale University Press, 1993), while the scenes at the Consumer Electronics Show are from Willem R. DeGroot and Matt Rundlet, "Neither Adult Nor Entertainment," *Premiere Magazine*, vol. 11, no. 13 (1998).

The quotations from law professor Catharine A. MacKinnon are from Catharine A. MacKinnon, *Toward a Feminist Theory of the State* (Harvard University Press, 1989), pp. 195 and 202.

About the Author

Scott Douglas Gerber, a former law clerk to a federal judge, is a law professor at Ohio Northern University. He received both a Ph.D. and a J.D. from the University of Virginia, and a B.A. from the College of William and Mary. His previous books are *The Declaration of Independence: Origins and Impact* (2002), *The Ivory Tower: A Novel* (2002), *First Principles: The Jurisprudence of Clarence Thomas* (1999), *Seriatim: The Supreme Court Before John Marshall* (1998), and *To Secure These Rights: The Declaration of Independence and Constitutional Interpretation* (1995).